WARD OF THE REDSKINS

Also by Sheba Hargreaves
The Cabin at the Trail's End
Heroine of the Prairies

WARD OF THE REDSKINS

SHEBA HARGREAVES

CUTTING EDGE

ISBN-13: 978-1-957868-71-4

Published by
Cutting Edge Books
PO Box 8212
Calabasas, CA 91372
www.cuttingedgebooks.com

CONTENTS

CHAPTER ONE

"THE COLUMBIA RIVER FISHING AND TRADING COMPANY"

THE cabin was in wild disorder and very dirty. Jim Faxon, straightening up from the saddle he was mending, surveyed his domain with a grimace of disgust—a single room, sixteen feet square, built of logs with the bark on, its two small buckskin-covered windows letting in the faint creamy light of a dun morning in late January. The stick-and-clay fireplace was choked with the ashes of many bachelor fires, the huge oak backlog nearly burned in two, and the ash-covered embers just faintly tinged with the last glow of red. A cluttery mess!

He turned in disgust from his bunk in the corner with its tousled buffalo robes and red-and-black-striped blankets. Sundry unmended garments hung limply over the one chair, a chair that bore eloquent testimony to having been made by hand to fill in the tedious leisure of a rainy Oregon winter.

The table, too, was a masterpiece—a huge fir puncheon with carefully fitted legs set at a straddling angle to insure its stability. But now its white, smooth-grained surface bore a sordid mass of soiled tin dishes and smoke-blackened pots and pans. All the culinary utensils the cabin afforded had been drawn by a force as mysterious and compelling as gravity to that table.

The puncheon shelf on the wall where the dishes should have reposed in scoured between-meal chastity was bare except for a tangle of dried fish, ends of jerked venison, greasy bacon rinds, and small hempen bags of meal and bits of this-and-that.

Jim's dog, Briar, a rangy black-and-tan animal nearly as large as a calf, was curled up on the warm hearthstones. She wagged a friendly stump of a tail as she caught his eye.

"Why don't I keep this cabin clean?" he inquired of the sleepy dog. "I'm a joke on myself, running clear across the North American continent to escape New England housekeeping, and now loathing my dirty cabin. I've been free of petticoat rule here, but I honestly believe that I am willing to submit to living in a scraped over-clean Boston home just to be near white women like mother and the girls. I'll keep this place clean, once Auxica clears up the infernal clutter," he promised his dog. But Briar had heard many similar declarations; she thumped her tail on the floor to show she was listening, but resumed her fitful dozing.

Jim Faxon laughed at the irony of the situation in which he found himself. He had fled to the remote wilds of the Pacific coast to attain freedom, and now his very freedom was becoming intolerable.

Life would have been unbearably dull and gloomy had it not been for his ability to find real humor in the grim pranks that fate had continually played upon him during the two years that he had spent at Fort William on Wappatoo Island. A nature unsweetened by laughter might easily have given way to blank despair under the vicissitudes attending the first attempt of Americans to establish a trading-post on the Pacific coast.

Jim Faxon was a born explorer. He had achieved a great distinction for his time, having made two overland trips from Boston to the Columbia River in an era when Americans on the smug Atlantic seaboard considered such journeyings almost as foolhardy as did the countrymen of Columbus when that visionary was endeavoring to interest a scoffing populace in the northwest passage to India.

He had spent his boyhood in a square white house next to the home of that intrepid adventurer, Nathaniel Wyeth, on the shores of Fresh Pond in the outskirts of Cambridge. Nat, the young daredevil, had been his boyhood idol, worshiped from afar, for Wyeth, with his five years' seniority, had paid scant attention to the small boy who followed his every escapade on Fresh Pond with breathless interest. As time went on, five years came to be not such a discrepancy in age, and, to Jim's overwhelming joy, the venturesome Nat came to recognize a kindred spirit in him.

Nat Wyeth flatly refused to attend Harvard College, where all his forebears had been educated with the dignity that became their station in life. Cambridge raised horrified hands at his behavior, and when, in his turn, Jim Faxon showed signs of rebellion, the combined efforts of a very determined widowed mother and a no less determined uncle were required to force him to follow in the path worn smooth by the decorous footsteps of his father and grandfather.

The day James Richmond Faxon was first placed in his deeply carved mahogany cradle, his mother, in spite of her overpowering physical weakness, had solemnly ordained him for the ministry, and ordained he must remain, with no swerving to right or left. With lagging footsteps Jim entered Harvard College, and for three tedious years had endured Latin and Greek in spite of his inward struggle to follow his boyish inclinations.

One bright strand of joy ran through the fabric of his irksome days. Thomas Nuttall, the celebrated English botanist, came to Harvard to serve as curator of the botanical gardens, and Jim Faxon, always a lover of growing things, fell under the enchanting spell of the microscope. Here lay the adventure his avid young soul craved. Under the gentle tutelage of this gentlest of natural scientists he gathered and classified the flora of Fresh

Pond, marveling, after the intense fashion of boyhood, at the wonders of root, stem and bud.

Matilda Faxon, Jim's mother, with the instinct of the New England housekeeper, rebelled at the clutter of weeds, as she sniffingly termed them, that rioted in her orderly clean-scoured house. This was just another evidence of the worthlessness of young Jim, wasting precious hours, when he should have been fitting himself for his mission in life, tramping through muddy swamps after putrid vegetation, tracking her spotless floors and filling his attic bedroom with worthless plants that he was forever analyzing and classifying. More than once she threatened to destroy his carefully-made herbarium, and in desperation he was finally forced to hide his treasures in the barn, and to continue his botanical study by stealth and subterfuge. He came to feel himself sort of a fugitive from justice, and yet for the life of him he could not take up the study of theology.

Jim Faxon's final revolt against maternal authority came one memorable morning when Matilda Faxon, in the course of a stormy interview, announced that the time had come for him to marry and that she had selected the proper wife for him, one who would settle him and bring him to the saving sense of his responsibility to the Church and his duty to his fellow-men if anything would, which she doubted.

Martha Judson was his mother's choice. She was eminently suited for a minister's wife. Her church activities showed her inclinations. She came of a family of God-fearing men and saintly women. She was—here Matilda Faxon paused and scrutinized the agonized Jim over her square shell-rimmed spectacles—she was a good housekeeper and thrifty.

This was too much to bear. Jim had instant vision of another house where his precious specimens would be rudely despised and he would suffer constant reproof for tracking in the mud of Fresh Pond on clean floors. He reasoned with himself in his refuge in the barn that it was not that he disliked Martha Judson;

he admitted that he was girl shy, yet he had always liked Martha after an indifferent fashion, but when it came time for him to take a wife he would choose her himself. Even in his callous soul he marveled at his rebellion, but his decision on that point was unalterably made. He loved his mother and she loved him, but from this time forth he must exercise a man's right to live his life in his own way.

At this juncture there was stirring news being whispered by the yearning youth of Cambridge. Nat Wyeth was planning bold adventure. Nat was now twenty-eight years old, safely married to his cousin, and the father of two children, and yet here he was swashbuckling again, just as he had in his reckless boyhood days. Not content with his business of cutting ice on Fresh Pond, he was mustering a company of very young men to travel across country and establish a huge trading enterprise on the Pacific coast.

"The Columbia River Fishing and Trading Company" would barter American goods for furs, raise tobacco on a grand scale for Indian consumption, and pack salmon on the Columbia River to ship to the Atlantic seaboard. A wild scheme. So far the Hudson's Bay Company held undisputed sway over the Pacific coast, though by the treaty of "Joint Occupation," signed in 1818, the United States maintained equal rights to colonize or trade on the western coast of north America.

Come what would, Jim Faxon resolved to be of this gallant company. Here was release from feminine tyranny once and forever. He hoped in his rebellious heart that he might never come under the sway of a woman again, and it was known that no white woman had as yet penetrated that vast wilderness lapped by the gentle waters of the Pacific.

Thomas Nuttall sighed when Jim Faxon told him of his resolution to join Nat Wyeth's company. His duties at Harvard had lately become irksome. He longed to examine the flora of a region where so little classification had been made.

"Go on, James," he said with yearning in his gentle voice. "When the trading-post is established, perhaps the way will open for us to explore the Pacific coast with a microscope together."

History records the outcome of Nathaniel Wyeth's venture in establishing an American trading-post on the Pacific coast. Jim Faxon was one of the twenty-three young men who made the trip overland with him, starting in the spring of 1832, while his vessel, *The Sultana*, fitted out by Boston merchants with supplies, made the long voyage "around the Horn."

An unkind fate dogged the footsteps of the gay young adventurers from the very first. They learned, on arriving at their destination, that *The Sultana* had been wrecked on the reef which today bears her name. All the supplies, the geegaws for the Indian trade, the cherished tobacco seeds—everything was lost.

On the long perilous journey across the "Great American Desert" many of the young men had turned their faces homeward. One poor boy died on the way. Only eleven of the twenty-four remained with Captain Wyeth to reach the coast.

Captain Nathaniel Wyeth could only spend the winter of 1833 in exploring the country with a view to determining his permanent location. There was nothing to do but return to Boston as soon as a crossing could be made in the spring. Jim Faxon, still faithful to his idol, and full of hope in the ultimate success of the venture, together with another young man, accompanied Nat Wyeth home to Cambridge.

Wise heads wagged when, disheveled and weary, Nat Wyeth and Jim Faxon returned to Fresh Pond in the fall of 1833. Jim feared that a second expedition could not be managed, but nothing daunted Nat Wyeth; what he started he finished or stood ready to die in the attempt.

Nat's persuasive powers were wonderful. The Boston merchants listened with interest and, while lamenting the disaster to *The Sultana*, forthwith invested twenty thousand dollars in "The Columbia River Fishing and Trading Company." Hard-headed

Yankee business men saw no reason why a second attempt to establish a trading-post on the Pacific coast should not succeed when the first had failed through "an act of God."

Jim Faxon was inspired by his idol's confidence. With such ample financial backing they could not fail. Now they knew the lay of the land. The company would pack salmon for shipment to Boston, trade with the Indians, and gradually develop large agricultural holdings on the Pacific coast.[1] Wappatoo Island where the great Multnomah River[2] joined the Columbia a few miles above the Hudson's Bay Company's post at Vancouver was to be the headquarters of the company.

The Wyeth expedition had attracted great attention on the Atlantic coast. The churches had for some years been planning to send their missionaries to the Western Indians. Here was an opportunity for safe conduct not to be overlooked. Jason and Daniel Lee, of the Methodist faith were detailed to labor among the Pacific coast Indians. The American Philosophical Society and the Academy of Natural Sciences of Philadelphia commissioned the naturalist, Dr. John K. Townsend, to explore this vast region to study and collect its bird life.

In spite of his mother's pleading, Jim Faxon was among the seventy picked men who accompanied Captain Nathaniel Wyeth on his second expedition to the Columbia River region in the spring of 1834. Jim's cup of joy overflowed when Thomas Nuttall announced that he was joining him to study the flora of the country. The great botanist had asked for leave of absence from Harvard College, and, when this was refused, had resigned.

---

1 Wappatoo Island, now called Sauvie's Island, was renamed for an employee of the Hudson's Bay Company, who operated a large dairy there when the company secured possession of this valuable holding.
2 This is the original name for the Willamette River. The latter name came into use a few years later.

But again fate took a firm hand in affairs. The brig *May Dacre* had been fitted out for trading and sent "around the Horn" with supplies. Her crew were to pack salmon that spring and be in readiness to sail back to Boston soon after the arrival of the overland party in the fall, but she was struck by lightning and limped into the Columbia River the day after the Wyeth party reached their destination.

Now it was January of 1836. Thomas Nuttall, who had lived with Jim in his cabin, sailed the week before to California to complete his study on the Pacific coast. Jim was lonely and discouraged—lonely with the desolation of loneliness that assails even the stoutest hearts at times. This dull day and the messy condition of his cabin made the longing for human companionship almost unendurable to him.

"I'll go for Auxica, and when she finishes a regular New England housecleaning, I'll turn a new leaf, Briar, honestly I will," he told his dog. But Briar wasn't interested. She strolled nonchalantly over and put her forepaws on the table as a hint that it was mealtime.

Jim called the dog and strode down the path to his boatlanding. His objective was the cabin of Jed Withers, the trapper, on the western bank of the Multnomah River, almost opposite his home on Wappatoo Island.

Auxica, a very large picture in a narrow frame, stood watching Jim Faxon from the doorway of the cabin as he moored the canoe. She was that most comfortable of all complacent comfortable human beings, the Indian wife of a white man.

Her papoose, nine months old, swayed in his *t'cash* from the limb of a near-by tree. She did not speak as Jim made his usual request of her, just unswung the cradle-board and, adjusting it to her back, scrambled into the canoe with an agility that belied her bulk.

"Ugh!" she grunted in disgust as she surveyed the littered cabin. "You need-um wife. Squaw better no *kloochman* [woman].

You not keep cabin clean; Indian *kloochman* take care her man. Wash-um clo'. Mend-um buckskins. Cut-um wood. Catch-um fish. Bake-um bannock."

She moved swiftly about, followed by the beady black eyes of her papoose hanging from his peg on the wall. She ran first to the creek for a closely-woven basket of sharp white sand to scour the dishes and scrub the floor.

Jim ignored her monologue, busying himself with sorting dried specimens and making notes as he placed the carefully mounted plants in his herbarium. The floodgates of Auxica's being were loosened; she continued to talk, so at last he turned and, shaking a dubious head, pointed to grease spots on the dirty puncheon floor.

"You no keep-um clean," Auxica scolded.

"I know that," he admitted, ruefully. "Mother's kitchen floor was always white and looked sort of fresh-scrubbed like, so that grease marks never showed on it. I must learn how to keep grease marks from showing on my floor."

"You mamma no give-um dog fish skins to chew on floor," Auxica told him with a fine edge of scorn in her voice, pointing an accusing finger at Briar calmly working on her fish skin by the hearth. She drove the protesting dog outside with the toe of her moccasin and applied herself to scouring the floor with a wisp of grass and sand.

This task completed, she moved on the tinware with a practiced elbow, and in an incredibly short time the little cabin shone with order and sweet cleanliness. Then before a freshly swept hearth she composed herself cross-legged to mend Jim's Indian breeches.

Briar ventured back with extreme caution and for a time there was no sound but the steady scratch-scratch of Jim's pen as he worked on his notes. He was sending specimens east by the next boat, and this meant steady work.

But Auxica was in the mood for speech, and Jim, nothing loath for her companionship, drew his chair up to the fire. She was quick-witted, and always quaint and amusing with her pride in her English speech and the airs she took to herself because she was the wife of a white man. The blinking papoose on the wall added a pleasing domestic note. Strange, he thought, that even a bulging fat squaw sitting cross-legged by a hearth makes home out of a bachelor's cabin for the time being.

Knowing her way, he waited for her to speak and she returned to the subject uppermost in her mind, a wife to share his loneliness. "I find-um young squaw," she announced, and paused for the weight of her offer to sink in. "I make clean. I show-um cook. You teach-um Boston talk."

But Jim frowned angrily. "No, Auxica." His gentle brown eyes held sparks of fire. "White men do not marry women just to keep their cabins clean and to do the heavy work for them. There must be love and companionship in marriage."

Auxica threw back her head and laughed in the full enjoyment of the joke.

Jim's frown deepened. He ran his fingers through his tangled auburn hair, a habit he had when perplexed or angry. "I'll just keep clear of Indian entanglements, anyway. No one shall ever call me a 'squaw man' while I'm in my right mind."

Auxica shrugged and resumed her mending in silence.

"Beside, mamma no like her only son marry Indian girl. Jim Faxon marry girl before live with her." He mocked Auxica's tone and manner.

"Then find-um white squaw," gibed Auxica.

"Where?" Jim inquired with elaborate curiosity. "You know as well as I do that there are no white women in the Oregon country."

Auxica's jelly-like being quivered with suppressed laughter. She arose and looked out the open door to satisfy herself that there was no one about, then closed the door with great caution before she spoke.

"Multnomah," she said, dramatically. "You ever hear of Multnomah?"

"Multnomah? Of course I've heard of Multnomah. The Multnomah river and the Multnomah tribe." Jim was a little disgusted with her elaborate secrecy.

"No, Multnomah, 'Rose-on-the-Water.' You see rose look in water when freshet come in moon of berries?" she inquired, stamping an angry foot. "Multnomah she little white squaw. So high." She placed her finger on the door frame to indicate the height. "Hair all same new buckskin." A comprehensive gesture indicated two braids reaching nearly to the knees, braids the color of golden buckskin.

She opened the door a crack, pointing to a small patch of intense blue sky between rifts of clouds. "Eyes same like blue sky." At Jim's look of incredulity she snatched back his sleeve, exposing a white forearm. "Face same like arm. Here pink same like rose looking in water," she said, pointing to her coppery cheeks.

"But, Auxica, what do you know about blue eyes and yellow hair? You never saw a white girl," doubted Jim.

"How you know what Auxica saw?" she inquired with fine sarcasm.

No white woman had ever penetrated the wilds of Oregon. That was a self-evident fact. Fancy a woman crossing the great American Desert. And yet, there was no telling. Strange things happened among the Indians. Jim longed for the sight of a white woman, and so eagerly entertained the vision conjured up by Auxica, even though he was sure she was just spinning a yarn for the sake of seeming important in his eyes. The Indian loves the mysterious, and nothing is dearer to his soul than the sharing of a secret with one whom he can trust.

Jim was silent a moment. Auxica evidently had knowledge that gave her extreme caution, for she had closed the door so carefully before mentioning her great secret.

She was watching him intently. Finally he laughed and shook a dubious head. "No, Auxica, you know you never saw a white woman. You've probably seen blue eyes in the head of a sandy-haired Scotch trapper, but a white woman you have never seen, because there aren't any here to see."

Auxica drew up angrily, then turned and busied herself on the hearth, with her broad back turned disdainfully toward him. She was raking out fine ashes and smoothing them down evenly. Jim looked over her shoulder as she drew with her forefinger. Finishing her design, she scanned his face for a sign of recognition.

A surprised exclamation escaped Jim as she completed her drawing.

"Where you see that?" she inquired. "Where you see-um?" She stood waiting for his answer.

"Why, yes, I have seen that picture," Jim admitted, thoughtfully and with a certain reluctance. "Last summer we saw that device on large smooth-barked alder trees in the mountains down to the south. Nearly always there was an arrow below, pointing toward the west. Nuttall and Townsend speculated a great deal about them while we were hunting specimens in the mountains."

"What you tink-um say?"

"We didn't know. Doctor Townsend knows Indian handiwork, and he was sure no Indian had drawn them. We came to the conclusion that some white man had carved the pictures in idle moments as he traveled. And yet," he asked himself aloud, "why did the arrow always point westward?"

Auxica frankly enjoyed his perplexity. "You go find-um Multnomah, Rose-on-the-Water. I show-um trail." But sudden panic overcame her as she seemed to realize what she had done. "No tell," she begged, anxiously. "Cause-um war, you tell."

"No, I'll not tell a soul," soothed Jim, noting the genuine concern in her face. He laughed to himself. "I'd never hear the last of it if I went hunting for a white woman down in the timber. I'm a butt of ridicule among the men at the fort now on account of my love for plants. No, you rest assured I'd never let the men know even if I should decide to search for a mythical white maiden."

Auxica knew intuitively that Jim doubted her story. "Ask-um Jed Withers if Auxica lie." Indignation in every line of her, she was adjusting her papoose to her back preparatory to crossing the river to her cabin. "White man no know Indian." Her scorn was withering. "White man not know ever't'ing in Indian country."

CHAPTER TWO
THE THUNDER STONE

WAPPATOO ISLAND is an alluvial delta, about fifteen miles long and from one-fourth to three miles wide, formed by the junction of the Multnomah River with the Columbia. Rich in high woodlands and lush plains, it furnished pasturage for numerous bands of fat elk. The jumping deer, called by the French Canadians, *le chevreuil,* and the larger black-tailed deer, made this island their permanent home.

Here the great white swans[1] wintered, migrating northward in April to return in great number in October. The Canadian wild goose, the gray or calling goose, and the small white goose fed in its sloughs. The wappatoo, or Indian potato, *Sagittaria latifolia,* a species of water plantain, grew luxuriously in the sloughs. Here the Indian women gathered their winter supply of this delectable tuber. Wappatoo Island was the pleasure ground of all the Chinook tribes.

Their medicine-men performed certain mystical religious rites about a curiously carved rock of black basalt half imbedded in the earth. Jim Faxon had chosen the site for his solitary cabin a few hundred yards below this sacred Thunder Stone, as the Indians called it, and the path to this shrine lay just below his door. From the first he had shown a friendly interest in the

---

1 The great white swans have long been extinct in the Oregon country.

Indians, and, much as they resented the building of Fort William on their venerated island, they recognized and loved a friend when they encountered one.

Jim was certain, though, that the American occupation of the island had a great deal to do with the Indian hostility to the Columbia River Fishing and Trading Company. An untoward circumstance in 1834 had incurred their enmity. David Douglas, the eminent English botanist, was then in residence at Fort Vancouver, and, noticing the rock, which was about four feet high and three in diameter, had called Dr. Townsend's attention to it. They were both of the opinion that it was a meteorite and decided to remove it to Fort Vancouver.

Even to touch this sacred stone was sacrilege to the Indians. They gathered in force, protesting vigorously, and Jim Faxon, out of sympathy for their distress, had finally prevailed upon the naturalists to leave the Thunder Stone in its place. This simple act of friendliness won him the lasting regard of every Indian in the country.

The evening after the attempt to remove the stone a terrific thunderstorm had suddenly arisen. Electric storms are so rare in the Oregon country that the Indians are filled with superstitious terror at their occurrence. They had explained to Jim that their gods were venting their wrath on the white men because they touched a stone which they declared had fallen from the sky. This tradition had been handed down to them from their remote ancestors who had witnessed its fall. The peculiar hieroglyphics on its surface they declared were the story of the will of their gods in regard to their destiny.

No-Lie, an old Indian who came often to view the Thunder Stone, told Jim at great length of the disasters that would shortly fall upon the Columbia River Fishing and Trading Company because of the violation of this sacred relic.

No-Lie (he must have had an Indian name, but no one knew it) had come into the country at about the time of the arrival of the Wyeth party in 1834. He was considered a great nuisance at Fort Vancouver and Fort William because of his insatiable curiosity about the strictly private affairs of the white men, and his habit of boasting of the prowess of himself and other Indians. He had been dubbed "No-Lie" by them because he prefaced his unbelievable stories with "Me no lie. Me tell-um trut'."

No-Lie would not have been tolerated around either trading-post but for the fact that he acted as agent for his Indian friends in bartering furs. He brought in quantities of prime beaver skins, really the best the country afforded, and, try as he might, no white man had as yet been able to trace the source of supply.

This mysterious personage had set up quite a pretentious establishment near the Tuality River, fifteen or twenty miles south and west of Wappatoo Island. Here he lived in Indian state with his numerous wives and children, waxing rich through his shrewd trade in beaver skins and cayuse ponies.

No-Lie was well above the Indian level of intelligence, and, curiously enough, he spoke English after a jerky fashion, never condescending to converse in the Chinook jargon, which is the trade language of the natives, a curious mixture of French, Spanish, and English idioms done over into the Indian dialect. Where he had learned English was the great mystery of the Oregon country, for he was not known previously to any of the trappers and traders of the region.

"Me no lie. Me tell-um trut'," he had told Jim Faxon. "Captain Wyeth him no catch salmon. Salmon no friend Wyeth. Salmon Indian friend. White man no make salmon medicine. When salmon come in spring, Indian chief first eat heart, make present to friend, no give first salmon to white man," he paused in horror. "Salmon feel much mad, you cut-um cross." He indicated with expressive hands the white manner of cutting fish in crosswise chunks, then proceeded to demonstrate to the amused Jim the proper manner of cutting up a salmon, first splitting the fish down the back and removing the backbone.

"White men try move Thunder Stone?" he indited. "Jim Faxon you heap big Indian *tillicum* [friend]. You stay in Indian country. You mind-um what No-Lie say. Captain Wyeth no stay. Go way soon. No can live in Indian country."

No-Lie's prediction uttered in 1834 had, by 1836, come all too painfully true. The Columbia River Fishing and Trading Company had dragged out a miserable existence. The Hudson's Bay Company was so securely intrenched that, while not openly opposing its American rival, it had been able to prevent the Indians from selling peltries to the latter.

The salmon catch in the spring of 1835, in spite of cutting the fish Indian fashion, was very light. The *May Dacre,* on her voyage to Boston, had carried less than half a cargo of fish and very little in the shape of peltries.

Plying back and forth from the Sandwich Islands, the brig had brought sheep, goats, hogs, and cattle for the farm at Fort William. Grafted fruit trees had been carefully set out and much land broken to the plow, but the odds were against the Americans from the start. Clearly they were not to succeed on the Pacific coast for some time. Nat Wyeth was a man whose vision was twenty years ahead of his day.

Jim Faxon had two alternatives. He could do fairly well by remaining in the Oregon country as an independent trapper and trader, or sail for home in inglorious defeat when the *May Dacre* made her final voyage in the fall.

Nat Wyeth had already started to Fort Hall, a trading-post he had established on the Snake River in coming across the country. From there he was going home by way of Taos, trusting his men at Fort William to attend to the salmon catch and the buying of peltries.

Small wonder that Auxica's fantastic story of a white girl waiting to be rescued intrigued his fancy, lonely and discouraged as he had been for so many weary months. With a woman whom he loved he would be content to spend his days here, living easily by trapping and trading, with a splendid leisure happily given over to botanizing.

He wondered whether he would fall in love with the first young white Woman he met, and did not know. And then, too, there was the possibility that the girl, if she existed, would have none of him. He had never had a taking way with girls back home.

Jim mused a long time by his evening fire after taking Auxica home. Multnomah, Rose-on-the-Water, what a beautiful name! The Indian was dirty and degenerate, but at soul he was a poet. His words were so happily chosen. A shy young girl with pink-and-white coloring and two braids of yellow hair and eyes like twin blue mountain lakes did resemble a wild pink rose drooping over the water. He grinned sheepishly to himself at his flight of fancy.

"A man might be happy to the end of his days in this cabin if Rose-on-the-Water could only be found and induced to share it," he told Briar. But in his saner moments he believed that Auxica's story was just a cruel joke that mocked him in his loneliness. He called himself a sentimental fool and tumbled into his bunk.

But in the morning he found himself considering the story again. Down in the depths of his being he knew there was only one reason for his returning to the States. At twenty-eight a man needs a wife, no matter how much disguising of the fact he may do.

And come to think seriously of it, there would be very little work for him at Fort William this next summer. He might make a casual trip of exploration. Perhaps he could secure some good beaver skins. He would be able to finish his classification of Oregon flora to his satisfaction before the *May Dacre* sailed in the fall if he started as soon as spring came. He hoped he would be able to discover all the orchids. Thomas Nuttall had agreed with him that there must be a few that had escaped them. David Douglas had searched in vain for *Monotropa uniflora*. Perhaps he could find this ghost flower, the rarest orchid in America.

He allowed his fancy free play. His quest for *Monotropa uniflora* could also be his quest for Multnomah and no white man the wiser if he failed. He wove romance about his last summer on the Pacific coast. He pictured himself rescuing a beautiful yellow-haired, blue-eyed girl from savage Indians somewhere back in the mountains and carrying her home in triumph after having married her according to the Christian ritual with Jason Lee, the missionary, performing the ceremony.

Then he came to earth. He laughed bitterly. Building air-castles would never do. Suppose there were a white girl secreted somewhere in the Oregon country. True, her eyes might be very blue, indeed, but mere blueness would not prevent their being crossed. Her hair, from Auxica's description, could just as easily be a pale ugly red as yellow like new buckskin. She might be, probably was, if she existed outside of Auxica's imagination, a slovenly, ignorant savage, as Indian in her habits and tastes as any blood Indian could be. Or if she were the celestial being his imagination pictured, she would not love him, and his romance would be shattered before it began.

Night after night as spring came in he mulled the situation over in his mind. Well, he could see no harm in inquiring casually about unknown white women in Oregon. If one existed, surely some mountain trapper would have heard of her. He promised himself, a little sheepishly, that he would ask Jed Withers when he went over to see about buying his winter catch of furs. Word had just come that Jed was at home, resting from his labors. The Yankees must be shrewd to make Jed an offer high and well ahead of the Hudson's Bay Company.

Jed Withers' cabin was a pleasant place. Auxica in her Indian way was a stickler like his mother when it came to housekeeping. Jed was enjoying himself by the fire, teaching the papoose to dance. He held him out in his little buckskin shirt with his bare feet just touching the floor, and as Auxica hummed a monotonous Indian tune—a-hum a-ha, a-hum a-ha, little Jed Withers laughed aloud, and to the fond parents seemed to be making an effort to keep time with a pair of lively little feet.

Auxica, catching sight of him from the doorway, made an excuse for an aside before Jed turned from his exercise with the papoose. "You no tell?" she inquired, anxiously.

"No, I haven't told a soul," Jim assured her, "but I'm going to ask Jed about it if I may."

"Jed not know. We tell-um now," she agreed.

Jed, a great hulk of a man clad in dirty buckskins, with worn moccasins on his huge splay feet, laughed immoderately when Jim asked him if he had ever known a white woman in the Oregon country.

"Spring air shorely a-comin'," he chortled. "All the young men air out a-huntin' o' wives."

Jim flushed a dull brick red through his sunburn, and Auxica flew instantly to his defense. "Jim Faxon no live with Indian woman; find-um white squaw," she declared.

Jed slapped his buckskin sides and laughed until the tiny cabin reverberated with sound. "Whar ye goin' ter find 'er, Jim?" he asked when he could speak.

"Auxica says she knows where there is a white girl," Jim told him with a little show of confusion. "She asked me not to speak of it, and I haven't, but I'm naturally curious."

"I hain't never heerd o' no white woman this side o' the Rocky Mountings," Jed declared.

"Jed Withers, when Auxica lie? You know I tell-um trut'. Indian hate lie. Lie all the same like steal. Like kill." Her black eyes held an appeal in their depths which sobered Jed instantly.

He ran two horny hands through an unkempt shock of coarse red hair in perplexity. As he turned to Auxica his eyes shone with a mingled love and pride that surprised Jim. That a white man could really love an Indian woman had never occurred to him. "Squaw man" alliances were commonly supposed to be just matters of expediency.

"Yep," he said after a long ruminative pause, "Auxica air a truthful cuss. But, man alive, don't ye be a-goin' out fer ter hunt trubble. Ef ye know fer sartain they's a white gal livin' amongst some o' the tribes, ye leave be. Ef ye want a wife, find a Injun gal. Me," he waxed eloquent, "I'd leifer hev a Injun woman ez six white uns." He waved a gracious hand in Auxica's direction. "My ole woman keeps keer o' me, an' nary a word back. I skipped from Kaintuck an' left a wife, 'cus why, she war allus a-wantin' o' me ter do somethin' I warn't minded ter do."

Jim laughed in spite of himself at Jed's case against the fair sex. Always wanting a man to do something he didn't want to do. He, too, had run away. But his laugh died as he glanced at Auxica. She was gazing at clumsy Jed Withers with adoration, the adoration that he had seen in the eyes of Madonnas in the art galleries of Boston. The love of woman for man shone forth in the eyes of that primitive woman, a holy thing, akin to the love of God.

The talk turned to peltries, and Auxica busied herself with some cooking until he rose to go. "Go ask-um No-Lie where find-um white wife," she admonished. Jed and Jim both burst into laughter at her words.

"Ef a Injun don't lie, hit hain't becus he cain't," roared Jed. "No-Lie's got all the white varmints in the kentry plumb beat when hit comes ter handlin' the truth. He'll shore tell ye all erbout hit—jest whar the white gals air, an' how ter fotch 'em inter the settlement."

"I'll go over to Tuality in a few days and see No-Lie," Jim said, half laughingly. "The early flowers are beginning to bloom, and I'll bring in some specimens and there should be a stray goose or two left on the sloughs. No harm in going hunting in that direction, is there?"

Jed was pondering deeply. "Wal, come ter think on't, they's a good yarn goin' round about some red-headed Injuns over onto the coast. Thar mout be a white gal over thar somewhares."

"No harm in drawing No-Lie out on the subject, anyway," Jim grinned.

"One thing thet allus puzzled me," Jed came out of his reverie as a thought struck him suddenly. "Ye ever notice how Auxica talks Boston? Wal, I know thet she hain't never been roun' the post at Vancouver, an' she hain't ever lived with no white man afore. She swears ter God she hain't, an' I believe her. She hails from somewhares over Tillamook way. I found her in the mountings down in the Umpqua kentry whar I war a-trapping the winter o' twenty-nine or thirty. She had well nigh perished o' cold an' starvation. She said she had strayed off from a root-gatherin' party o' squaws. Whar she l'arnt Boston talk allus war a puzzlement ter me."

"Did you teach her Boston ways of housekeeping?" Jim inquired.

"No, I hain't l'arned her nothin'. She war clean right from the start an' knowed white ways, but she hain't pestered me none erbout bringin' in dirt like a white woman allus does."

Jim pondered as he went home that evening. There was mystery about Auxica. Could it be that she had known white people before she came to live with Jed Withers on the Columbia?

CHAPTER THREE
NO-LIE'S LODGE

E VERY young man carries in his heart his ideal woman, secretly hopes to find the flesh-and-blood realization. After hearing Auxica's story, Jim Faxon's dream woman took a name, Multnomah, Rose-on-the-Water. He reasoned against reason that it was sheer folly for a lone white man to go seeking a white girl clear off on the edge of nowhere on the say-so of an Indian woman; just as often as he scouted the very idea, just so often he began formulating plans for an all summer's exploring trip. He found plenty of reasons to justify him—peltries to be secured and botanical specimens to be gathered in the far-western reaches.

Paying a friendly visit to the Hudson's Bay Post at Vancouver, Jim casually brought up the subject of white people in the unexplored regions of the Pacific coast. There was much discussion around a comfortable fire that evening. Dr. McLoughlin said he had heard rumors of a white man among the Indians who never spoke but made his wants known by signs. None of the men lounging about the room believed Indian stories, though they beguiled the long evening with such fanciful tales. But, somehow, after listening to the gossip of the post, Jim was more than ever inclined to believe Auxica's story had at least some slight foundation in fact. He thought perhaps he credited it because he wanted it to be true, but night and day he thought of Multnomah.

One morning in late March he started for Tuality, ostensibly to bring in a deer and a few wild geese for the table at Fort

William, but his real objective was the lodge of No-Lie. He made his pack very carefully, including a six-inch rope of the Brazilian trading-tobacco from the storehouse which would afford him a royal welcome in the Indian camp. He thoughtfully provided vermilion for painting the cheeks of the dusky females, as well as beads and small mirrors.

There had been a light rain during the night and a warm spring sun was hastily wiping up the excess moisture along the Indian trail over the hills. Jim traveled leisurely, exulting in the beauty of the morning, pausing to enjoy fresh swelling buds, or to search among last fall's carpet of oak leaves for some delicate spring blossom. *Claytonia lanceolata* (spring beauty) lifted delicate lavender cups to the sun from every copse. Insects hummed, small birds were setting up housekeeping in their favorite trees and bushes. Briar nosed out a silver-gray squirrel, or barked shrilly at the base of trees where black crows rested from their labors, and over all was an intense blue sky with fleecy clouds like white sheep pasturing on it. His nature-attuned soul knew ecstasy. God walks on Oregon hillsides in early spring.

All the landscape had turned a festive pink at the blazoning of the flowering currant, *Ribes nevadense.* He broke a spray, rubbing it between long sensitive fingers the better to inhale its exquisite tangy fragrance. The flowering currant, he decided, was his favorite among Oregon flowers. He had made this same decision many times during the long delightful season. The last rarely beautiful bloom was always his best beloved.

The gibes and sneers at the queer ways of "grass men" which made life so hard at Fort William were erased from his mind. He was six feet of virile manhood in his native environment with the dream woman, Multnomah, walking by his side through an enchanted forest.

Tuality in its wild fertile beauty broke on his vision as he reached the crest of the range of hills. Tuality—the Indian word for Paradise—was a Garden of Eden that rain-washed, sunlit morning. The broad expanse of richly grassed valley scrolled before him, the course of its numerous small streams well defined by the willows and vine maples that broidered their sides in tender green.

The fifteen miles of his leisurely journey passed all too quickly. He was nearing the establishment of No-Lie. Nothing but an avid appetite for information could have forced him to visit a smelling Indian camp on such a day. The din of the lodge reached his ears long before the odor insulted his senses. There is always noise about an Indian camp. The aborigine shouts both in joy and in sorrow, as well as in his level in-between moods. But today it was not mere noise, it was a literal hell of sound. Terrible blood-curdling shrieks rendered by high-pitched female voices were added to the yelping of many dogs and the shrill calls of the children at play.

Jim debated turning back before he rounded the turn that would bring him in full sight of the assembled Indians, but was too late; Briar had gone on ahead and grossly insulted the mongrel dogs that infested the place.

There might, from the din, be civil war in progress, but he was discovered. He must show a bold front and come up to the lodge.

The entire population of No-Lie's village was seething on the small plateau. Something terrible must have happened. Women screamed in either panic or derision, and braves bellowed their orders to them. A group of six calico ponies surrounded by appraising Indians grazed peacefully in a little hollow, but the center of attraction was a struggling young Indian girl securely lashed to a clay-bank pony held in leash by a decrepit one-eyed old Indian.

During the lull occasioned by Jim's approach, the girl paused long enough in her demoniacal shrieking to lift an agonized face from the pony's flank. He was moved to pity as he noticed that her arms and legs were securely lashed under the cayuse's belly with buckskin thongs.

The squaw was No-Lie's daughter, Wopcelia, noted around the trading-posts for her comeliness and her winning ways. Her keeper, he who held the pony's lash, was the old rapscallion, Cultee, a subchief with one foot in the grave and a body maimed and scarred by fierce battles among his fellow braves.

He was notorious for his shrewdness in trading horses, or stealing them. His methods of securing coveted riches were open to question among the Indians and the trappers. But Cultee was justly celebrated for his nice taste in wives. He had six or eight and was constantly adding to his seraglio by sharp trading with designing fathers.

Jim Faxon took in the situation at a glance. He had rudely interrupted a wedding party. No-Lie had disposed of his greatest asset, the charming Wopcelia, knocking her down to the highest bidder. Six sound cayuse ponies were a small fortune in the valley; they were secured by barter with the "horse Indians" east of the Cascade Mountains.

Opinion was evidently divided in the camp. No-Lie and several of his supporters at the moment of Jim's approach had been assiduously engaged in kicking and beating off three squaws who were protesting with what he took to be Indian cuss words unbecoming to the soft lips of women. Three other squaws, judging by their gibes and taunts, were in complete accord with the master of the household.

A primitive wedding, indeed, in the spring-saturated valley of the Tuality. Jim's first impulse was to protest, but long experience had taught him the folly of interfering in Indian affairs. His unexpected advent precipitated matters. Cultee and his cohorts moved off with what dignity they could command. Wopcelia, in passing, turned her imploring face to him, and the drama was finished.

Jim seethed with impotent indignation, but sternly held his peace. Wopcelia had visited Fort William many times. She had taken a girlish fancy to Briar, and had more than once offered him nicely woven baskets or a dressed elkskin for the dog, but he had steadfastly refused.

No-Lie was in no position to entertain visitors, but with elaborate Indian hospitality he invited Jim into a small teepee well to one side which was evidently kept for entertaining guests. He motioned grandly for the peering crowd of bucks, squaws, and children to retire, aiding the laggers by well-directed blows from the toe of his moccasin.

The tepee was comparatively clean, the floor almost covered with beautiful new mats of the squaws' weaving. Without a word No-Lie seated his guest. Jim produced a rope of tobacco and his host quickly filled a large curiously carved stone pipe and smoked in silence. One must wait patiently for the stolid Indian to open conversation.

"Wopcelia no mind-um papa," No-Lie volunteered at last. "Cultee much good Indian. Give-um six ponies for wife."

Jim offered no comment and his host resumed: "Indian squaw she no good. Make-um trouble for her mans. Fight-um in lodge. All time fight-um. Me no like."

Jim was familiar with the difficulties encouraged by the heads of good-sized camps. The custom was to bring in young wives by barter, and there was constant bickering and jealousy among the women. But if the coppery Eves brought the apple of discord into Eden, that was none of his affair. He was wondering how best to broach the subject of Multnomah without appearing too anxious. Fond as No-Lie was of prying into the personal affairs of white men, Jim knew that any undue curiosity about Indian relationships would drive his host immediately into his shell.

"White squaws make trouble for their men, too," Jim comforted. "But there's no living without women, so we must bear with them. I would give ten years of my life right now to find a white wife, but there are no women of my race in the Oregon country. I must go clear back to the land of the Boston's to marry." He congratulated himself on his adroitness in sounding out No-Lie.

No-Lie smoked in silence. Jim waited with carefully concealed anxiety. If he knew of Multnomah there was a good chance that the Indian would boast of his knowledge.

Laying down his pipe, No-Lie assumed an omniscient attitude. "Me no lie. Me tell-um trut'. You no go back Boston. You no tell, me find-um white wife. Me show-um tlail." He resumed his smoking.

"Then Auxica was right," Jim burst out in his excitement. "She told me to ask you about Multnomah. She said her Indian name meant 'Rose-on-the-Water.'"

"Auxica not know much as me," No-Lie boasted. "Multnomah send-um word find-um white mans. You no tell?" he inquired again.

"I'll not tell," Jim promised.

"Me no lie. White girl live with my people in Nehalem country. White girl friend Auxica. Friend No-Lie. Big *tillicums* [friends]. You ever hear of Nehalem people? Nehalem country down by big water."

Jim shook his head. The name Nehalem was new to him.

They were interrupted by a squaw bearing a wooden platter of smoking meat. Having no taste for Indian cookery except when pressed by hunger, Jim had not intended to remain to dinner. But now he must accept the hospitality with graciousness, though he knew dog meat was invariably served at wedding feasts. To refuse food was a deadly insult. Many times in his trip overland his party had been glad of dog meat. Provided the dog was young and fat, it was not so formidable as the uninitiated might be led to suppose.

The meal ended with dried salal berries pressed into a cake. When it was finally cleared away No-Lie made sure that no keen feminine ears were open to hear his story, before he resumed his monologue.

"No will tell much 'bout Multnomah," he declared, cautiously. "Make-um war in lodge of my people. You go find-um?" he asked, hopefully.

"If I felt sure there was a white woman I certainly would find her," Jim declared, emphatically.

No-Lie nodded approval, turning the subject over and over in his canny mind as he smoked.

"Me no lie, me tell-um trut'. You no believe." His tone showed the resentment he felt.

"I don't know what to believe," Jim answered, slowly. "How does it come that no white man has heard the story?"

"What Boston man know about Indian country?" No-Lie countered. "Indian no tell white man ever't'ing. He tell-um, white man say he lie."

He produced an elkskin pouch from a remote recess in his clothing, pausing with a finger on the draw string as he noted Jim's eagerness.

"Tomaniwus show-um. Tomaniwus no lie. Indian know."

Jim carefully concealed his eagerness. Tomaniwus is the great all-pervading spirit of nature. The Indian believes that he may draw this force to himself by certain mystical rites and practices and thus gain knowledge of the hidden side of things. No-Lie, then, had some connection with the great medicine cult. He was fingering his medicine-bag, preparing to practice divination.

Yes, this was a medicine outfit, held in a strong bag about a foot square, elaborately embroidered with threads of finely spun wild flax beautifully colored with native pigments. Breathlessly Jim leaned forward. He had often seen medicine-bags, but never had their contents been revealed to him. The medicine-men guarded their secrets jealously.

"I ask Tomaniwus." No-Lie carefully placed the contents of the bag on a clean mat on the floor, bending over in reverence.

Jim's eyes were riveted on the objects on the mat. A dozen round black pebbles worn smooth by much handling. "Just like the Thunder Stone on Wappatoo Island," he ejaculated.

"Yes, Thunder Stone, him fall from sky. Other stones no make medicine. I ask Tomaniwus you find Multnomah." No-Lie was picking up the stones lovingly as he spoke. He uttered strange gutturals in his native tongue as he placed them in a circle on the ground. "Tomaniwus tell if you go find Multnomah." He drew a few dried green leaves and some odd twisted roots from the heap on the mat, making a tiny mound inside the circle of stones, and carefully lighted the pile with a spark from his pipe.

With closed eyes he waited for the blaze, then on his knees swayed back and forth, inhaling the stupefying smoke. Jim turned dizzy as the lodge filled with the fumes. The pungent odor nauseated him, but he resisted an impulse to lean over the tiny flame and inhale deeply as No-Lie was doing.

No-Lie's face was terrible as he swayed, like a priest before the Delphian shrine in the Greek temple at Ephesus, weaving mystic figures in the air and uttering strange cries. Finally he began speaking slowly in jerky English, evidently describing visions conjured up in the thick white smoke.

"I see Multnomah." Jim looked with straining eyes, but could see nothing. "She cry. She sad. She watch trail for white man. He no come. She say come before hunting-moon. After hunting-moon, no good come. White man no tell. He tell, he no find Multnomah. Me see you on trail, Jim Faxon."

Waiting for the embers to die, No-Lie brushed out the ash with the palm of his hand and tenderly replaced the stones in the bag after examining each in turn, as if in search of further revelations from his Tomaniwus. Then he picked up a smaller bag that had lain unnoticed on the mat, fingering it speculatively and making as if to open it, pausing with finger on draw string. Jim was fascinated, but made no sound as No-Lie eyed him intently. He knew that the Indians practiced a species of necromancy, but he had never taken much stock in it, and here he was falling under the sway of a superstitious savage. He shook himself angrily, but the small bag still drew him irresistibly.

No-Lie muttered to himself, evidently deliberating as to whether he should reveal the contents of the second bag. Jim held his breath in his tense interest, though he dared not utter a word to hasten the Indian's decision, lest he should withhold his confidence.

"You go find-um Multnomah?" No-Lie asked, explosively, pausing in his fingering of the bag. "You no tell? You swear-um? You do like what No-Lie say?"

"I'll go, No-Lie; I'll do just as you say," Jim promised under the strange influence of his eye, but, recovering himself, he instantly regretted his hasty decision. He had made a promise that he realized, too late, must be kept. The Indian holds a vow sacred and scorns its violator. He had walked straight into the trap that No-Lie had so neatly baited for him. "I'll go," he repeated, "but if you've lied to me about the white girl I'll simply annihilate you when I get back. I'll sift this thing clear to the bottom if it takes all summer."

Without a word No-Lie opened the bag and handed the contents to Jim, a small package done up carefully in a sheet of paper torn from a large notebook or ledger. On its face it bore the rose with the three wavy lines underneath drawn delicately with black ink.

Jim untied the hempen cord, and in the palm of his hand lay a small white linen nightcap and a piece of creamy printed wool delaine bearing a delicate design of small pink rosebuds and green leaves. Of just such material the Sunday dresses of the girls at home were made. Too astonished to speak, he turned them over and over in his sunburnt hand. The nightcap was hemmed with infinitesimal stitches and edged with narrow thread lace. Some fastidious woman had made it, of that he was certain; here was no hint of Indian workmanship.

The fragment of woolen stuff appeared to have been cut from the ruffle of a dress; the scallops were intact and bound with narrow black silk. This, too, showed dainty stitching.

Jim stood like one transfixed, while No-Lie looked on solemnly. He was for the moment back in Cambridge and it was a Sunday morning in spring. The girls were coming into church in high-waisted dresses made of just such wool delaine, the flounces bound with black silk.

He returned the pathetic little trifles to the bag and deposited it tenderly in the bosom of his blue flannel shirt. He was glad now that he had promised to search for Multnomah. Surely, surely she existed.

No-Lie was business-like at once. "No tell-um when go," he promised. "You fix-um swap pack. Hunt-um flowa. No tell-um Indian you hunt white girl," No-Lie admonished as he turned to leave the lodge.

Briar was waiting patiently outside and, shouldering his pack after making his little gifts to the squaws assembled at a safe distance from the tepee, he strode off toward home through the sweet evening, entirely forgetting that he had set out to bring in a deer and some geese.

CHAPTER FOUR

NO-LIE MAKES
TEN DAYS' MEDICINE

W HEN Jim Faxon announced at Fort William that he
intended to spend the summer on a fur-trading expedition, a loud derisive laugh went up. "You'll get a lot of beaver
skins, yes, you will," they sneered. "We're on to you. You're going
off root-digging. There's no holding a 'grass man' when the dai-
sies are blooming," the superintendent laughed.

Jim was accustomed to their banter and quietly ignored it.
"Well," he said, slowly, "the Indians before now have sold peltries
to me when they turned their backs on you smart traders. There's
a possibility of bringing in a few skins. Why should I loaf around
here all summer? I'll probably be back in a couple of months.
There's time to get things in shape after that before the *May
Dacre* sails for home."

Jim's thrust about their failure to secure skins struck home.
He had, through his friendliness to the Indians, become their
most successful trader, securing good peltries where the red
men had turned an insulting back upon the other agents of Fort
William.

He paid no attention to their asides and the covert sneers of
the company's men when he announced his thinly veiled intention of spending the summer on a botanizing expedition. He
would fulfill his obligation to the Columbia River Fishing and
Trading Company at the same time, so there could be no valid

objection. Captain Wyeth, when in residence at Fort William, encouraged the botanists—he was interested in flowers and birds himself—but the main body of his company had made Jim the butt of ridicule, not because of his lack of bravery, but because they recognized that he was different from the ordinary workaday type. The dreamer always pays dearly for the privilege of dreaming.

There were cries of "Let me go with you," in assumed eagerness from a dozen of the jokers in unison. "I'll tote in yer beaver skins fer ye," burly Tom Hankins announced.

"Thanks, I'm going alone," Jim quietly told them.

There was a significant tapping of foreheads at his announcement, but under their chaff there was a forced admiration. Bravery was a quality they respected, and "grass men" had an uncanny fearlessness. Not a man among them would have dared venture out alone to trade with the Indians.

"You can't go alone," the superintendent said, doubtfully. "I'll detail six or eight men for a three months' trip up the Willamette Valley."

"I intend to go alone," Jim reiterated, and his tone carried conviction. "Captain Wyeth left Bang-up for me to ride this summer and I'll take a pack horse and all the goods the two can carry. The furs can be cached and sent for later, or else I'll bargain with the Indians for delivery at the fort."

"I hate to risk Bang-up; he'll sell for a good price this fall," the superintendent demurred. "He's worth ten of those ornery cayuses."

"I'll be responsible to Captain Wyeth," Jim rejoined, and nothing more was said.

Jim's declaration sobered his taunters. Much as they poked fun at the naturalists, they admired bravery when they encountered it. To go fearlessly into a hostile Indian camp was a supreme test of courage to which they were not equal. They could not comprehend the bond of sympathy between the red men who were children of nature and the gentle students of animal and plant life. They had marveled when a haughty Indian brought some rare specimen for Nuttall's collection.

To the consternation of the factor at the Hudson's Bay Company, David Douglas, the eminent English botanist, had insisted upon going up to the falls of the Multnomah River without a guard in 1825, when the Indians were quarreling over the fishing concessions. This was an unheard-of risk. No party had ever before ascended the river without an armed guard of at least sixty men, but Douglas had been well received and aided in his explorations by all the tribes.

Dr. Townsend had been rather more cautious, always going well armed, but had never met with disaster. He complained to the chiefs about the onslaughts of the mongrel dogs that infested their camps, and threatened to shoot them if they molested him. After that there was a stir in the villages at his approach, and cries of, "Iskam kahmooks, iskam kahmooks; kalak'alak tie chahko" ("Take up your dogs, take up your dogs; the Bird Chief is coming.")

The unmerciful chaffing went on, but there was a set to Jim Faxon's jaw that brooked no opposition. His spring pruning of the orchard and the gardening were finished. They admitted that there was nothing to hold him at the fort, but still the disapproval of his going off alone was general.

"Where are you going, Jim?" the superintendent asked; but Jim was evasive. He had no intention of giving his destination, and, anyway, he was not just sure of it himself, though he had gathered from No-Lie that the Nehalem people lived somewhere near the ocean.

Jim spent a happy week collecting the trading supplies. He took six feet of the twisted rope of Brazilian tobacco hanging in the storehouse, and gathered up all the small nails and bits of iron from about the forge in the blacksmith shop. Coarse blankets, beads, mirrors and flat disks of pierced copper, nose and ear ornaments, and a few cheap knives and brass bells made up his stock, not forgetting a quantity of vermilion to enhance the charms of the Indian belles. With his books and paper for field notes and the ever-present botanical press, this was all two horses could safely carry, for ammunition is heavy and he must take enough to carry him through the entire summer.

He was in the habit of pasturing his horses on the mainland near Jed Withers' cabin, so he carried his pack over and left it in Auxica's keeping. In a week his preparations were made; he was now waiting anxiously for the appearance of No-Lie with his traveling instructions, but the old Indian did not arrive. Nearly a month passed on leaden feet; the men at the fort were sneering covertly and still he lingered.

Could it be that No-Lie was living up to the name he had earned and had never had the least intention of telling him where to find Multnomah? He spent hours picking the ridiculous story apart, alternating between entire disbelief and then on looking at the bit of wool delaine and the nightcap in the buckskin bag, declaring to himself that he would get at the truth of the absurd story if it cost him his life.

"You wait-um. No-Lie come soon," Auxica comforted as he impatiently cooled his heels in her cabin. "Moon of leaves [May] not gone. You come Nehalem in moon of berries [June]. No-Lie heap big *shaman* [medicine-man]. Him know ever't'ing."

Excursions to the woods after specimens and hunting were resorted to to fill time. A week, two weeks passed, and no No-Lie. The delay was becoming too hard for Jim Faxon. Time was precious and it was passing with nothing accomplished. If Multnomah existed in the first place, she might be dead before he could reach her. His usual cheerful grin had died a lingering death, due to the eating out of his soul by waiting and the constant questioning from the *attachés* at the fort. "Where ye going, Jim, and when're ye starting?" was hurled at him from all sides. He could only shake his head and tell them with a levity he was far from feeling that he would steal off 'most any day now.

Waiting wore Jim Faxon nearly out. Time was precious if there was really a white girl to be found. He was on the point of worming as much as he could out of Auxica and making an effort to find the Nehalems.

Jed was fully as perplexed. "Ef Auxica sez they air a white gal among her tribe I'll take her word on't. Me, I never onct heerd o' them thar Nehalems, and I bin over this kentry right smart. She sez they're sort o' cut off from airy other tribe hereabouts, but they're all Chinooks. An' Injun air secret about his doin's, an' hit's best not to take airy chanct o' gittin' mixed up in their bizness. Close-mouthed they be, but mostly friendly ter trappers. I aim ter keep a shut face abouten this here ter-do. I hain't got no call ter take a hand inter their affairs. Auxica air a good wife ter me."

"There is no reason against my going among them to trade if I keep my mouth shut and my eyes open, is there?" Jim inquired.

Jed spat reflectively into the fire and shifted his enormous quid to his other cheek before he spoke. "No, there haint, but you-all 'ill come out no wiser nor when ye went in, ef they got ten white wimmen livin' down thar. Go on, sonny; ye'll likely git some good skins. So fur as I know, no trader air ever mixed with them thar Nehalems."

But Auxica was obdurate. "You no find Multnomah, you go now," she warned him over and over. "My people keel you, t'ink you hunt-um white girl. Soon No-Lie come. He off making medicine, make talk to Tomaniwus."

But just as he had decided to go on his own the next morning, No-Lie stood in his cabin door. But a sadly changed No-Lie. His hair, which he always wore smoothly braided and anointed with an evil-smelling viscid pomade expressed from the seeds of the wild cucumber, *Micrampelis fabacea,* hung matted about his shoulders. His buckskins, usually so immaculately chalked, were unbelievably soiled and hung in dank folds about his emaciated body. His moccasins, worn to shreds, were hanging to his torn and bleeding feet by the thongs that bound them to his bony ankles.

"You 'fraid, Jim Faxon," he greeted his host in a voice faint from weakness. "You go now to Nehalem country, find-um Multnomah?"

"Starting in the morning," Jim assured him, joyfully.

But No-Lie sank down by the hearth in utter weariness, and, suspecting that he was hungry, Jim hastily stirred the fire and set a generous bannock to bake over the coals, at the same time broiling a venison steak. He made strong tea and placed the meal before No-Lie. The gaunt Indian wolfed the hot food, then took the pipe of tobacco Jim handed him.

There was not a word spoken until the food had strengthened him and the tobacco soothed him.

"You 'fraid?" he asked, anxiously again. "Trouble in Nehalem county. Heap much war. You go find Multnomah, mebbe my people keel. Multnomah plenty much hard for find."

"I'm not afraid. If there's a white woman among your people I will bring her home with me, or die trying," Jim said as his jaw set in a rigid line.

"Ugh!" No-Lie grunted in approval, shrugging a pair of thin shoulders. "Now me show. Ten sleeps me no eat. Me no sleep. Make medicine. All time ask Tomaniwus. Tomaniwus say Jim Faxon find Multnomah." He assumed an attitude. "Heap big shaman me.

"Me no lie. You take-um Indian tlail. Auxica show-um. Ten sleeps you go. Mebbe twenty sleeps. You pick-um flowa. You kill-um meat. Long time you come wycoma [ocean]. You see-um heap big mountain out in water. Mountain, home of piah [fire] Tomaniwus. My people call Neah-Kah-Nie mountain. There lodge of Nehalems, my people.

"You no tlust Indian. Make-um show sign." He drew the rose with the three wavy lines underneath just as Auxica had done.

"Katoosh, him *tyee shaman* [chief medicine-man]. Him send Indian for meet you."

Jim looked at him incredulously. "Did you send a messenger to your people?" he asked. The delay could easily have been occasioned by No-Lie's waiting for the return of his emissary.

The old Indian was angry. "Me no lie," he declared, emphatically. "Me no go to Nehalem countly. Me no send Indian. Me make medicine. Me tell Katoosh in dleam after me no eat, no sleep."

Jim was eager to hear more, but No-Lie arose in great dignity, preparing to take his leave. "Me no named No-Lie. Cultus [no good] white man call-um No-Lie. T'ink-um Indian lie. T'ink-um Indian steal. Me named Yallup." His voice betrayed his resentment.

Jim followed him to the door, loath to allow him to leave without hearing more about Multnomah, but No-Lie changed the subject abruptly. "Cultee him cultus Indian, steal-um six ponies. Keep-um Wopcelia. Wopcelia heap smart squaw. Cultee find-um tlouble." There was a gleam of humor in his shrewd black eyes.

Jim was puzzled and angry as he stood alone in the cabin after No-Lie's abrupt departure. If only an Indian would come out in the open like a white man and tell all the truth. He strode after the old man, intending to question him further, but gained nothing.

"Auxica show-um tlail. Auxica skooum [wise or valiant] squaw." He tottered from weakness, but with a grunt of farewell started off down the path.

Well, that was that. Jim set about putting his cabin in order preparatory to making a very early start in the morning. He would be miles on his way before the inquisitive men at Fort William were about. No reason for allowing them to conjecture his destination. They had assumed that he was going up the Willamette Valley, and he had not corrected their impression.

CHAPTER FIVE
THE ANCIENT INDIAN ROAD

J IM reached Jed Withers' cabin about three in the morning. Auxica was bustling about, but Jed turned sleepily in his bunk as he entered. The papoose had also risen and was taking a lively interest in affairs.

Auxica had prepared to take a journey. The cabin shone from its recent scouring and there was a quantity of food in readiness to tide her lord over until her return.

"You going with me, Auxica?" Jim was pleasantly surprised. He had expected that she would lead him for a few miles and then give him his directions.

"Me show-um tlail. Go one sun. Come back one sun." She was packing a bundle tightly and securing it about her waist with a cleverly constructed buckskin thong. The papoose had graduated from his cradle-board. She secured him in his elkskin harness astride her back and went for the horses.

"Take keer o' yerself, Jim," was Jed's farewell from the bunk. "Auxica hain't nobody's fool at locatin' trails. I'd trust thet thar squaw with my life, any time. She's right peart. Nothin' ever gits by her. Hope ye work out thet thar puzzlement, Jim," he turned over to resume his sleep.

Briar sat waiting anxiously while the horses were being packed. Jim was undecided about taking her, but at the last moment he relented as he looked in her sad eyes. At his whistle her joy burst all bounds; she gamboled ahead with a frantically wagging tail.

Auxica led the way in complete silence. She had scarcely spoken that morning. Furtively she made a wide détour to avoid the Indian camps in the vicinity. She evidently intended to keep the matter of Jim's destination a secret from the Indians.

"You wait-um." She handed the horse's lead rope to Jim and went ahead to pick up the trail. The first rosy fingers of light were pointing up the sky. Tethering the horses, Jim gave himself over to a rapturous hour of dreaming, awed by the solemn beauty of the approaching sunrise. Birds murmured sleepily in the near-by copse of dogwood trees, and the aroma of dew-drenched flowers filled the still air.

A little below, a bank of mist tinted to rose and mauve by the first rays of the sun raveled upward in thin wisps. Against this ethereal background he painted a picture, Multnomah, as she existed in his imagination, a slender girl clothed in soft bright buckskin, with light tangled in her yellow hair. He was in the first vigor of young manhood, and today, he told himself, shyly, he was starting on his love quest. If he never found the object of his dreams, and in a workaday world that was a great deal to hope for, at least he would always carry the vision in his heart.

Panting from her struggle with the matted vine maple, Auxica returned and, taking her horse, led the way with unerring instinct up a slope where the going was tedious and difficult. With a grunt of satisfaction she at last picked up an almost obliterated Indian trail leading westward. They traveled in silence for a couple of hours in single file. Once the Indian woman stopped and listened, motioning to Jim to halt.

In a few moments a small company of squaws passed along the trail, the camass hooks over their shoulders. They were chattering and laughing among themselves like children on an outing, and so went by without noticing them. But Auxica waited until they were well around the bend in the trail before they resumed their journey.

"Squaws all time wa-wa [talk]," she grunted, disgustedly. She placed her hand over her mouth with a decisive gesture.

Sometimes they lost the way entirely and Auxica was forced to reconnoiter, but she picked it up with uncanny precision. Young Jed Withers, unaccustomed to such extensive traveling, whimpered. She nursed him by throwing a pendulous breast over her shoulder.

By noon they reached the summit of a ridge of hills, pausing to rest by a rill that tumbled from a steep bank. Without exchanging a word they ate the bannocks that Jim had baked at his fireside the night before, and some strips of dried fish that Auxica took from her pack. Content stole over Jim as they rested, a content marred somewhat by Auxica's sullen mood. Would the obstinate creature never speak? There were questions he longed to ask but wisely forbore!

Two hours more of strenuous going over a tortuous bush-tangled path and Auxica emitted a huge grunt of satisfaction. Stretched before them on the crest of the ridge was an ancient road, an Indian road that generations of moccasined feet had made. There were but few of these highways in the Indian country. The red man does not explore unknown territory unless driven thereto in the search for food. All the arteries of travel converged in the fertile valley of the Multnomah river, which teemed with salmon, with wappatoos and camass filling the lowlands and sloughs.

The Indian is an engineer in road-building. He chooses the easiest grade in the ascent of mountains, by a natural instinct going through the passes, but keeps invariably to the ridges. He has a sound reason for this—trees fall downhill, so his highway is always comparatively clear. An occasional tree across his path does not disturb him; he walks around it, so after a few centuries the thoroughfare becomes tortuous.

There are other reasons for elevated roadways. From the hilltop the Indian can keep a sharp lookout for his enemies and is always in a position to resist attack. Then, too, the valleys and lowlands are marshy in places. His highway never threads through a plain unless the necessity is absolute.

In most of its length this road was wide enough to admit of six horses traveling abreast, and, where the soil was sandy, worn down to as much as six feet below the surface, but packed like macadam with the constant travel. Even projecting roots of trees along the sides were worn smooth by the friction of the moccasin.

Jim estimated that they must have made between fifteen and twenty miles, and yet the sun was not more than three hours on its western descent. Trust a fat lumbering squaw with her shambling loose-kneed gait to eat up the miles and yet not appear to be making very remarkable progress. The steady going, going, looking to neither the right nor the left, unless an unusual sound strikes the ear, is the secret of covering distance.

The way was smooth and open; the whole country lay below them; to the south the enchanted plains of Tuality, its half-ripened grasses shimmering greenish-gold in the mid-afternoon heat; farther south a smooth velvet carpet so darkly green as to appear black; in the shadowy folds stretched mile after mile of unbroken Douglas fir forest blending remotely with the serried horizon in a luminous purple haze. To the northward tantalizing bits of the blue Columbia glimmered through gaps in the trees.

Jim was for pausing to admire the view and had in mind descending a few feet down the north side of the slope, where a large colony of *Erythronium parviflorum*, the graceful avalance lily, or dogtooth violet, nodded a welcome to him. Again he saw in fancy the girl Multnomah standing among them; she smiled and waved there among the lilies. The girl had spent her life among the flowers, in all probability. The Indians had a name for every wayside plant; of course she had learned them all and she would tell him of the blooms she loved. But the vision wrought upon his senses by the exotic perfume wafted on an idle breeze was rudely dispelled by Auxica's angry jerking on the lead rope. She had a destination in mind and would on no account pause until it was reached.

Jim, half angry, plodded on behind her for another half hour, when Auxica turned abruptly off the road into a grassy glen sheltered by a copse of salmon-berry bushes higher than a man's head. With a single motion she tethered Bang-up to a sapling, unstrapped the weary young Jed Withers and set him on the grass, then threw the pack at her waist on the ground. Eyeing her, Jim decided that she intended to make camp. Not for the world would he have questioned her. He tethered his pony, a mean bit of cayuse horseflesh who rejoiced in the name of Early Piety and was called Pite for short. If this was her mood when traveling, he secretly thanked his lucky stars that she declined to accompany him farther.

Slowly unwrapping her pack, Auxica spread the blanket on the ground and placed its contents upon it. Jim was rather surprised with the objects that lay revealed. She was sorting them with her back turned rudely toward him. At last she turned, holding in her hands a length of screeching red calico pied with what Jim took to be enormous yellow squashes, just such yardage as the Hudson's Bay Company kept for their Indian trade. She had a strand of gay beads, a small knife, and a set of copper nose and ear ornaments.

"You give-um mamma." She broke her day-long silence by handing them to him. "Soon you see-um mamma. Mamma t'ink Auxica memaloose [dead]. Tell-um 'bout papoose. Him so beeg." She made measurement with her two hands to indicate little Jed's height. "Jed Withers. You tel-um mamma ever't'ing."

Relieved that Auxica's taciturn mood had passed, Jim placed the gauds near his pack. Her tongue loosened at last, she was going to give him his traveling directions.

"You know kloske [good] Indian. You know cultus [bad] Indian?" she queried. "Some Indian you trust. Some Indian you no trust. You shut-um mouth. You open eye. You open ear. No trouble. My people make kap-swal-la [honest]. No lie. No steal. No keel. Cultus Indian in evely tlibe."

Just like a squaw, Jim thought, angrily. Refuse to utter a syllable for half a day and then spend an hour moralizing on the perfectly obvious. Auxica had nothing of importance to tell him, after all.

"Tell me about Multnomah before you go," Jim implored. "How did the Nehalems find her? Did she have people? Are they all dead?" In his eagerness he poured out a torrent of questions. "No-Lie wouldn't tell me a thing about Multnomah and I asked him over and over. You must tell me."

Auxica turned her attention to the papoose, taking him on her knee and crooning an Indian cradle song to him, though he showed no signs of sleep.

Jim tried again. "Will this road lead all the way to the lodge of your people?"

"No," she answered, curtly. "Him stop-um when la-mon-tai [mountains] stop. Then you see-um tlail. Katoosh send-um Indian. Him show sign. You know-um. Kum-tux [understand]? You safe on oo-e-hut [road]. Mebbe you trade. You make-um potlatch [gift]. On trail, no can trust. Use-um eye. Use-um ear. No use-um mouth. No eat Indian muck-a-much [food]. Kum-tux?"

She spoke rapidly, as if in great agitation, lapsing unconsciously into Chinook, a thing he had never before known her to do. Her vanity over her command of the English language was amusing. She had a habit of enunciating as if each word held a sweet hidden flavor that she desired to prolong on her tongue.

She averted her face, busying herself with rolling her pack and fastening it on her back. She set the papoose in his saddle on her shoulders, taking an unnecessarily long time for the trifling business. If Jim had not known Indians he would have been sure she was crying, but the face that she turned to him at last was composure itself.

She was going, with none of his questions answered. "Who is Katoosh?" he asked in a last effort to draw her out? "How am I to know him?"

"You mind-um business. You know Katoosh when see. You know-um Auxica's mamma when time come." She scowled angrily. "You 'flaid," she taunted in scorn. "Kwass, kwass [coward]." She fairly spat the words at him. Kwass is the deadliest insult an Indian can hurl.

Jim Faxon flinched as if she had struck him, his eyes fairly blazing in his white angry face. "I've had just enough of this Indian foolishness, beating about the bush and making a dead secret of every trivial thing you know and do! You and No-Lie you're two of a kind. I don't believe a word you say about a white girl down in your God-forsaken country. If I didn't know you were my friend I'd say you were baiting a neat little trap for me and that I am deliberately walking into it. But what your object is in sending me off into your country I damn well can't figure out. If you've been making a fool of me, I'll beat the living camass out of old No-Lie and fill his worthless old hide full of buckshot and tack it on the side of Fort William, when I come back."

He was fairly out of breath with his tirade. While he was about it he intended to tell Auxica what he thought of her, too, but he chanced to look her full in the face after his flash of blind wrath.

She was holding her fat sides with her two hands, and as he stared at her peal after peal of wild elfin laughter escaped her. She fairly shrieked in her unholy glee. When recovered sufficiently to speak, she said in the casual tone of one bidding a friend goodbye, "You tell-um Multnomah Auxica send husband to her."

Before Jim could answer she was off through the thicket on a jog trot, papoose and all.

He paused for a moment, too astonished to comprehend what had happened, then wave after wave of hot shame surged over him. He had been a cad. He had relaxed into the nasty vernacular of the mountain men. He had used profanity before a gentlewoman. No matter if her skin was coppery instead of white, there was no excusing his action. He had mistreated a woman who had been heavenly kind to him. And, in a way, he did believe their story; at least he took enough stock in it to go off alone at the risk of his life to make an investigation.

He was always full of contrition after a mad outburst. Now he stood uncertainly contemplating hurrying after Auxica to beg her pardon. She was a kind woman, kind as his own mother in taking care of him, and he had wounded her. The bushes parted and Auxica's drawn face peered forth.

"Jim Faxon"—her voice was a moan of anguish wrung from a tortured soul—"you come back Fort William. You forget-um Multnomah. You hunt, trade in Umpqua country. Me show-um tlail."

"No, Auxica, if Multnomah exists, I'm going to find her. I couldn't go home this fall with the belief that a white woman was living in misery somewhere in the Oregon country and I had made no effort to bring her to her people."

Auxica made a queer guttural sound deep in her throat, muttering words in her native tongue, a tongue no white man will ever learn in its entirety. She held out her hand. Jim pressed it silently, his face working.

"I'll always be sorry I spoke angrily to you, Auxica," he said, contritely. "You've been a good friend to me. If I do not come back, tell the story to the superintendent at Fort William and see that he sends word to my mother."

"You come back after long time, Jim Faxon," Auxica assured him, gently. "No-Lie make medicine. Ask Tomaniwus. You come back some day. Me t'ink mebbe you find Multnomah. No can tell."

She backed off a step or two, then raised her two hands above his head just as a minister does in benediction, speaking strange words that Jim knew instinctively were an agony of prayer for his safety.

A tired, bent old squaw, bearing the heavy burden of her race on her back, tottered down through the underbrush.

48

CHAPTER SIX
A BIT OF DEVILTRY

JIM hastened to make camp for the night after Auxica left. He was, for the moment, rather perplexed and uneasy. He had confidently expected to have the whole story of Multnomah and full details of the situation in the country of the Nehalems, and yet, here he was committed to a rather hazardous adventure among an unknown tribe without the least foreknowledge to guide his actions.

As he viewed the ludicrous situation, he laughed aloud and hoped that no inkling of the story ever reached the men at Fort William. What a capital joke they would make of it! But he sobered a little, recalling Auxica's offer to guide him into the little-explored Umpqua country to the south, where good peltries could be secured. Auxica had, at the last, weakened, a rare thing for an Indian woman; she feared for his safety, or, he reasoned, perhaps she repented of her part in baiting a trap for an innocent and well-meaning white man. But what object could No-Lie have in luring him into the Nehalem country? Jim could see no reason except the one the Indian offered—to bring the white girl out. He could not for a moment entertain the thought that there was treachery afoot.

No-Lie was known for sharp dickering and for his preposterous stories, but when it came to keeping his word he was the soul of honor. And try as he would, Jim could not find it in his heart to doubt Auxica. And the two were agreed. Surely there was something in their story.

Reason told him to dismiss once and for all the fantastic hope of finding a white woman in the remote wilds, and blind intuition bade him go on and make the search.

As if searching for a clue, Jim examined the scrap of wool delaine and the dainty linen nightcap. Could No-Lie in some way have gotten them from a trapper or trader who carried these tender mementoes to solace his lonely days? Possible but hardly probable. A rough man who cherished such sentiment would have taken the utmost precaution to conceal the fact from his jocose fellows. Such a trophy would have been soiled by much handling, and while the nightcap was yellowed with age to an old ivory, it bore no evidence of having come in contact with grimy hands.

And was it coincidence that the wrapper bore a delicate pen-and-ink drawing of the wild rose with the three wavy lines beneath? He could hardly believe that the sign they had seen on the alder trees and the sketch here were the work of some mountaineer.

How could a white girl have reached the coast without the knowledge of some trapper or trader? News travels rapidly in an isolated country and even faint rumors persist for years.

A white woman or girl among the Indians east of the Rockies would be within the range of possibility. St. Louis was a thriving trading-post, and already white settlers with their families were pushing westward. The fear of abduction was a very real one to women and children. The Indians of that region often stole white children and brought them up in their tribe, concealing them so carefully that they were almost never traced.

But the Rocky Mountains barred intertribal relations between the plains tribes and the Pacific coast Indians so there was not the faintest possibility of the Nehalems having secured a white child by purchase or capture.

The territory of the Nehalems bordered on the ocean. Could Multnomah have been washed ashore from some wrecked vessel?

But this idea, too, had to be dismissed as he reasoned upon it. White men might have survived wrecks—there were unfounded rumors of Englishmen who had spent their lives here as castaways. But seafaring men did not take their women and children with them when they set out on whaling and fur-trading voyages. The Pacific Ocean was infested with Spanish pirates. No sane man would risk the lives of his womenfolk on its treacherous uncharted waters. Jim felt perfectly safe in assuming that the girl Multnomah had not come in by way of the sea.

So far only two white women had set foot on the Oregon coast. Jane Barnes—he smiled at the recollection of the story as he had heard it recounted so many times. Jane Barnes, the adventuress, had been a lively barmaid at an inn in Portsmouth. She had sailed from England in 1812 as the mistress of one of the mates of the *Isaac Todd,* bound for Fort George, as Astoria was renamed by the British.

This blue-eyed, yellow-haired daughter of Albion had attracted considerable attention among the Indians, who flocked around her, fingering her clothing and admiring her hair and eyes. She had fled precipitately to China when the son of Concomly, the principal chief of the Chinooks came to the fort attired in his richest dress, his face fancifully bedaubed with red paint and his body redolent with whale oil, and insisted upon taking her for his head wife. He had four already.

Jane had liked China. An English gentleman connected with the East India Company had offered her a place in his establishment, and no doubt she was still living there at her ease. But perhaps Auxica had gotten her idea of blue eyes and yellow hair from seeing or hearing of Jane Barnes. Only twelve or thirteen years had passed, and the memory would be one long cherished by the Indians. Strange that he had not thought of this before. Indian imagination could construct a vivid picture of a white girl from the memory of a blue-eyed, flaxen-haired Englishwoman.

The minister of the Church of England, Herbert Beaver, had come with his wife, Jane Beaver, to minister to the spiritual needs of Fort Vancouver last fall. Jane Beaver had not liked the country, either. Jim had never seen her, as she had held herself haughtily aloof. The Beavers were planning to return to England at the first opportunity. The white women on the Pacific were all accounted for in Jim's mind. Multnomah had no existence, and he must accept the fact now that the evidence was all gone over.

Once on the way, he realized that he was foolhardy to attempt to go into the Nehalem country. Who were the Nehalems, anyway? Jed Withers had never heard of them, and he had been in Oregon ten or twelve years and knew every inch of the territory.

Jed had conjectured that they were some remote branch of the great Cinookan family. The very word Multnomah attested their origin. A small tribe of Chinooks bore that name, and then there was the Multnomah river, lately renamed Willamette by the Hudson's Bay Company.

A small clan might easily go aside and become detached from the main body of their people by geographical barriers. Indians are singularly reticent about tribal affairs, and traders were not in the least interested, so Nehalems might be numerous enough and still not be known as such. The coast Indians were known as the Tillamooks and, as near as Jim could make out, Nehalem was somewhere in their country. He felt a large curiosity in regard to them.

He did some hard thinking that night, but could reach no conclusion, so decided to sleep on the problem and decide whether to abandon his foolish quest and return to Fort William, or follow the will-o'-the-wisp and satisfy himself once and for all about Multnomah. The latter plan intrigued him, though he felt no violation of his promise in returning, in the face of the failure of its sponsors to furnish him sufficient information to warrant the venture. He felt somehow that both No-Lie and Auxica would be secretly relieved at his coming home.

"O-ka-lee, o-ka-lee," sang the blackbird from the thicket; the flash of red under his wings as he flew was like a tongue of flame in the morning sun. Silver-gray squirrels were up and about their business when Jim woke, and before him the Indian road stretched like a ribbon of delight. He was going to the Nehalem country in search of Multnomah. He knew that before he was fully awake. What if Multnomah *did not* exist? He was going.

Why should any man harbor black anxiety in his heart alone in the forest? He laughed at his trepidation of the night before. So long as he kept out of Indian politics—and he had never had a taste for interfering in the affairs of others—he was as safe in the Indian country as in a New England church on a calm Sunday morning. He came in friendship and in friendship he would be received.

He had long since come to understand and in a way respect the Indians. He recalled with a smile Nat Wyeth's assertion that out of twenty white men more downright rascals could be taken than from a thousand natives.

Nature was in a gentle mood when she made the Coast Range; the mountains here are not like the Cascades, all tortuous bluffs and crowning crags, but just low rounded hills, one gracious swell with a valley-like depression through which runs a sparkling stream and then another undulating slope. Jim reached the summit on the fifth day of his leisurely traveling. He imagined that the air was different and the streams whose course had been northerly now seemed to be running uphill.

He could not resist exploring each stream. Alder trees shaded the banks and it was on alder trees that Multnomah's sign had been found. Odd that he could not relinquish the hope of coming onto some faint trace of the white girl. But the trees yielded no sign.

He met but few Indians, and these were on the march to the berry fields on the west slopes of Mount Hood, or to the camass and wappatoo beds on the sloughs of the Columbia. They were friendly; the process of shaking hands with every man, woman, and child was tedious, but they offered him roots and herbs, salmon pemmican, and jerked venison, in exchange for trifles from his pack.

When he inquired for beaver skins they shook regretful heads; their catches had been sold long before, but they were effusive in promises to trade at Fort William the next season. The trip did not promise much in the way of financial gain. The Hudson's Bay Company were too securely intrenched in the Indian heart to admit of a rival company gaining a foothold.

Early one morning Jim came upon a camp of Indians. Long before he sighted them around the bend of the road the commotion told him of some disaster. From the wailing of the squaws he took it to be death or illness.

His fame had gone before him. The wailing ceased as they caught sight of him, and cries of "Kloske tipso squintum" ["Good grass man"] went up. A lane cleared for him as the milling men, women, and dogs stood aside. An old squaw sat with a naked child on her knees, a quivering child who had just been trampled by a horse. With the pity and the helplessness that he always felt at the sight of human suffering, Jim knelt and ran his hands carefully over the little body to determine the extent of the injuries, just as he had often seen Dr. Townsend do in the trip across the plains. There were numerous contusions, but no indications of internal injury.

One leg was broken between the thigh and the knee. In rapid Chinook he asked for hot water and, taking a cake of soap from his kit, gave the baby what was in all probability his first warm bath. He set the leg carefully and bound it with hastily made splints. He had often helped the doctor and knew what to do in a case of simple fracture. For the want of liniment he covered the bruises with wet clay from a near-by spring and bound them with clean buckskin. Eased, the little one slipped off to sleep.

Jim stopped long enough to give careful instructions for caring for the child and to help prepare a travois to trail behind a pony so that he could travel in a recumbent position, then passed on, carrying an embarrassing shower of gifts and blessings from the whole assemblage.

He grinned sheepishly as he went. If the child did well, his reputation as a *shaman* was assured, but should he die, he would probably be hunted out and dealt with, such was Indian nature. A sudden parallel smote him, such was human nature.

No, this trip did not promise even a thrill of danger, not that he courted danger, nor wished for thrills or hair-breadth escapes. He had had plenty of that in crossing the continent. Recalling his most narrow escape from death in the country of the Blackfeet, he shuddered. He had wandered off on horseback in search of meat for the camp, when three murderous savages came yelling upon him. To provide a defense he had been forced to stab his horse in the neck with his hunting-knife, jumping clear as the faithful animal fell, and shooting from behind the defense offered by his dead body. He had killed two of the Indians, and the third had beaten a hasty retreat after wounding him in the shoulder with an arrow.

Killing and gloating over the untimely end of his enemies was never to his liking. He went in peace. He was a "grass man." He killed only for food or in defense of his life, and remained silent and regretful over the necessity.

Search as he did, he found no sign of Multnomah on the alder trees. Afterward he regretted having made no inquiry among the Indians whose child he had befriended about the Nehalems, but perhaps it was just as well. Auxica had warned him to keep his mouth shut and his eyes open on the road.

The road began to fade out toward the end of the tenth day, showing a tendency to divide into numerous puzzling trails. He was sure, from the time he had occupied in his journey and from changes in the flora of the country, that he was nearing the ocean. The failing of the road gave him but little concern. He decided to bear a little to the north and then come down the coast, thus making sure of his destination. He took no stock in No-Lie's promise that an Indian would be sent from the Nehalem country to meet him.

Early one afternoon Jim made camp. He had a number of specimens that he must mount, and there were little matters needing his attention. He must not run the risk of illness through a too constant meat diet. He gathered a quantity of woolly lamb's-quarters, humble member of the *Chenopodiaceæ,* or pigweed family, boiling them for "greens" in his iron pot, while he prepared a salad of *Montia parviflora,* the "cow cabbage" or miner's lettuce.

On a sunny hillside late strawberries were ripening. He gathered nearly a quart. What a granary of good things the forest was, and yet men had nearly starved to death in the summer because they had no knowledge of the plants that could be used for food! A man might subsist here even through the winter, and come out in spring enormously hungry but nowhere near the starvation point, if he but knew roots and herbs.

Filled with peace after his dinner, he felt no particular hurry about making his preparation for the night. He had hobbled the horses and tethered them to graze near his fire. He smoked contentedly, watching the stars prick out one by one to light a dark blue heaven.

When bedtime came, still filled with peace, he decided to leave his packs by the fire, retiring to the shelter of a large maple tree to sleep. The tree would protect him from the heavy dew, and, besides, no sane man would lie down in the circle of light from a rousing camp fire when on the march, even in the country of friendly Indians. He threw on some large pine knots in order to enjoy the effect of the firelight playing against the night. Briar, always the faithful watchdog, took up her station near the horses.

He slept after a time of musing upon the beauties of the trail with its overhanging canopy of green, and brooding rather pensively upon his unfulfilled wish to find some trace of Multnomah. He chided himself over and over for his folly in hoping that a blue-eyed girl lived in this country, and yet he looked for her sign every day and continued his hope.

Briar, wagging a sociable tail, at the same time poking a cold wet muzzle in his face, woke him the next morning.

As was his custom, he first replenished the fire and put on the water to boil for breakfast. He started in astonishment as he chanced to glance at the packs. There beside them lay a bale of beaver skins, neatly corded. Briar, catching Jim's eye, wagged an enthusiastic tail as if expecting to be praised. Thoroughly alarmed, her master turned to look to the horses. They were gone, hobbles, tethers, and all.

Bang-up and Piety—Nat Wyeth's horses—had vanished off the face of the earth without a sound and within twenty feet of where he slept. He, Jim Faxon, trained to mountaineering, had slept while some soft-footed rascal had invaded his camp. And here was Briar, who never allowed a stir without notifying him instantly, wagging her confounded tail, expecting to be praised.

His breakfast forgotten, Jim ran wildly down the side of the hill. Tracks of horses' feet, three of them, were plainly visible in the dewy grass. His had evidently been led behind some one on horseback, for there were no moccasin tracks. Their trail ceased to be visible as they entered the timber. There was small hope of overtaking the thief on foot, even if he were successful in picking up the trail; they may have visited the camp three or four hours ago.

Befuddled, Jim Faxon sat down on the ground to think. His first inclination was to punish Briar. She had failed him, but why? Then he paused to mourn his loss. Bang-up was stolen, the best saddle-horse in the country. He was worth twenty of the ugly-tempered native cayuses. Pite, he did not grieve over. His full name, Early Piety, was not given him by chance; he was known to be the meanest horse in all Christendom.

"If Pite had the power he would go off by himself, and lead Bang-up, just to express his meanness," he told Briar, furiously. "But Piety would never have left a large bale of prime beaver skins by the camp fire, nor yet get away, much as he would have enjoyed doing a dirty trick." Jim shook his head in perplexity. Some one had visited the camp before daybreak, and that some one was clever, mighty clever.

There was nothing to do but sit and swear, which he did until he was sweating with the exertion. Such is the first recourse of the man whose horses escape him. Always has been, always will be.

His unique store of cuss words, which he very seldom used, completely exhausted, he spent twenty minutes in inventing forceful invectives. Some, he felt, were good. He would remember them when he had occasion to swear again.

When he had finished to his complete satisfaction, he rose and set calmly about preparing breakfast, just as if the sun were shining on a Jim Faxon steeped in peace. He made a satisfying meal on jerked venison and wild strawberries.

"Briar, you're one good watchdog, you are," he commented as he gave her the remains of his breakfast. Briar agreed with him. She finished her meal and sauntered off to fill in a few idle moments in digging out a gray squirrel. She had never yet caught one, but never intended to give over the effort.

CHAPTER SEVEN
AN UNEXPECTED
ENCOUNTER

JIM FAXON smoked by his dying breakfast fire for an hour or more, pondering over the deplorable situation in which he found himself. His first impulse had been to go in search of the horse thief at once, but on sober second thought he admitted reluctantly to himself that this would be useless. The packs might be rifled in his absence. He may have been shadowed for days. The coup of his hidden adversary had been carefully planned and admirably executed.

This was clearly Indian work. No white man would have left a bale of prime beaver skins either by accident or by intention. There was no ordinary thieving here. The packs could have been easily taken. He went over and examined them carefully, but there was no indication of their having been molested.

Pressing matters demanded his immediate attention. He did not even attempt to formulate a theory. He must first make a *cache* to protect his goods, and then, if the horses could not be recovered, reluctantly make his way home, and either come himself with fresh horses or send some one to raise the *cache*.

The return would be humiliating. Jim felt equal to the gibes that he would have to parry, but the loss of Bang-up was a real grief to him. He was suddenly a little bitter at fate for dealing him such an unexpected blow. This was of a piece with all the other efforts of the Columbia River Fishing and Trading

Company. Certainly the venture had been launched under an evil star; nothing but loss and misfortune had ever attended the Americans on the Pacific coast. No matter; they were men who had followed their vision. They had struggled and failed honorably. Worse things could happen in life, but for the moment he could not think of them.

Locating a suitable site for the *cache* and preparing it took the remainder of the day. Another day was fully occupied in sorting the packs and carrying the goods the five hundred yards up the hill on his back.

Fresh courage came with the morning. Under a gentle exterior Jim Faxon had a stratum of hard granite in his nature. He habitually clung to his purpose like a crab, unable to loose his hold even when morally certain that the cause was lost. Perhaps, after all, it would be best to continue on his journey to the coast. He judged that at the outside he could not be more than twenty-five miles from his destination. Perhaps only ten or twelve. He had been told that the Coast Range hugged the shore, and that one sometimes, in crossing, glimpsed the surf before realizing that the ocean was near.

A man could easily carry a sixty-pound pack, and Briar, whose negligence had caused this disaster, should bear her share of the burden, though this never before had been required of her. A rangy muscular dog would not suffer under fifty or sixty pounds in traveling such a short distance. There might be an opportunity for trade if he encountered a remote band of Indians.

His selection was a careful one. In sorting the goods he came upon the small package Auxica had sent as a gift to her mother. Rather contemptuously he placed it in his pack, thinking that when he returned he would have a few remarks to make to the Indian woman who had so grossly deceived him. He took all the tobacco and as many trinkets as his load would possibly bear, rather scanting the ammunition on account of its weight. He could easily live on roots and wild vegetation, with berries for dessert, when he had no further means of killing his meat. He stopped once, undecided about carrying his press and the paper for preserving specimens; the pack was intolerably heavy. Yes, the press must go. The flora of the region was strange and interesting. How else could he preserve his record of it?

Two unfruitful days were occupied in the effort to track the horse thief. But not so much as a trace of an Indian encampment could he discover. Climbing to the crest of a knoll, he had an uninterrupted view of the surrounding country, but so far as evidence of human life was concerned he might have been the last human being alive in the world.

The rich plant life amply repaid him for the lost time. He found variations in the habits and form of even the flowers common to the Columbia River region. On a rocky hillside exposed to the afternoon sun grew a distinct variety of shooting-star. He exulted in his find. Nuttall had always maintained that there were four forms of *Dodocatheon* commonly called wild cyclamen or American cowslip. He fairly reveled in the lilies-of-the-valley, *Maianthemum bifolium*, as he chanced upon large colonies in the moist shade when he was scanning the alder trees.

Never had he given over looking on the north side of every alder that he saw, often searching the vicinity where a particularly smooth-barked one spread its ample green branches, or a small cairn of rocks where a message might have been hidden, but never a trace did he find. Being alone for such a stretch of time, he had fallen into the habit of dreaming of the girl Multnomah again, though he told himself he was childish to build castles in Spain when he knew that he had not even the flimsy foundation of a supposition for the underpinning. But the dream that had dimmed in his bitter disappointment at Auxica's failure to provide it sustenance was taking definite form under the spell of the forest.

The heady fragrance shaken from the bells of the lilies-of-the-valley by a vagrant breeze acted as an opiate to his reason.

Multnomah walked by his side through the cool glades, just as she had done on the morning when he set out on his unacknowledged quest of her. He saw her in the wistful pink of the wild bleeding-heart, and her dainty moccasined feet brushed the drops of dew that trembled on the ferny leaves of the meadow-rue. Where was the wrong in enjoying his brief dream? He must come back to the world of stern reality soon enough. Visions were powerless to harm a man if he kept his feet on the ground.

Coming slowly back to his camp near the trail, a thought struck him with the sharp impact of a blow. Suppose, just suppose, there *was* a white girl within twenty-five or even fifty miles of him and he turned back without making an effort to find her. She must spend the remainder of her days among dirty Indians. What degradation! The thought of her would haunt him the rest of his life. He would go to the village of the Nehalems, as he had first planned. He could surely follow down the coast and reach their country in a week, and what was a week out of a lifetime? No one need be the wiser if he found the Indian story false; a miserable lonely woman might be saved from her fate if the tale were true.

In the elation of his mood he made the final adjustments of the packs next morning, finding plenty of justification for pushing on. Even a week's delay in returning crestfallen to Fort William was soothing to his spirit. The prospect of seeing the ocean after two landlocked years brought Jim a solemn joy. He had spent his life near the sea and loved its moods. Taken altogether, another week or so before starting home would serve as balm to a spirit that had been sadly lacerated of late by the blows of fate.

At first Briar made strenuous objection to the indignity of carrying a pack, but finally submitted surlily, and the two veered off to the northwest. The first day's travel was a scant eight miles over trails almost obliterated in places, but the indescribable throb of the ocean filled the night air, and a fog so dense as to have the effect of rain drenched them. Jim felt a homesick hunger for a sight of a rugged coast line with an incoming tide tearing at the rocks.

The third day at noon sudden rapture was his. The trail had by this time become so faint that he frequently lost it entirely and was forced to steer a course as best he might by the sun, making many wide détours over the steep hilltops. The Oregon coast is frowning in its severe rock walls jutting into the ocean.

Briar had panted after him as he ascended a sharp incline, clinging to the salal bushes to pull himself up. Before he realized he stood on the crest of a bluff overlooking the ocean. The broad Pacific burst upon his delighted vision. The fog had lifted toward noon and there before him lay the salt water, smooth and blue, with the surf creaming on a long stretch of hard white sand that glistened with a silvery sheen in the sunlight.

Entranced, he stood for a moment, filling his lungs with air that was salty and smelled of seaweed and driftwood. Reverently, Jim spoke a beautiful word that Auxica had taught him—"*Wycoma*" [the ocean]. Still another word replete with poetic meaning came to him—the effort of a primitive people to express with sound and inflection the processes of nature and the life about them—*Okalum* [the roar of the surf].

The better to inhale the bracing salt air Jim cast off his pack, noting as he glanced below that he would be obliged to retrace his steps to reach the beach. He stood on the sheer edge of a precipice. A rough path led down, to the sand below where a flock of gulls screamed over the remains of a fish cast up by the waves. The path, he judged, was impassable, probably just a deer-run around the face of the cliff. It grew faint, seeming to end where the tenacious roots of a stunted storm-worried tree hugged the rock to endure the constant wind. How brave a tree was to live gnarled and distorted through the countless centuries. With a trained eye he scanned the crevices in the rocky wall for signs of plant life. Yes, below the exposed root he noted a small yellow patch, without a doubt *Sedum Douglasii,* or Douglas stonecrop. After he had rested a bit he would clamber down and investigate.

Briar's bristling and growling recalled him. She was inclined to resent her pack in making a hard climb. He eased her burden, but took the precaution of tying her to a near-by tree. She might complain bitterly of weariness, but the instant she was free off she dashed after a bird or a ground squirrel, sometimes objecting to coming back when he called her. The way must be retraced over the trail they had so laboriously climbed and Jim had no taste just then for searching for her when he wanted her.

He turned for another prolonged view of the ocean and the enchanting shore line, drinking in the rugged grandeur of tor and tide like some cooling draught after a long season of thirst. He was measuring the distance to the coveted patch of yellow bloom when an angry growl from Briar caused him to wheel about in sudden alarm.

Two Indians stood facing one another directly in front of him. One, a tall, nobly built man of middle age with a decidedly Roman cast of features, was handsome in his savage way in spite of his flat head. He was remarkably clean in person for an Indian, and dressed in new, well-made buckskins. A fantastic design in red and blue native pigments was embroidered on the breast of his fringed jacket. Clearly he was a person of considerable importance.

The other was not a Flathead, which went to show that he was a slave or a person of very inferior rank, but as Jim's glance fell from the leering malignant face to the body of the savage, he could scarcely conceal his shudder of horror. Clad only in a pair of decrepit buckskin pantaloons that threatened to drop off at the slightest movement, his chest and abdomen were bare and gruesome to behold. Twenty or thirty large red marks he bore, some of them raw and oozing blood and others in various states of healing.

Not by the flicker of an eyelash did Jim betray his surprise or that he felt the least apprehension in regard to his precarious position—two Indians effectively cutting off his retreat and a sheer precipice at his back. From the tail of his eye he noted that his gun, where he had carelessly thrown it over his pack, was out of reach. Briar was securely tethered; he had no weapons for defense but his clasp-knife and the small hatchet that he always carried in his belt.

But he was not particularly alarmed; neither Indian was armed, and they appeared for the moment at least to be much more interested in each other than in him. Nonchalantly he stood waiting. The only method of dealing with Indians, either friends or foes, was to hold the peace until they chose to open the conversation.

They stood motionless, glaring into one another's eyes for an unconscionable time, while Jim viewed first the lofty Flathead and then his despicable companion. When it seemed impossible to bear the silence another moment, the Flathead spoke to his fellow, fixing him at the same time with a baleful stare under which he quailed, rallied with a show of bravado, and then quailed again. With arms folded across the breast of his embroidered jacket, the dignified one held the slave with the fascinating gaze of a coiled snake about to spring upon its charmed victim.

At length the terribly scarred Indian spoke rapidly with an apparently forced courage, and there ensued a lengthy pow-wow, angry on one side and calm but defiant on the other. By their tones they were quarreling violently, and he sensed that the altercation was over him, but whether they intended to kill him, take him captive, or simply rob him of his goods he could not determine. The language was a dialect of which he was entirely ignorant. Listening with all his ears, he could not recognize a single word.

Jim stood waiting with an outward semblance of calmness, but he was running over his chances of escape, and they seemed very slight indeed. He did not dare to turn down the sheer face of the cliff. Any sudden movement would instantly precipitate matters and end his slender chance of reaching his gun.

The dignified one, never taking his eyes from his opponent, made a gentle movement in Jim's direction. Jim remained impassive. Insinuatingly the Indian ran an appraising hand over the sleeve of his blue flannel shirt. This was nothing unusual; the native is naturally curious. To resent the familiarity would have been an insult.

With a gesture so quick as to be almost sleight-of-hand he reached into the bosom of Jim's shirt—he had unbuttoned it at the throat as he felt the heat of the climb—and drew out the buckskin bag that No-Lie had given him. With a jerk the bag opened and the nightcap and bit of wool delaine were held up in triumph before the face of the leering Indian with the livid scars.

The malignant expression on the slave's face changed instantly to one of diabolic fury. He made a furtive movement toward the fringe of his trousers and drew forth a small knife that was concealed there. Before Jim's fascinated gaze he swiftly gathered up a handful of the loose flesh on his scarred and bleeding chest and without a tremor or the least change of expression cut it off. Jim gasped in horror, but the Flathead watched him in complete indifference, saying something derisive in his guttural dialect. For another long period the two glared at one another, the blood streaming unnoticed down the chest of the slave.

At length the Flathead began hurling some terrible curse at his companion; it was a curse, that was clear by the fury of the guttural tones, at the same time fixing him with a terrible stony stare, a stare that made Jim's blood run cold. Never in human eye had he seen such a look of hate and vengeance. Covered by now with blood, the other Indian returned the gaze somewhat feebly after an uneasy shifting and a reluctant return to the face of his charmer.

Then with an unexpected yell that curdled Jim's blood he made a lunge. Taken completely off his guard, Jim was thrown backward clear off his feet. As he fell, the Indian pushed him with his bloody hands to the very edge of the cliff, where he balanced precariously for an instant, but before the Flathead could reach his side Jim had lost his grip on a small shrub and had fallen clear of the wall of rock, headlong into space.

CHAPTER EIGHT
THE TLA-QUILL-AUGH

J IM FAXON lived an eternity in the moment between his fall over the edge of the cliff and his striking the earth. He clutched at an overhanging hazel bush and broke the force of his momentum, almost turning over in midair as he lost his grip.

Unrolling scroll-like, his whole life passed before him as his memory had etched the events. This, then, was death; he felt a vast indifference; then his head struck something hard and he knew no more.

He came gradually back to earth. Now he was at home playing ball with the boys on the common, but something struck him; Slippy Winters had thrown his bat again; he'd been told often enough that he would hurt somebody. His head hurt him horribly.

He drifted off into a fitful sleep. Mother was frying her weekly batch of doughnuts. How good they smelled! He wondered if he could snitch a handful when she turned her back; he had often managed it; but he decided not to make the effort, it hurt him so terribly to move. He slept again. Always wandering and perplexed, sometimes he was in the great cathedral and candles were burning on the altar and there was music and swinging censers giving off pungent fumes.

He must be ill; he was in his clean white bed in his attic room at home, and mother was bending over him; he felt her cool soft hand on his burning head. In terror he lifted himself up on his elbow. He was in the Blackfoot country and the Indians were attacking their party. He saw Nat Wyeth, but try as he would he could not reach him to give warning of the peril. No use, he was burning with thirst.

He heard Auxica laugh. What was it she had told him about a white girl over on the coast? The effort to recall the incident was too great. Just as well. Indians were always telling wild stories to make the white men notice them. He never had liked Indians, anyway. Couldn't trust the red devils. Dr. Townsend had said that a man should never go unarmed even if they were friendly; there was no telling when an Indian would take it into his head to kill a man. He must be on his guard. He was too careless about dropping his gun out of reach.

Queer how his head kept hurting and how difficult it was to connect his thoughts. Just now he could not be sure where he was and thinking was such a bother. There was a girl somewhere he was going to find, but no matter; he sank at last into the deep sleep of utter exhaustion.

He awoke on a dull foggy morning. He felt curiosity at first, then memory came slowly back to him. That hideous Indian with the scars and the blood streaming from his chest had pushed him over the bluff. He must be dead now and lying on the rocks. Mildly interested, he looked about. There were no rocks in sight. He was prone on a bed of soft clean Indian mats, and the light was strangely dim like a gentle twilight. This was an Indian tee-pee. In bewilderment he noticed his hands; they were strangely bleached and shrunken. He must have been delirious for some time. A cool refreshing odor stole up to his nostrils. Balm of Gilead, the soothing yet penetrating aroma of bursting buds in early spring when the wind blew through the trees by the water; he recognized the healing ointment under the swathing bandages of buckskin.

Briar was unconcernedly chewing on a bone near his couch. When he spoke to her he was surprised to notice the weakness of his voice. She came joyfully and thrust her soft cool nose under his relaxed palm.

Very slightly interested, he glanced idly about. Here in the teepee was his pack just as he had left it when he caught his first glimpse of the ocean. His hard white hat and his gun lay upon it. He was glad he had not lost his hat. Briar's pack was there, too. He drifted off into restful sleep again.

A slight stir woke him this time, and he opened his eyes to find the dignified Flathead in the act of entering the teepee. Yet he experienced no alarm as the Indian, squatting on his heels, bent over him, just a calm sense of well-being. Nothing mattered particularly.

The Indian examined his swathing bandages and, finding them to his satisfaction, left the wigwam as quietly as he had entered. Jim was not worried in the least. If the Flathead meant him harm, he was completely in his power; there was nothing that he could do about it. With the receding of physical power, the mind often takes on a calm clearness that cannot be attained in the thick of the battle of life.

When his nurse came again he held in his hand a stalk bearing dark blue flowers that he had pulled up root and all. Jim roused as he noticed the bloom, and the first faint twinge of alarm shot through him. The plant was monkshood, *Aconitum Columbianum*. The turnip-shaped root is most deadly poisonous, so wolf-bane is another name by which it is known. Monkshood has certain medicinal value in allaying fever. Dr. Townsend had predicted that aconitum would at some future date be grown commercially on the Pacific coast. He remembered, too, what the doctor had said about every poison having its dose and its rightful place in the healing art. Well, just the same, he hoped he was not going to be dosed with aconitum by an ignorant savage!

The Flathead picked up a small stone mortar and pestle and carried them outside. By now Jim was mildly interested in his surroundings. Raising himself painfully on his elbow, he looked out through the turned-back flaps of the teepee. A thin spiral of smoke was rising from a small cooking-fire and a nicely dressed deer hung from the limb of a tree. A water-tight cooking basket and various native culinary utensils were scattered about. Evidently they had been in camp for some time. He glimpsed a spotted cayuse grazing peacefully at the end of his tether.

Here was a mystery indeed. How had he reached the teepee and was the Flathead a friend? Previous circumstances did not justify that comforting conclusion. The actions of the two Indians had certainly been most open to suspicion. In vain he looked about for his assailant on the cliff, but he was nowhere in evidence. Jim smiled grimly as he came to the first realization of his position, resolving to say nothing but to be constantly on his guard.

The Indian entered soon with a drinking-cup, one of those curious utensils so highly prized by the natives, made from the horn of a mountain sheep, the *mouton gris* or gray sheep of the voyageurs. Jim brightened, hoping it might be broth; he felt enormously hungry, but his face clouded again. He was going to have a dose of something; just as likely it would be aconitum.

Seeing that he was awake and really rational for the first time, the Flathead spoke. "Heap plenty sick; no die," he announced in a casually conversational tone.

Thank Heaven he spoke English, Jim thought. Some of the remote tribes did not even know Chinook. The language the two had spoken on the cliff might have been Chinese so far as his understanding it was concerned. At least he could question his captor and perhaps gain an inkling of the situation, though a working knowledge of English in a native did not necessarily mean that information could be extracted from him unless he chose to give it.

"Me Tilki. Tla-quill-augh. Make heap much medicine." He was being lifted on a lean sinewy arm while the horn cup was set to his lips.

Jim shook his head and refused to drink.

The Indian carefully set the cup down so that its contents would not spill and then came to urge him just as a mother coaxes a sick child.

"You dlink-um, you heap well soon. Seven sleeps now you sick. Soon you strong."

"Have I been here a week?" Jim exclaimed, incredulously. "How did I come here? That bloody fiend pushed me over the bluff. Where is he?"

"No here. Him gone." He made a large inclusive gesture southward. "Cockqua velly had mans. Tilki good mans. Tilki friend. What you name?" His face beamed with benevolence. There was a simplicity and yet a dignity that made Jim trust him in spite of his suspicions.

"I'm Jim Faxon," he told him. "I'm a 'grass man.' I come on a friendly visit to your people. I have tobacco and a *potlatch* [gift]. You see my pack? Why did you try to kill me?"

"Tilki no keel. Tilki make-um well." He was proffering the cup again, and Jim drank the bitter dose at a single draught, sampling the terrible mixture afterward, as the taste remained long in his mouth. Yes, it probably contained aconite, but there were a number of other ingredients. The infusion contained dogwood, and who could mistake the lingering misery of cascara? He could identify a number of tinctures through his habit of tasting twigs as he examined specimens. And did he detect *Berberis repens*, the root of the Oregon grape? Well, if bitterness had any connection with medicinal virtue, this was certainly a potent dose. He decided to die fighting rather than swallow such another.

In mercy Tilki gave him a dried camass to chew as he saw the cold sweat beading his forehead, though Jim gave no outward sign that the draught was in any way unpleasant. After this he had broth, the most delicious broth he had ever tasted, he was sure, even if he had watched Tilki making it in the cooking-basket, after the ancient manner of his race. The skill with which he lifted cool stones from that basket with a looped willow and replaced them with red-hot ones from the fire bordered on the miraculous.

There was no more talk that day. Tilki coolly ignored Jim's questions. At night his bed was straightened and his bruises carefully dressed with the soothing balm, but never a word did Tilki utter.

Jim slept without disturbing dreams. In the early morning he was awakened by sounds like the wailing of a lost child. He listened, then understood. The camp must be near the ocean. The sea gulls were about.

Tilki brought broth and camass, baked on a bed of leaves in the ashes. Jim felt that he was well on the road to recovery. He was hungry and the zest of life had returned to him. He felt all over his body, and knew that no bones had been broken, though sore spots showed that he had been bruised terribly by his fall. His head was tightly bandaged. He decided that he had suffered a concussion of the brain. His hard white hat was all that had saved him, for he must have struck the roots of that gnarled tree when he fell.

Lovingly he surveyed the hat on his pack. He never took it off his head except to sleep. This was all that remained of the proud uniform that the Wyeth party had worn in crossing the country. They had boasted that these felt hats were hard enough to stop a bullet.

"How did I come here?" he inquired of Tilki, in the effort to make conversation.

"Carry-um on back." Tilki made a staggering motion as if bearing a burden almost beyond his strength up a steep path.

"You killed the other Indian, didn't you?" Jim inquired.

"Me no keel. Me no lie. Me no steal," Tilki informed him with a smug satisfaction in his own virtue. "Me *tla-quill-augh*. Make-um well. Me use-um," he paused as if searching his mind for an English word to express his meaning. "Me have evil eye. Rule-um with eye. Scare-um bad Indian. Help-um fliends."

Jim understood. He had heard of the *shaman,* or head of the great medicine cult, who was also sort of a high priest. And lower in rank came the *keél-al-ly* and then the *tla-quill-augh.* There were fine shades of distinction between them. The *tla-quill-augh* was, so to speak, the general practitioner, the man or woman who gathered the herbs, set the broken bones, and acted as midwife in the village. Every tribe boasted three or four of these general-utility folk.

They were all members of the great medicine cult, that indirectly determined the policies of the tribe and in reality ruled over them by right of their claim to supernatural powers of divination and magic. They claimed the ability to detect the witch; Indian witches are greatly feared, and if caught are summarily executed. While the chief is the nominal head of government, his powers are in the main persuasive; he seldom exercises any real authority, but is, in most cases, completely under the domination of the powerful medicine cult.

The power of magic is a very potent force in Indian life. Jim had seen so-called exhibitions of necromancy, but had detected that in the main they were the most obvious fraud. He had little faith and less patience with medicine cults. But still there were baffling happenings in the Indian country. The white men had just shrugged their shoulders and made no attempt to explain many of them.

Savages living close to nature do have a highly sharpened sixth sense, something like dogs, he was sure of that. He had so often marveled at the rapidity with which news traveled among the Indians. Remote tribes sometimes had information that could not be attributed to the runner or messenger. And no doubt, some of them were gifted with a grossly exaggerated prophetic sense.

But the talk about the evil eye was silly. Yet here was a grave, dignified Indian calmly claiming supernatural powers, and his stare at his horribly gashed and scarred companion indicated that he wielded a terrible power over him, though this could be easily explained by the terror of the primitive man who had an implicit belief in the potency of witchcraft.

Still superstition is ingrained in the human race. He recalled the little unpleasantness in Salem, Massachusetts, when a few innocent women had suffered death at the hands of intelligent white men. Everyone now admitted that with their enlightenment they should have known better, but there had been a belief in witchcraft. Jim smiled a little to himself. How alike human beings were at the bottom, always ready to believe the impossible. Credulity neither began nor ended with savages. He himself would not care to sit down with thirteen at table. Mother would never have permitted that, yet she hushed grandmother when she spoke of haunts and warnings and various other supernatural happenings in which she must have believed.

Perhaps, after all, he believed in magic, though he was loath to admit it, even to himself. Was it possible that Tilki was the Indian who No-Lie had promised would meet him when the trail faded out? How else could he have had knowledge of the contents of the buckskin bag? He would have liked to ask about it, but felt a bit reticent. Better wait a few days before attempting any questioning. Perhaps in the meantime Tilki would tell him of his own accord. But he meant to secure that bag.

The daily examination of his injuries was carefully made. Jim was progressing wonderfully. With hands strong but soft in their touch as any woman, Tilki rubbed and kneaded with an amazing skill, picking up sore muscles and working out the stiffness. The cut on his head was dressed. Tilki with an arm under his shoulderblades lifted him to his trembling feet.

Though swaying from weakness and forced to lie down again immediately, Jim found that he could walk about in spite of the pain the movement caused him. He spent the day rising to limp a few steps and then resting from the exertion, with Tilki hovering in the background with bowls of steaming soup or a nourishing porridge made of the crushed seeds of the yellow pond lily, *Nymphœa polysepala.*

In a few days he would be able to travel, and, though Tilki had nothing to say on the subject, Jim felt sure that he would take him to the lodge of the Nehalems. There was no turning back now, even if he had wished to do so. Escaping from Tilki would be extremely difficult. There was so much of the mysterious in the whole matter that he felt a growing curiosity, even though there was an element of danger. Somehow his hope of finding the white girl, Multnomah, had revived until at times he felt certain, and then he was assailed with doubts.

Tilki talked freely now, though he confined his remarks mainly to the subject of plants and herbs. He told Jim that his people knew just why the Great Spirit, the Tomaniwus, had placed each growing thing on the earth. He promised to instruct him in the magic properties of certain flowers and to tell him the meaning of the signs and omens that Tomaniwus had taught the Indian. They were kindred spirits, the bond between them an intense love of nature.

Jim felt that he owed his life to Tilki and was grateful to him for his kindly ministrations, and this alone was disarming. By his second day of walking he found himself, in spite of reason, trusting the Indian implicitly, and more and more inclined to an open mind in regard to his magic.

Eager questions were constantly forming on his lips. Once he asked Tilki if he knew No-Lie, but the Indian shook his head and did not answer. Neither would he speak again of Cockqua.

Jim promised himself that he would have the information he desired before he moved a step in the direction of the lodge of the Nehalems. Evil eye or no evil eye, magic or no magic, Tilki should answer his direct questions or he would know the reason why. In the morning he would have it out with him.

CHAPTER NINE
INDIAN NECROMANCY

"TOMOLLA we go," Tilki announced as he attended the camp duties after breakfast. "No far. You walk-um. You ride-um cayuse." He pointed to the calico pony grazing near.

"Just where are we going, Tilki?" Jim asked in a casual tone. He must use the utmost diplomacy in dealing with Tilki, for he intended to pin him down and extract the whole truth from him by hook or crook. The opening was promising.

Tilki came over and squatted in his usual posture by the tiny fire, producing an enormous stone pipe ornamented with a carved bird that served as a receptacle for the tobacco that Jim was quick to hand him. He had some difficulty in making it draw properly; he fussed over it for quite a time before he answered. "Neah-kah-nie," he grunted at last between strenuous puffs, rocking back and forth on his heels. The interview was opening auspiciously. Jim possessed his soul in patience. Tilki was the most promising Indian he had yet encountered.

"I was on my way to the country of the Nehalems when I met you," Jim volunteered, cautiously. "Neah-kah-nie is down that way, isn't it?"

"What for you come Nehalem countly?" Tilki asked, closing his eyes and blowing out a great mouthful of smoke.

"I have an errand down there," Jim said, a bit lamely. "I—er—I was intending to trade a little with your people. My horses were—got away one night, and I had to come in without them. I have a *cache* of goods on the road." He was weighing every word before he dared give it utterance.

"What Yallup tell you?" Tilki inquired, his face an inscrutable wooden mask.

"Yallup?" Jim said, wonderingly, then remembered. "You mean No-Lie?"

"Yallup say you go find-um Multnomah," Tilki answered his own question, smoking as if his very life depended upon it. "Yallup say Indian meet you when tlail no clear. Yallup give-um buckskin sack." He produced the sack and held it up for Jim's inspection.

Jim reached for the sack and Tilki handed it over without a remonstrance.

"How did you know where to find that sack?" Jim asked him, vexedly. He still resented Tilki's method of relieving him of it.

Tilki's face widened in the first smile Jim had seen him wear.

"What for you want know?" he laughed.

"There're a lot of things I want to know," Jim told him, heatedly.

"Mebbe me tell, mebbe me no can tell," Tilki said, cautiously.

"How did you know I was coming down here?" Jim leaned forward in his eagerness.

"Me watch-um tlail with medicine. Ever day me watch-um tlail. One day medicine him no good. Lose-um tlail. Then me start-um on tlail. Cockqua him ver' bad Indian. Him watch-um. Him follow. Me go back. Cockqua him ver' bad Indian. Him keel. Him steal. Mebbe him lie." Tilki was off on his favorite topic, the degeneracy of Cockqua.

"Who is Multnomah?" Jim asked, suddenly, by way of cutting short a monologue that threatened to become tedious.

"Multnomah," Tilki spoke the word slowly, rolling it lovingly on his tongue. "Multnomah little white squaw. Nehalems her people. Multnomah flaid. Multnomah sad. Nehalems go for find-um white husban'. Yallup long time hunt-um white mans.

No can find ver' long time. You come take Multnomah?" he inquired, hopefully.

"If there is a white girl living among the Nehalems I'm certainly going to take her out," Jim said, with his jaw set in an unwonted firmness. "Are your people willing to let her go with me?"

Tilki was silent for a moment before he answered. "My people ver' good people. Cockqua him ver' bad Indian. Tly keel you. Him steal. Mebbe him lie. No can trust Cockqua. You like-um see me make medicine?" he asked brightly.

Jim knew he was just diverting his attention from the main issue, but he nodded a rather ungracious assent.

As if rid of a disagreeable subject, Tilki rose with alacrity and strode to the small stream near by, making an elaborate ceremony of washing his face and hands. Cupping his palms, he threw water over his hair and smoothed it down carefully, shaking his body back and forth to dry off the moisture. He stood for a time contemplating the design on the front of his jacket, tracing out the lines with a forefinger. Then he raised both arms above his head and began whirling in rapid circles, uttering hoarse gutturals that Jim took to have some ritualistic meaning.

When at last he returned to the fire he held a shining black stone in his two hands. The stone was curious, half of a sphere about the size of an apple. The flat side had been ground until it shone like a mirror in the sunlight.

"A thunder stone," Jim queried, eyeing it in fascination. He made a move as if to take it in his own hands for a closer examination.

Holding the stone tenderly, Tilki backed away with a forbidding frown. A thunder stone must not be handled by the unholy, Jim read in his glance.

"Where did you get it?" Jim asked.

Tilki composed himself by the fire in his customary squatting position.

"Thunder bird him shoot-um," he explained. "Make-um bow with wings. Thunder stone all-same arrow-heads." He was considering the sphere in his cupped hands with reverential awe.

Jim remembered the story of the thunder bird. The Indians had loved so to recount his miraculous doings. He made the lightning by the movement of his gigantic wings. These stones, then, were meteorites that had fallen at the time. Small wonder that the savage paled in superstitious terror when a thunderstorm occurred. Its very rarity on the western coast added to its horror. The rain that fell afterward in huge spattering drops was from the agitation of a lake that this mythical bird bore on his back.

"You talk, spoil-um medicine," Tilki warned. He began polishing the surface of his stone with a square of clean buckskin, then sat for fifteen minutes motionless, peering into it through half-closed eyes. He moaned at length, uttering grunts of disgust and disappointment, then tried again. Now there was satisfaction in his face.

"What you want Tilki see?" he inquired, as if anxious to oblige.

"See my mother. What is she doing this morning?" Jim ventured.

Tilki shook his head. "No find mamma. No live in Indian country. Too way off." He inclined his head toward the east, indicating great distance. "Indian only see-um in own country."

"Then see No-Lie." Jim was a bit disgusted; he felt no particular interest in hearing of the personal affairs of the Indians just then.

Tilki peered again. What he saw evidently amused him. He laughed outright. "Yallup him ver' mad Indian. Shake-um fist. Stamp-um foot."

This was silly. "Find Auxica," Jim commanded, his tone tinged with disgust.

Tilki started as if he had been struck, then dejection settled over him.

"No find-um. No more see." He crouched lower in a sadly meditative mood, then turned suddenly to Jim as if inspired by some new idea.

"Who speak-um to you?" he asked, sharply.

"Why, Auxica——" Jim began, but Tilki silenced him with a look. For some reason he could not bear to hear Auxica's name spoken.

"Well, then, see who stole my horses and tell me where to find them."

Tilki turned the stone first to the right then to the left, reversed his position by the fire so that he faced the south and peered intently again.

Jim watched him amusedly. This magic business was all of a piece. The stone-gazer never answered a direct question nor put himself in a position where his vague statements could be disproved.

Tilki was perfectly safe in telling of his vision in the stone. No-Lie was a mad Indian. Of course. He was mad most of the time. A horde of his poor relations had given a great *potlatch* early in the fall, and that was just a polite way of quartering on him for the winter. Having given away everything they owned, the recipients of their scanty gifts were in duty bound to provide for them afterward. No-Lie must keep a semblance of peace between five or six wives, and added to all this, Cultee had given him six horses in payment for his best-looking daughter, and then had stolen them from him within the week.

But Jim persisted in his investigations. Here was his first opportunity of studying the "black art" at first hand. He had been taught that any form of divination was wicked, but surely there was no harm in whiling away a few hours of his tedious convalescence.

Tilki was speaking again. Here was a chance to test his powers.

"Me see," said Tilki, weighing every word—"me see-um horse. Him big black horse. Him no cayuse. Me see-um cayuse.

Him much mean cayuse. Bite-um. Kick-um. You know-um horses?" he asked as if to confirm his vision.

Jim admitted that he did.

"Me see-um far way off." His inclination was toward the south.

"But who stole them?" Jim persisted.

"Horses no stole. Me see-um heap big bale beaver skins. Buy-um horses." Comprehension dawned on the seer. He rocked back and forth with merriment.

"What do you see?" Jim was inclined to indignation. "Where can I find my horses? Let me catch the thief and I'll show him whether he bought my horses or not. What good does a bale of skins do me when I have no way to move my goods. How he ever got away with those horses is beyond me. You say your people never steal. You call sneaking up in the night and riding off horses without permission buying them?"

Tilki sobered at his accusation. "Me not know ever't'ing. My people no steal horses." Laughter overcame him again, but he refused to divulge the cause of his mirth.

Jim was overcome with sudden anger. "What good does all this do me? You say the horses were taken by some one who left a bale of beaver skins in their place. I knew that before. Now if you will tell me where to find them I'll be more likely to believe in your medicine."

Offended at his brusque manner and his lack of faith, the Indian glared at him without answering, then quietly put the stone in his pocket.

"Me *tla-quill-augh*." He spoke with dignity. "Kawok [guardian spirit] show me, long time ago. Show now. No tell-um tomolla. You laugh-um. Tink-um lie. Tilki's tongue no forked, him straight. No make more medicine."

"I'm sorry, Tilki. You did make good medicine, only it didn't go far enough. What good does knowing the past and the present do if you can't know the future? What you've just told me I knew already. Just try to tell me how I can find the horses," Jim urged.

Tilki shook his head. "See-um horses far off. Mebbe some day you find-um. Mebbe save-um life. Me not know. You no can use horses now. Long time, two moons, t'ree moons, then find-um horses. No can tell."

"Can't you ever forecast the future with that rock of yours?" Jim questioned.

"No," Tilki answered. "T'ree sleeps me no eat-um. No sleep-um. Make-um heap much smoke. Me know. Not now. You well. You strong. Now we go Nehalem countly."

"Yes, we can start in the morning," Jim agreed. "I can walk slowly, but first you must tell me just what you are running me into. You tell me in one breath that your people are friendly, and in the next admit that one of them tried to kill me. How am I to be sure he will not try again?"

Tilki transfixed him with the piercing eye he had used on Cockqua as they stood on the cliff. Jim returned the stare in kind. No use to try the evil eye on him.

"Are your people willing to give me the white girl, Multnomah?" Jim was looking the Indian directly in the eye.

Tilki's gaze wandered off to the ocean, then turned to the near-by hills. He brought his eyes back to Jim very reluctantly before he answered:

"My people good people. Love-um Multnomah heap plenty. Find-um white husban'. Cockqua him bad Indian. Him no like for find-um white husban'. Cockqua make-um war in lodge." He brightened. "You take-um Multnomah. Mebbe you kill-um Cockqua. Cockqua no take-um Multnomah."

Jim's spirit soared. Multnomah did really exist. He could no longer doubt, and yet in his exultation he had a sudden chilling premonition of evil. He was going on a perilous mission. He regretted his foolhardiness in not telling the men at Fort William a little more of his destination. Plenty of explorers had gone into a strange Indian country, never to return. Perhaps he would share their fate, but that was no reason for turning back. There *was* a white woman within a few miles of where he stood and he was going to bring her to Fort William or die in the attempt.

But this entanglement in the medicine cult was not to his liking. He knew that there were societies among the Indians, whose members belonged to the various tribes. These orders were said to have very much the same form of organization as the Masonic lodge, their secrets just as jealously guarded. He felt that he had been enticed into the Nehalem country by one of these mystic cults, and this alone was enough to strike terror to the heart of a white man. If he failed to rescue the white girl or came to know too much of the doings of the medicine-men, he would be killed, there was no doubting that fact.

The medicine-men were dangerous and often unscrupulous in their efforts to gain power over their credulous fellows, but their so-called powers of sorcery were not to be credited by an intelligent white man.

"You ver' smart young mans," Tilki told him, by way of compliment, as he set about roasting a haunch of venison for dinner. "You no tell what see, what hear. No tell-um white mans. Indian kill-um you tell."

"I'm not telling," Jim assured him.

"My people good people," Tilki reiterated, in his monotonous singsong.

He was going to launch forth again on a tedious discourse on the Indian code of ethics, but Jim cut him short. He had heard about good Indians and bad Indians to the exclusion of every other topic until the subject wearied him.

"If your people are good and honest as you declare they are, there'll be no trouble. Your tribe will find themselves in serious difficulty if harm comes to me. The entire force of Fort William will descend on the Nehalems and wipe them off the face of the earth. The Hudson's Bay Company will join them. This country is going to be safe for white men."

"No harm come you trust fliends. When you come lodge you find-um out much t'ings. You no be solly you come for Multnomah. You wait-um. Soon know."

Further efforts to draw Tilki out proved futile. He simply took refuge in sermons on conduct, or refused to hear. The situation had to be accepted just as it stood, and implicit faith placed in Tilki. But somehow Jim rested in contentment. As he watched the Indian preparing food for the journey he did trust him, though just why he could not have told for the life of him.

CHAPTER TEN
TILKI'S COUP

TILKI was breaking camp when Jim awoke from a refreshing sleep next morning. The enticing odor of broiled venison floated to him, and the trout baked on a bed of ferns was ready. Within an hour they were starting on the journey to Neah-kah-nie Mountain.

Jim strolled over the little knoll that shut them in on the west, rather surprised to find the ocean so near. Tilki had sought shelter from the sea winds in a small grassy recess between two hills. Perhaps he wished seclusion until his charge recovered from his illness. At any rate, they were securely hidden from view on all sides.

Breaking camp was simplicity itself. Tilki simply piled his equipment neatly and left most of it on the ground. Jim's belongings he packed on the cayuse and they were ready to start. Having no taste for the Indian horse, and feeling that gentle exercise would do him good, Jim preferred walking. Time enough to ride when the exertion began to tell on him. Tilki accommodated his pace to his, occasionally kicking or vilifying the pony when he drew back on his lead rope to snatch an inviting bunch of grass.

Travel along the beach was easy; the sand was hard and smooth and the ocean breeze stimulating. There was much to attract the attention. The nimble sea-duck, called the "hell-diver," rode the crest of incoming waves in quest of small fish. The way was strewn with the remains of curious fishes. Here and there, like a great lens, the crystal-clear jellyfish, caught the light. Sea anemones, reflecting the elusive colors of the deep, bloomed in coppery blue and green on the rocks lapped by the tide. Giant ropes of kelp and other refuse from the ocean floor made the going interesting to Jim. He was disposed to loiter a bit, but Tilki urged him on.

He seemed curiously on the alert, looking about constantly as if he half expected to encounter other travelers and had no taste for meeting them. Once he drew Jim hastily back behind some rocks and tethered the horse out of sight. In fifteen or twenty minutes three squaws rounded a point and passed on, talking and laughing. Jim was going into the Nehalem country without being detected, he was sure of that, though his guide made no comment on his furtive actions.

"One sleep we come to lodge of my people," Tilki told Jim. "Two sleeps you take-um heap big rest."

Jim wanted to take "heap big rest" anyway, and preferred to spend the time on the beach, but Tilki would not listen, though he noticed Jim's lagging step and shifted one of the packs to his own back so that there was room for Jim on the horse.

They passed a shell-heap, or kitchen midden, and in spite of Tilki's objections Jim insisted upon inspecting it. Finally the Indian grumblingly consented, and stationed himself in a position to scan the full length of the beach.

Dr. Townsend had spent considerable time exploring these ancient kitchen heaps; they were to be found all along the coast. He had collected many valuable specimens of Indian handicraft for the Academy of Natural Sciences. The kitchen midden is nothing more or less than a gigantic garbage heap or dumping-ground of the aborigines. The complete history of the race may be read in them by the archæologist.

Taking life as easily as possible, primitive peoples of every race made their homes at the confluence of streams or on sightly promontories where rivers ran into the ocean. Fish were easily taken here. Gaining a livelihood requires a minimum effort. In the most remote times refuse was probably left to rot where it fell, but as the tribe progressed, it developed a rude sense of order. The north side of the lodge was sunless and the space not in use, so the habit of dumping here became at last a fixed rule. Clans lived in their villages generation after generation, and after a few hundred years the heaps grew troublesome. The lodges gradually moved southward, so that oftentimes the tumuli covered a number of acres.

From the shells of sea fish, the bones of animals, and such broken tools and household utensils that were thrown on the kitchen midden the complete domestic life of a people may be reconstructed. Under ordinary circumstances nothing short of physical force could have drawn Jim Faxon away, but today his interest was curiously divided. Now that he had come to believe that Multnomah was a reality instead of a figment of his imagination, he was eager to reach the lodge of the Nehalems, but as the day drew so near he felt a reluctance—the shyness of adolescent boyhood.

The frankness of the Indians could easily prove embarrassing to them both. Tilki would probably tell Multnomah outright that he had brought her in a husband; while the whole tribe stood about grinning. There would be obscene jests that the poor girl, familiar with the Nehalem dialect, would understand. How a sensitive nature would suffer! How could he hope to win the love of a woman under such circumstances? His courtship was starting out on the wrong foot. But no matter. Even if there were no love on either side, his duty lay clear before him. He would take Multnomah into the settlement at Fort Vancouver. Dr. McLoughlin's wife would look after her, and steps would then be taken to find her people if they could be traced.

He set his teeth at the thought of the duty before him, regretting that he had not paid more attention to girls when he was at home. What a romantic fool he had been never to have given a thought to the practical side of the matter. Cold sweat broke out in beads on his forehead. The shell held no further interest. He motioned to Tilki and mounted the cayuse in clammy silence.

They had followed no trail. Tilki seemed to be avoiding beaten paths, though they had crossed several. The way now veered sharply inland. An hour's going over rolling country timbered with magnificent firs brought them at last to the top of the ridge.

"Neah-kah-nie," Tilki exclaimed, sudden rapture lighting his somber countenance. "Neah-kah-nie. Over there my home." He indicated a mountain; its sharp northern slope, deeply wooded, loomed almost black against a cloudless blue. The promontory ran clear out into the sea. They could hear the roar of the tide dashing in fury at its rocky base.

Jim wondered how they were to skirt the mountain, but could elicit no information from Tilki, who began in haste to set out food for the noon meal. He was impatient when the meal was over, kicking the cayuse under the belly as he faced him about to help his charge onto the back of the surly animal.

Turning and twisting over the hills, they came at length to a ravine where a small stream tumbled over the rocks in its swift race to the ocean. Tilki led the protesting horse into the icy water, following the course for nearly a mile, except where he was forced to take the bank by impassable boulders. Jim suffered from the splashing of the water about his feet, shivering as the spray drenched him almost to the waist. The day had been comfortably warm where the sun shone on the hills, but here there was an eternal chill and semidarkness. The overhanging trees prevented either light or warming rays from entering the tunnel formed by the rocky sides.

The way grew steeper and narrower, the passage in places where the descending water had worn through the rock was scarcely wide enough to admit the horse. Jim swayed from weakness and the numbing chill, wishing that they had delayed their start a few days until his full strength had returned, but he bore the agony without a sound.

After an hour that seemed a year, Tilki led the horse to the bank and motioned for him to dismount, which he did with all the haste that his stiffness permitted. They stood before a giant boulder that a tree with its infinite patience had split in half. At first this seemed to the exhausted Jim an impassable barrier, but his guide stepped to one side and began removing a heap of stones that lay piled against it.

He worked swiftly, and at length revealed the mouth of a tunnel large enough to admit the horse. They passed through, though Briar whimpered and protested until Jim called her from the other side. This passageway between the rocks was roofed over as if placed there by nature, but Jim saw the careful hand of man in it as he surveyed it. Once through, Tilki returned and Jim listened as he replaced the rocks. A little later he appeared in the top of the tree, letting himself down from limb to limb. The pass into the Nehalem country was closed.

"Why," Jim exclaimed. "I never could have found my way in here alone! The pass is a secret. No wonder No-Lie sent a guide to meet me."

"Boston man no find Nehalem countly," Tilki grunted. "Indian no find tlail. Nehalem know. Him no tell-um."

He was helping Jim on the horse again. Another hour of travel seemed to him more than human flesh could endure, but the path through the timber was broad and soon they emerged upon a grassy sun-warmed slope.

Tilki almost lifted him off the horse and, placing him on the ground, helped remove the sodden clothing. He was the solicitous nurse again after his apparent indifference to the welfare of his patient. He produced an elkskin bottle and poured some dark, evil-smelling liquid into Jim's tin cup, and held it for him to drink. Nauseous as the dose was, it produced a glow of warmth in his numb body almost immediately. After rubbing and kneading

Jim's whole body, the Indian got his extra pair of shoes and clothing and then left him rolled in the buffalo robe for a short nap in the sun.

Jim awoke feeling none the worse for his drenching, and announced himself able to walk along the smooth trail up the side of the mountain. A most enchanting panorama was the shore from the top of Neah-kah-nie. To the south below them lay a small emerald-green valley, sheltered lovingly by a rim of mountains on three sides, with a placid ocean lapping its sandy beach on the fourth. Small wonder that traders had never heard of the Nehalems. They lived in a little world of their own. No chance wanderer could ever discover the secret of that pass. Tilki told him even friendly Indians of other tribes had never been admitted to this sacred ground. For here, he said, pausing reverently before he spoke, the Fire Spirit was at home. In the Nehalem dialect, "Neah-kah-nie" meant "Abode of the Fire Spirit," who guarded and prospered his chosen people.

He explained that once a long time ago, so long ago that his grandmother had it from her grandmother, to whom the story had been handed down through numberless generations, there was loud noise and a great white light all over the heavens. This heralded the coming of the Fire Spirit to dwell among them. The south slope of the mountain had at that time been densely wooded, just as the northern side was, but with the baptism of this terrible white light it became a solid sheet of flame, starting at the base and sweeping upward, consuming the trees. But when the fire reached the top of the mountain a curious thing happened. The blaze did not descend the north slope, proving conclusively that the Spirit still lived among them. As a token that the Nehalems recognized the presence still in their midst, every fall the mountain was fired at its base. The flame ran to the crest and stopped there.

Jim listened politely to the lengthy tale of the advent of the Fire Spirit, looking about from the height for some natural explanation of this strange phenomena. From the position of the promontory in regard to the prevailing winds, the reason was perfectly apparent. Sheltered from the gale, the fire ran to the top and there encountered a strong head wind that drove it back, leaving the north slope intact.

The coming of the Fire Spirit had of course been a severe thunderstorm; lightning had started a fire at the base of Neah-kah-nie, and the fertile imagination of the Nehalems had evolved the explanation. Jim smiled to himself but made no attempt to enlighten Tilki. Why destroy a really beautiful myth and create doubt in the mind of a simple Indian? If he reverenced the Spirit of the Flame and gloried in the certainty of its presence, there was beauty in the worship, which, after all, was but the adoration of a great force of nature.

The circling of the south side of Neah-kah-nie was a trip never to be forgotten. Jim rode and walked alternately along the smooth trail. The afternoon was clear and very warm, with light clouds on the western horizon at sunset. They paused to watch the glory of gold and crimson fade slowly to tender violet and mauve, standing bathed in the heavenly radiance that illumined the sea and the gentle valley.

Tomorrow the people of the Nehalem would be encountered. Jim felt the chill of a dire foreboding as his eye swept the valley. Getting out of there might be much more difficult than entering, and that had not been so easy. He cursed his folly in not laying careful plans before undertaking such a hazardous adventure, yet how could one make definite plans when one was entirely in the dark about the situation?

In spite of his seeming bravado Jim was certain that Tilki entertained grave misgiving. Well, he had unwittingly placed himself in the hands of the Indians, and must rely on their faithfulness to protect him. But should Tilki and his confederates, if he had confederates, prove unable to manage matters, he would be in a serious predicament, so serious that he did not dare allow his mind to dwell upon it. To show trepidation would never do now. He would face the music with head up, depending upon his wits to see him through.

Well, what was done was done. Nothing to do now but take the day as it came. He would just call this the spice of life, this element of danger that was always present even in dealing with the most friendly Indians.

This mystic stuff bothered him, though. He had no taste for knowledge, if it were knowledge, gained through supernatural power. But after all there was nothing mysterious about a polished black stone. A sudden thought struck him forcibly. He had been delirious for a week. No doubt in his ravings he had disclosed the whole story of his trip over the Indian road. The stolen horses and the bale of beaver skins had been much on his mind; of course he had babbled of them. There was, somehow, a great relief in this reflection.

Tilki was merely a cunning Indian vainly exhibiting his powers. That was natural enough to Indian nature. The question was how far could he go in controlling his people with the evil eye. High dignitaries of the medicine cult were frequently deposed from their high office and killed offhand. Tilki might meet a similar fate at any time.

There was serious trouble brewing among the Nehalems. Jim pondered over the whole matter until his brain was weary. He was not disturbed by Tilki, who appeared to be deeply engaged with his own problems.

Tilki walking ahead, leading the horse, with Jim following slowly, they made their way halfway down the mountain as the sunset faded and the long summer twilight deepened. They were not to enter the lodge of the Nehalems that night and Jim was thankful. A bad situation was easier to meet in the clear light of the morning.

They made camp near a large spring of sparkling cold water. Jim was rather surprised that Tilki made no cooking-fire, and his surprise turned to consternation when he found that the Indian was making preparations to leave him on the mountain for the night. After their meal he took the buffalo robe and handed it to him, with a haunch of roast venison and enough dried camass for the morning meal.

"You sleep-um here." Tilki's tone was a command. "Me go. You no light-um fire. Next sun you come lodge. Me take-um cayuse. Me take-um dog."

Jim remonstrated, but the Indian seized his gun and faced him angrily.

"When sun so high"—he pointed directly overhead—"you come lodge of my people." He indicated the downward trail. "You find-um fliends." With these terse directions he took the horse's tether and the leash with which he had secured Briar, who growled and squatted on her haunches. The path he chose led off eastward.

Full of distress, Jim stood helplessly for a moment. He had not sensed Tilki's intention until all his preparations had been made, the whole thing had happened so quickly. The Indian's tone of command filled him with rage. He was not accustomed to being ordered about, but here argument would have been useless.

He had a mind to try to make his way back to Fort William for reinforcements to investigate and take the white girl by force of arms if she could be found, but he dismissed the idea at once. He had no gun and was entirely without food and still in a weakened condition from his illness. He could not travel a day without being overtaken by Tilki or his confederates.

He cursed himself for a prize fool to allow an Indian to bamfoozle him so completely. He had, from the first, been nothing but a pawn in some game Tilki and No-Lie were playing. And yet heretofore he had thought rather well of his native resources and the quickness of his wit. Well, life certainly took the conceit out of a man!

He was spent with the terrible exertions of the day, and the night was made for sleep. He wrapped his buffalo robe around him and lay down. Time enough to meet trouble when it faced him in the path. He'd die but once, not every day through anticipation.

CHAPTER ELEVEN
THE COUNCIL

THE ocean fog drifted in smotheringly in the morning. Beads of moisture stood on Jim's hair when he awoke, and he ached with the penetrating cold. He could have no fire, so he decided to climb to the summit of Neah-kah-nie, where the fir trees on the north slope would protect him somewhat from the chill. The fog would lift about ten and then he must take the trail down to the lodge of the Nehalems.

He was in a chastened mood, brought on by the cold breakfast and the dull ache in his stiff limbs, as well as by a certain anxiety as to the outcome of his encounter with the Indians in the valley below. Before starting out on this adventure he had felt an easy assurance in his innate ability to deal with the natives. In his opinion, they were just like simple trusting children with minds developed perhaps to the capacity of the white child of six or seven years, easily won over by flattery and delighted with evidences of friendship in the shape of small gifts and trivial kindnesses. Firm statements, promises few and faithfully kept, and above all a calm eye and the ability to conceal the least qualm of fear were all that was necessary to win their respect and confidence.

But while the mass level of intelligence was low, favored individuals, both men and women, possessed keen minds. These giants of a primitive race exhibited a shrewdness that would put the average white man to shame, and added to this an aboriginal cunning that made them powers to be reckoned with.

Tilki had been master of the situation from the moment he appeared on the scene. Jim admitted this to himself rather shamefacedly. But there were in this case extenuating circumstances. A week's delirium had placed him completely in the *tlaquill-augh's* hands. He was forced by weakness to obey just as a patient must obey his doctor or nurse. The decisions of a man who is desperately ill must be made for him without his for the moment suspecting that he is being skillfully managed. Tilki's bedside manner was that of the physician the world over, but Jim resented the healer's tyranny after the need for it had passed.

Jim was more and more at a loss to understand Tilki's abrupt departure the night before, and he had not gone directly to the camp, but had borne off toward the rim of mountains. Curious thing for him to do, but he softened a little as he thought it over, and in a measure his faith returned. Tilki must know what he was about; it was best to follow his instructions and keep his wits about him if he hoped to find the white girl. He intended to find her, and would march down to that camp like an army with banners.

What was done was done. He had made a serious mistake through his dread of bringing the ridicule of the fort down upon his head. A sane, reasonable man would have confided the story No-Lie and Auxica told to three or four of the more trustworthy men and enlisted their help in the search. There would then have been a reasonable excuse for going alone when they refused to have anything to do with his proposal. Still, they would have refused and probably would have taken extreme measures to prevent his going. And the white girl, Multnomah, would have lived her miserable life out alone among the Nehalems as the wife of the loathsome Cockqua. The thought was too horrible for him to entertain. Suddenly he exulted in the fact that he was here on the mountain within two hours of the village of the Nehalems. Qualms and misgivings vanished before a set determination to succeed in his undertaking.

With a lighter heart than he had known for days he strode up the mountain to fill in the time with a search for interesting plant life. The olive green of the salal tinted the whole hillside. How David Douglas had loved this glossy evergreen plant, a dignified member of the great heath family. *Gaultheria shallon* had been the plant he stooped to gather when he first set foot on the Pacific coast. In his opinion the great Oregon country should have been called Gaultheria in honor of the herbage that gave the shores of the ocean its magic green.

The memory of David Douglas sustained him today. David Douglas, a man ridiculed by his fellow travelers, but at the same time respected and loved. He pictured the gentle naturalist placed in his uncertain position. Just what would he have done if he had reason to believe that a white girl needed to be taken away from a tribe of Indians who were divided in their willingness to part with her. Why, just what he intended to do. A thing a trader or trapper, for all his bravado, would never so much as think of attempting.

He stopped just before he reached the edge of the timber to admire the scarlet flame of the Indian paintbrush *(Castilleja miniata),* thinking ruefully that there was no use to take specimens. Tilki had his paper and presses, and like as not he would not recover them soon.

There were no evidences of uncommon plant life about, so after taking his bearings very carefully—it would never do to lose the trail in the fog—he stooped where the outer fringe of the firs almost brushed the ground. The temperature was most comfortingly higher under the trees and the fog did not penetrate to any great degree. In the dim twilight he walked along, enjoying the carpet of needles that was soft under his tired, aching feet. Vegetation could not gain a foothold on account of the turpentine the falling needles held. He walked rapidly to stimulate his circulation and to work the stiffness out of his sore limbs, and when just on the point of retracing his steps to the trail, his sharp eye caught sight of a patch of dead white about a hundred feet farther on. He started in sudden joy. Here was a piece of white cloth. Perhaps it was something Multnomah had placed there or dropped inadvertently. He fairly flew over that hundred feet of fir needles, and stopped in awe when he came up to what he had mistaken for a bit of white cloth.

He, Jim Faxon, an amateur botanist beside David Douglas and Thomas Nuttal, had accidentally stumbled upon the orchid that they had searched for in vain. Here was the "ghost flower" *(Monotropa uniflora).* He forgot that his teeth had been chattering with cold the moment before. His fall over the cliff, his illness, the danger of his quest for Multnomah, were in that instant as nothing to him. What was peril or the remote possibility of difficulty with Indians when compared with the discovery of a rare orchid? Even if the white girl, Multnomah, had no real existence—though he was sure she had—his trip to the country of the Nehalems had been a glorious success.

Monotropa uniflora is known to grow in favored spots all over the North American continent, but is so rare that it is seldom chanced upon, and the discovery of a clump by a botanist is the event of his lifetime. This saprophite lives, like the true orchid, on decayed vegetable matter, usually decayed wood, and is never found except in the semi-darkness of the fir or pine forest. The waxy, corpse-like whiteness of stalk, leaf-blade, and flower is due to the complete absence of chlorophyll, or the green coloring matter that plants by some mysterious alchemy of nature manufacture from the elements.

After his first burst of rapture, Jim scrutinized the clump from all sides to determine the best manner of taking it up root and all. He had often read in his field book that *Monotropa uniflora* had the habit, when disturbed, of changing very shortly from pearly white through shades of dull gray, finally turning completely black in the process of withering. How he wished he had enough alcohol to preserve it in all its pristine whiteness.

There were eight pipes in the clump. With the utmost caution he scooped away the decayed wood and was pleased to discover that the root mass just filled his white felt hat. It would never do to allow the heat from his hands to reach the sensitive orchid.

Realizing at last that he had spent more time than he had intended in the timber, he hurried to find the trail down the side of the mountain. There was no time to lose if he were to be on hand at the hour Tilki had appointed for him.

He hastily strapped his rolled buffalo robe on his back and descended, bearing the hard white hat containing *Monotropa uniflora* with all the tenderness of a vestal virgin carrying a brazier of sacred flame to light some bygone pagan altar.

At length the encampment burst upon his vision. There it lay, the village of the Nehalems, a dozen or more skin tepees, gleaming grayish-white now that the sun had dispelled the morning fog. The location was pleasant, a lush upland meadow, barely three hundred yards above the beach.

There was the usual activity around the camp. A number of squaws were engaged in digging clams on the shore, throwing them into huge baskets. Tilki had boastingly told him that the clams on this particular stretch of beach were larger, fatter, and to be found in greater quantities than at any other point on the coast. This he attributed to the Fire Spirit, who was the guardian of the tribe. To his sacred presence they owed their prosperity. Great numbers of beaver lived in their streams, deer and elk were always fat and plentiful, and the generous run of salmon in the river assured them that they never would lack for food. Owing to the mildness of the climate, the salal berries held on until late in the winter. Small wonder that the secret of this little valley, that literally flowed with milk and honey, should be so carefully guarded by the peaceful, contented Nehalems.

Jim felt greatly comforted by the pristine beauty about him. The apprehension had been driven to the background of his consciousness by his wonderful find, and it did not emerge. Pooh! He had been a child afraid of its own shadow. What did a little touch of Indian mysticism and hocus-pocus amount to in such a spot? He strained his eyes for the sight of a white woman who would be Multnomah. He could easily have detected her by her bearing among the other women, but she was nowhere to be seen.

He swung joyfully down the trail. At the head of the meadow he passed three old squaws who were engaged in gathering and pounding the sword-like leaves of the *Iris Douglasiana*. He had seen some very fine fishing-nets made from the tough silky fiber of this wild blue flag. They paused in their work to stare at him in wondering awe, and when they did not offer him a salutation he passed them in silence. They looked after him, chattering noisily among themselves before resuming their labor.

A good-sized clump of willow trees promised grateful shade, and he made for it, intending to rest a few moments before making his way to the village. He had pushed aside the low-hanging branches and entered before he realized his situation. There was some sort of a conclave going on in a cleared space inside.

He had attributed the slight stir he heard to the movement of small birds among the branches, as he parted them carefully so as not to brush the plant he carried in his hat. For a moment there was commotion in the circle of Indians, and then a death-like silence. After the glare of sun on sand, it took a minute or two for his eyes to become accustomed to the gloom, then he started in spite of himself, with mingled sensations of amazement and consternation. Twenty men, their faces as expressionless as wooden masks, sat staring at him. He had unwittingly disturbed a solemn council of braves.

Jim started and came near dropping his hat, but recovered it and his composure as to a man the assembly rose and began gesticulating and speaking together. They were evidently as greatly surprised as he was. He stood for a moment at the edge of the group, then, his ruling passion uppermost even in the face of danger, with a stride he reached the center of the group and carefully set his hat with *Monotropa uniflora* on the ground. He was not going to risk damage coming to it. He straightened up, and in spite of inward seething and uncertainty assumed an air of nonchalance that he was far from feeling. With folded arms he stood surveying the Indians.

There was but little doubt that the council in some way concerned him, for he recognized Tilki in a small group that stood a little aloof from the others. Not by so much as the flicker of an eyelash did his friend acknowledge his presence. The dignified men composing his group were medicine-men or at least belonged to the priestly order, for their regalia was topped with the enormous head-dress peculiar to the cult. Each carried in his hand the familiar medicine-mask of wood carved to represent some fantastic animal or bird.

The others were still more formidable. They were attired in full war dress, with the exception of one who kept well in the background. This was his enemy, Cockqua, who had pushed him over the cliff. He wore only frayed buckskin pantaloons, the better to exhibit his horrible red cicatrices. He was engaged in sharpening his knife on a stone with a V-shaped groove in it, and, this task finished, he ran his finger along the edge, then secured the weapon with a pair of wooden pinchers to his wrist. There was a subtle threat in his action.

Jim knew that a party holding a powwow in full war dress boded no good to him. The double robe of elkskin reaching to the heels, and the corset of narrow hardwood sticks interlaced with tough bear-grass was enough to daunt even the stoutest heart.

As the hubbub occasioned by his entrance subsided, each man again took his place in the circle. An unearthly quiet fell upon them. Jim waited for them to make the first move. Then one by one they advanced and shook his hand with a cordiality that he fancied was a bit forced. Cockqua did not come forward, but never took his baleful eye off him. Jim was devoutly thankful that he was spared shaking his loathsome hand. This would have strained courtesy to the breaking point. He returned the stare in kind.

Jim was motioned to a seat in the circle; the medicine group squatted on their heels near him. He was thankful for his tobacco pouch. As soon as it was produced the calumet, or medicine-pipe, appeared, passing from mouth to mouth, while the utmost good feeling prevailed.

Jim felt faint with hunger; his breakfast had been light and early, but he knew that the tedious powwow would last the better part of the day. As the spirit moved him, man after man arose and began a harangue. The medicine group broke into an occasional weird chant, to the general accompaniment of hand-clapping and swaying of bodies. At length a messenger was dispatched. He took this to mean that a feast had been ordered, and he breathed a thankful sigh. No matter what was offered, it would at least be food.

The summer heat became oppressive even in the shady inclosure, and the perspiring Indians in heavy double elkskin cloaks filled the still air with a sickening stench. The session ended just before sundown.

Jim could not understand a word of their dialect. The Chinook jargon had not penetrated to this mountain fastness. When his turn came to speak, being a guest, he was last, he told them his name and explained that he was a "grass man" and had come to make them a friendly visit. He expressed his delight at discovering the long-sought Indian-pipe growing in their country.

They nodded enthusiastic assent to this and began at once speaking in halting English to him, asking numerous questions and making protestations of everlasting friendship, while Cockqua glowered in the offing, putting in his time in sharpening the knife. Jim was rather exasperated to think that they understood English and still would spend a whole session in speaking to him in their own language, just another example of

Indian idiosyncrasy, though the fact that they understood him was conclusive proof that they had had contact with the whites. Very few of the natives about Fort Vancouver spoke anything except the Chinook, and not a chance word of the trade jargon had he heard the whole time, though he had strained his attention to catch their meaning.

The pipe plant reposed in state. No one so much as offered to touch it. As they rose at the conclusion of the powwow, Jim lifted his hat carefully to take the specimen with him. At this Tilki stepped to the front and led him out, while the others formed a solemn procession behind and moved single file in the direction of the village.

The occasion was one of the solemn ceremony. Tilki led the rather sheepish Jim to each tepee in turn, where the pipe plant was accorded a sort of adoration from the inmates. A hush fell over them as they gazed at it; then, as they departed, there were animated handshakes and merry quips and laughter. Holiday had been proclaimed in the Nehalem tribe. Jim wondered at this. War or some terrible mischief had been brewing when he burst upon the council, and yet here was cordial welcome and the utmost in hospitality. He felt secure, and yet his very security was shot through with uneasiness.

He had scanned each teepee as he entered for some signs of Multnomah, but had found no trace of her. Why had Tilki adopted the manner of an utter stranger to him? He determined to remain on his guard in spite of all the evidences of friendship. And there was Cockqua eternally sharpening his knife and running his finger along the edge of the blade to test its keenness. Cockqua would kill him if he could find the opportunity, there was not the least doubt on that point.

Dinner was ready—fat elk meat cooked in a large trough hollowed out of a block of cedar. The squaws were manipulating the hot rocks by means of the pliant loops of willow. They were busy removing the mats that had held the heat and piling wooden trenchers with the savory stew.

The Nehalems held quite advanced notions as to table etiquette. They served their foods on polished wooden plates and ate it with rather clumsy spoons made from the horns of the mountain sheep. They were cleaner in their culinary habits than any tribe he had visited before, though this was not saying much.

At the conclusion of the repast, a tall young man appeared with Jim's pack, Briar followed him, and rushed upon her master with delighted barks. She was duly admired by the tribe, whose dogs were the most miserable mongrel curs.

Jim thought Tilki showed rather an exaggerated surprise at the appearance of the pack. They gathered about it wonderingly. The squaws squealed with delight when he opened it.

Pleased that he had gifts to offer, Jim opened the packs and spread its contents on a clean mat, and proceeded with his *potlatch*. The women exclaimed in rapture over the beads and other trinkets, and made a meticulous division among themselves, draping the blue and white beads around their necks.

Jim noticed one wrinkled old beldame eyeing the handle of his tin cup. He had placed it in his pack when it fell off. He handed it to her ceremoniously. Her delight escaped all bounds. Seizing a small knife which had just been given one of the braves, she cut a gash in the lobe of her ear and inserted the gaud. With blood pouring over her face and neck she strutted and posed before her admiring sisters. This was too much, Jim laughed until weakness overcame him, and the whole tribe, catching the contagion, laughed with him.

At the conclusion of the evening's amusement his gun was handed to him, after being fingered and admired by all the men. There was a distinct relief in having the gun and ammunition by him and the faithful Briar at his heels.

The exertions of the day had wearied him terribly. Tilki rose at last, announcing that he would conduct their guest to the medicine lodge, where he was to sleep. There was more handshaking, and then his impassive friend led him up the hill. It seemed to the staggering Jim that they traveled a mile, but the distance was probably no more than a scant half.

The medicine lodge stood alone on the edge of the timber. A small hole just large enough to admit the body of a man formed the only entrance. Tilki led the way and Jim followed. The interior was as dark as a pocket. Tilki left him standing uncertainly in the middle of the blackness, to return shortly bearing a flaming piece of pitch wood, and by its light began making his guest comfortable for the night. First he doused the hard-packed earth with water to discourage the vermin, then spread new mats two or three feet thick for his bed. He produced a skin bottle and gave him a bitter draught, then began chafing and kneading his tired sore muscles. Never a word did he utter the whole time, silencing his charge's eager questions with a cautious finger placed to his lips.

"Me come in morning," Tilki announced in a voice loud enough to be overheard by a chance loiterer, and crawled through the hole, blocking it after him with a cedar slab.

CHAPTER TWELVE
THE LODGE
OF MULTNOMAH

WITH a sigh Jim relaxed in the depths of his soft bed. The day's exertions had wearied him. Sleep came at once, but his rest was short. After the first keen edge of fatigue had worn off, the night noises registered in his consciousness. The hoot of an owl, or the cry of some remote predatory animal, sounds to which he was ordinarily oblivious, disturbed him. Briar was actively engaged with the fleas that infested the lodge. She scratched, she bit, she growled, she changed ends with herself, pausing at his angry command, only to resume her work in a minute or two.

There was nothing but light dozing with irritating awakenings in store for him. He told himself in exasperation that his nerves were unsteady since his illness, and just now he needed a steady hand and a level head. He *must* sleep. But, half awake, visions of Cockqua sharpening his knife and staring at him out of eyes that were black pools of malevolence haunted him. Multnomah's frightened face rose from the mist of dreams— Multnomah cowering before Cockqua, who menaced her with his knife. He would be glad, tired as he was, when the blessed light of day broke, though it summoned him to further exertion and perhaps to danger.

The medicine lodge was a safe refuge for him. Here were stored the sacred implements of the craft. No member of the laity would presume to venture into this sanctuary. By the flare of the resinous torch he had seen the hideous masks, the ceremonial robes, and the gigantic head-dresses that hung on the walls. There were totem poles, carved in terrible representations of birds, animals, and fishes, looking down upon him, guarding his rest in the sooty blackness. Though nothing had been told him, he was sure that the place was guarded by some of Tilki's companions, to prevent Cockqua's making an attack on their guest.

Aside from Cockqua, Jim was certain that he had no one to fear. One significant thing, that in the excitement attending the feast and the *potlatch* had escaped him, was that Cockqua took no part. He had stood in the background, sharpening his knife. Cockqua's round head accounted for this. He was a slave and would take the remnants of food with the women.

But he had a large hand in the affairs of the tribe; his presence in the council proved this. Unusual, Jim reflected in the darkness, though the Indian slave is not the subservient creature that his bondage might seem to indicate. Slaves are merely captives of war, and while they must attend to menial duties, given superior intelligence or unusual bravery, they often rise in rank, sometimes gaining freedom and marrying into the clan. The greatest cross of the slave is that his head may not be flattened in infancy, neither can his children enjoy this mark of distinction.

Masters often married female slaves, and once in a great while the flattening of the head of the first child born to her was permitted, so that after a number of generations the blood of bondsman mingled with the free-born, tending to stimulate the clan.

Briar growled softly with a note of warning this time. A slight sound near the entrance to the lodge, and Jim sat up with every sense alert. He spoke to the dog, at the same time seizing his gun that he had placed at the head of his bed.

"Tilki come." The voice was scarcely audible.

Jim was glad of human companionship. He groped his way to the entrance as the Indian crawled in.

"No make talk," Tilki whispered. "Come now Multnomah's lodge, then me tell-um."

Jim lost no time. He had not undressed, not knowing what the night might bring forth. Briar rose to accompany them, but Tilki ordered her down, and she obeyed, whining.

Tilki took Jim's hand in the darkness and they left the lodge without a sound, barring the entrance after them. They kept to the shadow of the trees until they had climbed for a distance up a hill; then his guide led him bodily out into a good trail. A dog barked in the village below and Tilki froze to instant attention, but, deciding that nothing was amiss, he pushed on, stopping every few minutes to listen.

Jim was wondering. Now that he was really going to meet Multnomah, he felt that he should have been given time to brush his rumpled clothing and smooth down his rebellious hair. He longed for his white felt hat; it had been left in the village with the Indian-pipe plant reposing in it. This meeting would not be so trying as the one his fancy had painted with all the tribe as witnesses, but still first impressions made a difference.

His reflections were tinged with bitterness. Tilki was in command. How he resented obeying an Indian unquestioningly. But in his anxiety to find Multnomah he buried any feeling he had in the matter of his going. He would allow events to run their course until opportunity to become master of affairs presented itself and hope ran high. A huge object loomed in the distance at the crest of the rise; coming closer, he saw it was a house of some sort. In the moonlight it appeared to be built of slabs with the bark on, but he could not be sure. Light beamed from two windows, and, wonder of wonders, as they came closer he saw that the windows were of glass. Real glass windows! Multnomah, then, was not the only white person among the Nehalems. She had not built a house with windows. There must be a family here. He made a futile effort to smooth his hair with his fingers, then, excitement mounting, he broke into a run, with Tilki close at his side.

When they reached the door Jim hesitated and fell back a step, but Tilki advanced and drew the latch. In a daze Jim entered behind him. An old squaw rose from an easy chair made of barrel staves to greet them. Seeing Jim, she cautiously shut the door and drew a bolt of wood across it, before she spoke.

Her face lit with joy and tears streamed from her eyes as she grasped Jim's outstretched hand. The Indian woman seldom weeps, but drops wet his hand as she bent over it. "Thank God," she said. "Our prayers are answered!"

She spoke halting English, not like the Indian who has picked up a word here and there and joined them together piecemeal with idioms of his own dialect, but like one who had been most carefully taught to enunciate correctly. There was a throaty burr on the gutturals and a hesitation between words that betrayed her, but otherwise she might have been a gentle lady of his own blood so far as her speech was concerned.

"I am Celiast [pronounced Cel-i-'-ast]," in her emotion she grasped Jim's hand again.

"I am Jim Faxon. I have come from Fort William in search of Multnomah," Jim told her.

"Multnomah has been waiting for the white man who is to take her to her people. She has been waiting these last two years in faith that he would come. I who am old and have known much sorrow have not her trust in the goodness of the God of the white man. I have often doubted."

Tilki grunted his disgust. "What me tell-um. Last sleep me tell-um white man here. You t'ink-um Tilki have forked tongue?"

"No," Celiast assured him, gently. "I believed you last night. I have been waiting all day for news of him."

Jim was looking anxiously about for Multnomah. He felt a smothering disappointment. There was no one else in the single large room.

Ignoring him, Tilki began speaking rapidly in his own tongue to Celiast. Evidently he was rehearsing the events of the day, embellishing the tale nicely, for Celiast's manner changed, as she listened, from the anxiety of the deepest concern, her laugh ringing out like that of a delighted child as the story progressed.

Jim looked about him in joy such as he had not known since entering the Oregon country. Here was a real home. He paused in wonder at the lights that illumined the comfortable room. Candles, real candles, in carved wooden sconces on the walls, not gutturing tallow dips, but slender wax tapers, cast their mellow light.

Along one wall stood two beds neatly spread with blue-and-white-checked counterpanes. There was a shelf of books. A large family Bible had a small homemade table to itself. The walls were completely covered with beautifully colored Indian mats, and a huge fireplace displayed a well-set crane with three pot-hooks hanging on the iron bar. A fat black tea-kettle stood on a trivet by the smoldering fire. His gaze was avid. He could not take in the details of that wonderful room fast enough.

Joy of joys! This was like coming home. His unbelieving eyes fell upon shelves where pewter and crockery stood in shining rows. His mother had never maintained a more immaculate home. After the filth of the Indian lodge the room fairly dazzled him.

During the exquisite moments Jim spent in his scrutiny of the room, Tilki talked rapidly to Celiast. He seemed to be giving her directions. But when he at length turned to them her glance fell like a benediction on him.

Celiast was small for an Indian woman, and stooped like the aged squaws of her toil-burdened race. She was wiry, a slender wisp of a woman, with smooth hair parted in the middle and coiled at the nape of her neck, with wooden pins holding it in place. In spite of her buckskin skirt and jacket there was an immaculate daintiness about her that vaguely reminded him of his mother.

"You are surprised, Mr. Jim Faxon?" she asked in her halting speech.

"Surprised? I am astonished! I can scarcely believe my eyes!" Jim faltered, reddening under her indulgent gaze like a schoolboy. "But where is Multnomah?" he pleaded, afraid that, like the other Indians, she would refuse to answer his questions. "She has parents here? Where are they all?"

Celiast stiffened at his queries. "There are matters of which an Indian may not speak. There is much to tell. You will hear the story in good time."

"But Multnomah. Where is she? Surely you will tell me?"

"Multnomah went to the mountains with Katoosh. He is a great *shaman*. She was in danger. There was no other way. I trust in God that you will find her and bring her to safety." Her simple statement had the fervency of a petition to heaven.

Jim's spirits fell. Then he had by no means reached the end of his quest. He wondered dully how he could go on. So he was taking a hand in Indian politics, just as he had feared. There was danger in intrigue between the medicine-men and the members of the tribe. He acknowledged to himself that he was desperately weary of Indians. He doubted if he could bear with them for another day, but he knew at the moment that he would go on until he died in the effort to rescue Multnomah.

Her home was redolent with the lingering perfume of her presence. She was again the woman of his dreams, but the dreams had taken on the substance of reality. Could he dare hope to win her love? The room spoke eloquently of her. A man would love such a girl long before he saw her. He was certain of his own desire.

But whether she wished to marry him or not, his simple duty lay clearly before him. Multnomah must be found and taken at once to the safety of Fort Vancouver. Jane Beaver would look out for her; she was an Englishwoman. Or Dr. McLoughlin's wife Margaret was a kindly soul. If no other way opened, she could sail for England under the care of the Beavers, who were returning home in the fall.

Jim turned to Tilki. "We will go at once in search of Multnomah." He meant just what he said and the Indian was quick to recognize the note of command in his voice. "But, first," Jim went on, looking Tilki straight in the eye. "I must know all about this business. I am through with all this evasion and mystery."

Tilki returned his gaze in kind, then laughed indulgently. "Soon now tell-um ever't'ing. Now you know-um Indian no lie? One sleep, two sleeps, mebbe, we go. No can tell. Much for do." He rose quickly. "Me go. Watch-um tlail. You safe. Cockqua him bad Indian, ver' bad Indian. Him no come here." He spoke a few words to Celiast, and opening the door went out into the night.

"Tilki will come for you before daylight," Celiast assured Jim, who had cast an uneasy glance at the door. "Tilki has much to do before he leaves. You are perfectly safe among our people for a day or two, but you must not let them know that you have been here talking to me."

"When did Multnomah leave?" Jim asked.

"Ten days ago," Celiast answered with a sigh. "Katoosh waited as long as he dared, but Cockqua has been plotting mischief for a long time. Even a great *shaman* cannot always give protection. Multnomah is the idol of my tribe, but Cockqua is gaining power over them. Katoosh has feared he would take her by force." She shook her head, with her sad eyes full of tears.

So Cockqua, the unspeakable, was going to take a white girl by force, was he? Not while Jim Faxon lived to kill him. His fists clenched in his anger and his face whitened. He had never before felt real blood lust, but the urge to slay gripped him as he recalled the loathsome self-inflicted wounds of the depraved monster who had pushed him off the cliff. He was for hunting out his enemy then and there and shooting him as he would a mad dog, but Celiast's gentle voice recalled him.

"Tilki will soon come for you. There are things I must tell you for your safety."

"I want to get to the very root of this trouble," Jim's voice urged her to confide in him. "I mean to kill Cockqua. The thought of his coming into the presence of a white girl is enough to warrant his death, let alone his trying to take her for a wife."

Celiast stared thoughtfully into the fire. "Do you know that the council you broke into yesterday were deciding upon killing the white man immediately if he appeared as Tilki promised he would?"

Jim gasped in astonishment. "I knew there was something in the air, but had no idea they were as desperate as that."

"Tilki is shrewd," Celiast continued, admiringly. "He gave out two weeks ago that he was going into the mountains after his supply of simples. Day before yesterday he came back to the lodge saying that he had been fasting and had had a vision while he was alone in the mountains and that next day about noon the Nehalems were to receive the white man whom they had been told was coming to take Multnomah to her people. We all believe in Tilki's visions."

"Why, the old rascal!" Jim laughed. "So that's the reason he left me up on the mountain that night and told me to come in in the morning. I was good and mad at him for going off like that. He might have told me what he was up to. Drat Indians, anyway! They're too fond of being mysterious."

"Yes," Celiast admitted, smiling, "my people's ways seem odd to you, who cannot always understand. Tilki has good reasons for his actions."

"Cockqua was at the bottom of this decision of the council, wasn't he?" Jim asked. "He tried to kill me on the trail. Tilki saved my life."

Celiast started at this, but said nothing.

"Will they kill me tomorrow?" Jim asked, and laughed at the sober face of Celiast.

"Cockqua has been a trouble-maker since he was a small boy. He worked on our young men until they donned their war clothes to frighten their elders and the medicine council into consenting to keep Multnomah with us. Cockqua didn't dare tell that he had met you before. Tilki would have revealed the truth and he would have been dealt with for attacking you. My people do not kill!

"Do you know what saved your life?" Celiast asked. "The Indian-peace-pipe you carried into the circle. But for that you would not have left alive. The peace-pipe is sacred to the Nehalems. Seldom do we find one, though we need it sorely at times. The pipe brings peace to the lodge; it heals dissensions. You wondered why it was carried into every teepee and my people laughed and shook hands and made a great feast for you. I do not think they will kill you now. The omen was most fortunate. You will be accepted as the husband of Multnomah. The hand of God directed you," she added, softly.

"To think that I should chance upon *Monotropa uniflora* just in the nick of time to save my life, that does look like the hand of God," Jim admitted.

"While the peace plant lives you are in no danger here, but it turns black in a day or so, and Cockqua has not given over his evil schemes. Tomorrow you must mingle with my people to cement friendship. Tilki will take you away in the night. We were laying plans just now."

"I mean to kill Cockqua just the same," Jim persisted, stubbornly.

"White men kill; my people do not kill, only the very evil ones, and they are swiftly punished. Not in my time has a life been taken in our tribe." Celiast's tone was a rebuke to Jim.

"Cockqua, shall not have Multnomah," he reiterated.

But Tilki came to take Jim back to the medicine lodge. Celiast at the door gave him a parting instruction. "Come to Multnomah's lodge if there is trouble tomorrow," she said, and Tilki nodded his approval.

They reached the medicine lodge just before dawn. Jim lay down and slept like one under a powerful opiate until a smiling delegation of his hosts, among them the expressionless Tilki, waited upon him to convey him to the feast that was being prepared in his honor.

CHAPTER THIRTEEN
AN INDIAN HOLIDAY

THE tribe were in gala apparel when Tilki brought Jim down to the village next morning. All work had ceased for the day, and the Indians were making merry with games and contests of skill on their playground above the cluster of tepees.

Squaws were busy about the cooking-fires, following the directions of an aged crone who was head of the chief's household and thus held a position of authority among the women. There was to be a great feast late that afternoon.

Jim watched a good-natured squaw as she prepared breakfast for them. Anticipating their needs, she had already laid out choice bits of elk meat, which she now proceeded to place in the cleft of a split willow withe, tying the ends of the twig with a rush to keep the morsel from falling into the fire. She broiled her juicy steak over the live coals with the consummate skill of the culinary artist. The meal was delicious and satisfying. He felt fortified for enduring the tiresome ceremonies that made up an Indian holiday.

The tribe were not all at home, this being the season for gathering the winter supplies of meat, roots, and berries. Tilki had told Jim that they numbered about three hundred, but there were not to exceed seventy Indians in the village, and perhaps thirty of these were very old men, with a few boys too young to go on the hunt. The women too decrepit to garner foodstuffs in the mountains remained at home to carry on the dressing of skins and the other drudgery that the younger women forced upon them. The group of strong young squaws whose duty it was to dig the clams, of course remained at home on the beach.

Jim wondered how it came about that Cockqua and his band of young daredevils were loitering about the camp during the busy season. Then he began to understand, or thought he did. They had left their fellow workers on some pretext of their own and were making preparations to overcome the medicine cult while the majority were away. Katoosh had fled to the mountains with Multnomah to save her from Cockqua. No doubt Tilki and the other sympathizers of the medicine cult would follow, taking him with them that night. If his deductions were correct, the outlook was bad. There was the prospect of fighting, perhaps of being overtaken and killed before they could reach Multnomah.

Cockqua was wandering about this morning in the company of the young men, calling them aside to talk earnestly with a small knot, then covering their actions with loud laughing and engaging in some feat of strength or test of skill. Jim felt his eyes boring into his back most of the time, though he did not come near the group who were showing him the courtesies due a guest.

After breakfast he was escorted to a large teepee where the chief, Cassicass, in his ceremonial robe of rich sea-otter skin, covering him from head to heels was waiting to give him an official welcome to the country of the Nehalems. After an elaborate introduction Jim was left with him, one of the men remaining to act as interpreter. The chief was an old man, tottering and feeble, but he had a singularly clear mind for one of his years. He had a small smattering of English, which he seemed loath to use, though he understood Jim perfectly when he spoke to him.

Cassicass was childlike in his delight at having the white man for his guest. Jim was cordially offered the best the lodge afforded, and the hope that his stay among the Nehalems would be a long and pleasant one was expressed over and over. Jim was sure that Cassicass was sincere and friendly toward him, though he imagined that he detected a tincture of anxiety in the chief's manner.

Jim was hoping that Cassicass would mention Multnomah and that his consent would be given for taking her out of the country, but he felt, as the interview proceeded, that he was skillfully screening the issue in his long tiresome monologue dealing in glittering generalities, and plentifully sprinkled with trite Indian platitudes. He glanced keenly at the interpreter, wondering if he were giving him a correct version of the address and decided that he was honest.

The elaborate ceremonies began soon after. Jim surveyed the squaws with a critical eye, finding them a shade cleaner in their persons and rather more modest in demeanor than their sisters on the Columbia. Their habitations did not reek so horribly of decaying fish, but this could be attributed to the fact that the salmon run in the Nehalem River had not yet begun.

While their heads had been flattened, the young women were rather comely, though most of them had been horribly tattooed from chin to ear. Jim had always been fascinated by this primitive form of personal decoration, so painfully accomplished. The coloring was applied with a sharp piece of bone and a cinder from the fire. Blue predominated in the color scheme. The lines might run from mouth to ear. Some were done in spots, while a few were completely blue over the lower part of the face. The Nehalems considered tattooing a great mark of beauty, particularly when a little red or green clay mixed with salmon oil was applied to the upper part of the face.

The nostrils of many of the men and women were pierced. Those in opulence wore haiqua, a small cylindrical shell, white and of extreme hardness, varying from three to four inches in length, and from about three-eighths to half an inch in diameter. The wealth of a tribe may be determined from the display of haiqua, which answered for money among all the coast Indians. The price of various articles is reckoned by it, a fathom of the best grade of shell being equal to ten prime beaver skins. Judging from the display, the Nehalems did not suffer from poverty, and from the trinkets they wore it was very evident that they had some intercourse with the neighboring tribes and with white traders.

The labret was also in evidence among the men. This is an ornament worn in a hole pierced through the lower lip. The labret had its origin among the northern tribes, and haiqua is a shell only to be found in the neighborhood of Nootka Sound, so the Nehalems mingled freely with other peoples, even though they guarded the secret of their own rich country.

The holiday costumes of the men and women were elaborately ornamented. The women wore the summer dress—a skirt made from threads of the inner bark of the cedar tree, knotted in such a way as to offer protection and yet not interfere with their movements. They had on loose fringed jackets of buckskin and beautifully beaded leggings. The buckskins of the men were also adorned with fringe and beads.

All the jewelry they owned was in evidence. Heavy strands of beads, thimbles, disks of copper strung on elk sinews, enhanced the savage charm of the women and girls. Many of them had tiny hawk bells concealed about their persons, which tinkled as they walked. The ears of both men and women had been horribly gashed for the insertion of trinkets.

Jim Faxon never tired of watching the colorful play of life in an Indian camp, the numerous mongrel dogs, the spotted ponies, perhaps a bear or a fox tethered outside a lodge. There were babies in their cruel headflattening cradles, and naked children running about under the feet of the horses and in the way of everyone.

This occasion would have been an unalloyed delight to him under ordinary circumstances, but now Cockqua disfigured the colorful scene—a Cockqua who was in the festivity but not of it. He, alone, was unadorned, though he strutted about, wearing only his tattered buckskin trousers, calling attention to his terrible cicatrices as if they were medals given for bravery. His satellites dogged his footsteps, occasionally one of the bolder of them running inquisitive fingers over the half-healed sores.

Jim ignored his enemy, and yet it was an effort to keep his gaze from wandering in his direction. When Cockqua could manage he came as close as he dared without attracting attention and began sharpening the knife, running his fingers along its keen edge and then returning the weapon to the wooden pinchers on his wrist. The movement was slight and furtive and yet calculated to convey its subtle meaning. The strain of it through that long day was telling on Jim, though he maintained his air of nonchalance through it all.

First in order came religious exercises. Cassicass called his people to their devotions. Their gay chatter ceased instantly at the peculiar flute-like note, accompanied with the hoarse Indian drum. Silently they seated themselves in a large semicircle on the grass. The chief was feeble; leading the devotions fell upon Tilki, who took his position facing the assemblage.

There was fifteen minutes of complete silence, then Tilki began speaking to them. The interpreter at Jim's side told him a little of what was said. He reminded them of their object in assembling—to adore the Great Spirit who made the light and the darkness, the fire and the water. He told them that if they offered sincere prayers they would be accepted.

Tilki rose from squatting on his heels, then sank on his knees, and the congregation followed. His prayer was fervent. With eyes looking to heaven he asked a blessing on his people in short sentences, short and uttered in great rapidity. As he concluded each abrupt petition his audience responded in a few words, accompanied by moaning. The prayer lasted all of twenty minutes, then Tilki, still kneeling, began a sacred song in which all joined fervently. No intelligible words were uttered, just the syllables, ho-ha-ho-ha-ho-ha-a, beginning in the lower registers and gradually swelling to a full, round exquisitely modulated chorus. The clasped hands of the singers moved back and forth across their breasts, while their bodies swayed with the rhythm of the music.

The service occupied about an hour, then each Indian rose quietly from the ground with the rapt glow of religious exultation in his dark eyes and moved in silence to his tepee.

Jim felt a thrill of religious fervor which the two-hour sermons in the church at home had never excited in him. On the plains among the Blackfeet, wherever a group of Indians were holding their devotions, the men of the Wyeth party had never failed to join them with bowed heads and uplifted hearts. Always had come the realization that there is but one "Great Spirit," no matter by what name men may call him, and that those who seek him in simplicity and earnestness are for the moment lifted unto him.

The travelers had often remarked that, no matter in what tribe they happened to be, religious exercises were carried on at stated times. A day was set apart, whether one in seven as among Christian peoples or according to the phases of the moon they had not been able to determine.

After the religious observance there was half an hour's pause, then the dancing began. Two large circles formed, the men inside, women and children outside, moving in opposite directions, the men going with the course of the sun, the women contrary to it, the former turning from right to left, the latter left to right.

Music was provided by the raucous Indian drums and rattles in the hands of the medicine-men, supplemented by bone and reed flutes. The din was deafening after the dancers gained momentum and began their weird chanting. Faces were kept always to the sun. The body was held erect, the swaying and bending accomplished by the flexing of the knees and the alternate advancement of the shoulders, intended to interpret the movement of reeds in the wind. The heel and ball of the foot were lifted and brought down with great force and incredible swiftness, the changes of position being slow, but attitudes glided into one another with surprising rapidity and violence. This was no medicine dance, but just an expression of simple joy in life and holiday. Cockqua leaned nonchalantly against a tree, sharpening his knife.

Jim stood at the edge of the circle with the aged Cassicass, watching the dance with the delight he always felt in the poetry of motion with which the savage interprets the simple processes of nature. He sensed their mood and the joys and sorrows expressed in movement and sound. The dance ended only when the participants sank to the ground, laughing in their exhaustion. Men and women sprawled resting where they fell, while merriment reigned.

Games and tests of skill followed. Cockqua distinguished himself at archery by repeatedly shooting an arrow through a wooden ring that was tossed in the air. He scored again and again, while the whole assembly applauded.

Jim was invited to show his prowess in some particular way. He always elicited shouts of approval in every camp he visited by placing powder and dry twigs on the ground, and using his lens as a burning-glass to set fire to the tinder. As the wood charred and at last the tiny flame appeared the Indians drew back in superstitious awe. The white man had drawn fire from heaven. He must be some sort of a supernatural being. Tilki here seized the opportunity to explain that in the vision that had come to him in the mountains he saw the white man commanding the lightning. This was accepted readily. The white man had more power than the great *shaman,* Katoosh. Henceforth he was to be regarded with veneration.

Not to be outdone, Cockqua, who had been sulking in a little knot of his followers, announced that he would show them a feat that had never before been performed in the tribe, though their forefathers had known men, who could endure the ordeal. The interpreter was quick to give Jim the substance of Cockqua's speech.

All waited in breathless eagerness while Cockqua, wearing an exaggerated air of importance, motioned to a confederate to come forward. He appeared leading a cayuse by a plaited thong. Cockqua drew his knife and, handing it to the man, turned his bare back to him. Without a moment's hesitation the savage cut two gashes in the flesh just below the shoulderblades and, inserting the blade, slashed the muscles, making an aperture large enough to thread the horse's tether through. He secured it with a knot and Cockqua without a tremor led the animal all about the circle.

The horse was then untied, and to finish the exhibition he cut off two large handfuls of flesh from his chest. The spectacle was ghastly. Jim turned his face in sick disgust. From the throat to the waist the Indian was covered with blood, still he smiled in appreciation of the cries of *"Skookum! Skookum!"* ("Valiant man!")

This dreadful piece of self-inflicted torture had the desired effect upon every brave present; even the sedate medicine-men grunted their appreciation, while a few of the women cheered, but the most spat in scorn. A *skookum* is the envy and admiration of every Indian who treads the earth. His power over his fellows is tremendous; they will follow him to the death. In a terrible moment Jim realized that Cockqua had gained the ascendency over the medicine cult. They might all be killed by his followers who had witnessed the drawing of the blood that had made him a *skookum*.

Jim glanced in Tilki's direction, but he was talking unconcernedly with two of his friends. He showed no inclination to run, yet it cost Jim a mighty effort to keep his composure though he knew that the slightest indication of fear on his part would instantly precipitate matters.

Jim was anxious about the pipe plant. It was still in the chief's lodge. When the gambling began he went off to look at it. The heat of the day and the wind had played havoc with *Monotropa uniflora*. In a couple of hours it would be perfectly black. He gazed at it in sadness, then he removed the clump from his hat. He would hate to lose that hard white hat; he had worn it clear across the plains and he had scarcely had it off his head since, except when he slept. He might be forced to run for his life at any moment, but anyway he would take his hat along.

The feasting began a little before sunset. Cassicass took his place at the head of the circle, with Jim at his right, and the food was passed about. The repast was an orgy of gluttony.

All day the old women had been busy about the cooking-fires. The principal dish was elk haunches grilled on wooden *brochettes*. There were clams cooked in the shell, and trout prepared in the cooking-baskets. Camass was lifted from the bed of hot rocks where it had lain since the night before. The fleshy roots of the yellow sand verbena, *Abronia latifolia*, growing so plentifully on the shore, had been roasted together with a huge root six feet long and as thick as a man's body. Jim had noticed this root when it was carried into camp early in the afternoon. He recognized it as "man-in-the-ground," or wild cucumber—*Micrampelis fabacea*. In its raw state the odor is very disagreeable, but after roasting he found that it developed rather a pleasant flavor.

There were fresh black raspberries and the everpresent salal berries for dessert, and as a confection to end this Gargantuan meal the seeds of the yellow pond lily, *Nymphœa polysepala*, had been parched to be eaten like popcorn.

Cassicass ate like a gourmand. Jim was alarmed for his safety. He was old and feeble and had exerted himself strenuously through the long hot day, but he laughed and jested during the intervals of gorging.

As the twilight deepened huge fires of resinous wood were lighted. Anxiety was steadily mounting in Jim; every sense was on edge, expecting some sudden turn of events. Cockqua, being a slave, was served last. Even in his triumph the Indians would never allow him to forget his position among them, though the group of admirers hovered about as he ate.

Cockqua, too, was awaiting events. Jim felt his beady black eyes full of triumph and malignant with hatred upon him. The Indians were, most of them, falling into a semi-stupor from the unbelievable amount of food that they had wolfed in the last hour and the heat of the fires.

Tilki and the medicine-men were alert, too. Jim noticed the sharp apprehensive glances they exchanged. The very air was charged with an undercurrent of feeling. He felt the tension would be somehow relieved if he could only exchange a word with Tilki, but, try as he would, he could not find the opportunity.

At last Cassicass, stupid with food and fatigue, rose to his tottering feet to signify that the feast was at an end. But undue exertion and gluttony had done their work. He swayed uncertainly for a moment, then fell in the throes of a seizure awful to behold, writhing in agony on the ground.

Men and women, groggy with indulgence, roused in alarm and wild confusion reigned. In a bound Tilki reached the chief's side, straightening him out and feeling for the beating of his heart. Jim stepped aside to allow room for the medicine-men.

Here was Cockqua's great opportunity. He advanced boldly and thrust an insulting face up to Jim's, muttering some terrible imprecation in which he was joined by three of his most stalwart followers. Jim thought for an instant that his time had come.

Fierce anger rose in his heart. He would sell his life dearly. In a sudden onrush of strength he felt equal to killing Cockqua with his naked hands, if he attacked him.

But Cockqua retreated and advanced, waving his bloody arms to egg his companions on, keeping always just out of the circle of firelight, not quite rash enough yet to make an open attack, though the group about the prostrate chief were oblivious to everything.

Folding his arms on his chest, Jim backed closer to the milling group about the sick man. Two of Cockqua's companions, seeing this, merged at once with the crowd, but the third at a command from Cockqua struck viciously at Jim. He dodged. There was no science in the blow. Then catching the Indian completely off his guard Jim's fist struck him squarely on the angle of the jaw, sending him sprawling to the ground, where he lay an inert mass.

Pandemonium broke loose among the Indians at the outcry of the few who had witnessed the blow. Tilki, seeing what had happened, made a scarcely perceptible motion up the hill, at the same time covering the confusion by calling loudly to draw the attention to the writhing old chief. What he said caused them to gather immediately around the sufferer, and Jim instantly seized his opportunity. He flew up the hill.

He must find the lodge of Multnomah in the darkness. Celiast had told him to make his way there if anything untoward occurred. He knew that Cockqua was faint from loss of blood and the agony he must have endured, and his bold companion was temporarily out of the running, but the others would be on his trail as soon as they sensed the fact that he had made his escape. He stood but little chance against them, unarmed and unacquainted with the way, while they were familiar with every foot of the ground.

He could only guess the general direction of Multnomah's house, but he ran as if his life depended upon it. Out of breath, he stumbled over the fallen limb of a small tree and lay a moment listening to the medley of sounds from the village.

The sudden wailing of the women told him that Cassicass was either dead or at the point of death. He dared to hope that he would not be pursued immediately, but there was not an instant to lose. He gropingly made his way through a thicket and bore straight up the hill, and after a terribly anxious interval struck the trail that led to Multnomah's home, where he was sure Celiast awaited him.

There was not a flicker of light from the windows, but he tapped cautiously on the door. Celiast opened it for him, and he fell across the threshold, fairly spent and breathless with running.

CHAPTER FOURTEEN
CELIAST WAILS
FOR THE DEAD

CELIAST shot the bolt on the door before she spoke to Jim.

"Rest a bit," she said, as she lit a small candle over the mantelpiece. She had evidently been expecting him, sitting in the darkness, waiting for the turn of events at the village.

Jim noticed that the windows had been carefully screened with heavy elkskin curtains that did not permit of the faintest gleam of light being seen without. Briar whined her welcome to him. He stroked her head, silencing her with a gasping word. He had left the dog safely imprisoned in the medicine lodge; finding her here was rather a surprise. Still struggling to regain his breath, he noticed that his pack and gun lay by the hearth, together with another carefully made-up pack, its elkskin thongs in place ready for the shoulders. Very careful preparations for a hasty departure had been made during the day.

"What has happened?" Celiast had waited for Jim to rest a moment and to regain his breath before questioning him.

In a few words he told her, looking anxiously about as he concluded. "If that Indian I struck has recovered his senses they are on the way up here by now, but I doubt if Cockqua has strength to go very far. He has lost so much blood. Still, there are five or six of those young bucks who will do just as he says. He's going to rule the Nehalems after this or I'm very much mistaken."

"You are safe here for a time, anyway. Cockqua might dare to enter Multnomah's lodge, but the others will not. We will go as soon as you have rested an hour. I must guide you. I am sorry Tilki will not be able to take you to the great medicine mountain. Last night he told me exactly what to do. We could not tell what might happen at the feast. I made preparations for a long journey today." She indicated the packs lying in readiness.

"Cassicass is dying; I am sure he can linger but a few hours at the outside," Jim said. "Who will be chief?"

Celiast did not answer. She made a peculiar sound deep in her throat, a sound between a sigh and a groan, then covered her face with her hands and rocked back and forth, as if shaken by an uncontrollable anguish. But realizing Jim's position, she recovered herself immediately and in matter-of-fact tones began to acquaint him with her plans.

"Cockqua will seize this opportunity to kill the medicine-men. He will not follow us at once. Those rogues will try to take us at the south pass, I am afraid, but they will do nothing unless Cockqua leads them. He has two great ambitions—he hopes to be chosen chief of the Nehalems and to take Multnomah for his wife."

"Why, he is a slave! How can he be chief?" Jim exclaimed.

"He is proclaimed a *skookum* now. Most of our people are away. If he can overcome Tilki and the few medicine-men before they reach home, he will follow Katoosh into the mountains to kill him and take Multnomah. Without their *shaman* to guide them my people are powerless." She covered her face again with her hands. "I do not know. I do not know. There will be war among my people when they return to their lodges."

"We should leave at once," Jim rose and lifted his pack.

"Not yet; I must wait a few moments." She opened the door and listened for the noises at the lodges a mile below. A medley of discordant sounds came to them on the still night air.

"I can't forsee. Cockqua may kill Tilki. They may not try to overtake us for a few days if Cassicass dies. There is no way to tell."

"Who will be the next chief?" Jim asked. "I mean who is the hereditary chief?"

"Tilki is the son of Cassicass," Celiast answered with an effort. Her drawn face was working, though she struggled for composure.

A long-drawn wail arose from the village below, the hills sending back its poignant echo. Silence for a moment, and then another wail.

"Cassicass is dead." Jim bent to catch Celiast's whispered words.

The Indian woman rose without speaking again, and adjusted the pack to her shoulders with the elkskin thongs. Motioning to Jim to take up his load, she led him out into the darkness.

Celiast did not make the slightest sound as she picked her careful way up the hill. The carpet of fir needles hushed their footfalls. She had a sense of direction as well defined as some night animal.

Never touching a trail and keeping always in the dense timber, Jim followed her through the night. He lost all sense of direction, simply following in her footsteps without question. He was going to save Multnomah from Cockqua. This thought filled his mind. He kept praying—a wordless prayer—that he might fulfill his mission. Jim was not given to prayer—that is, to audible prayer on bended knees—but through that terrible night he came to understand what real prayer meant in the human scheme of things.

Following Celiast hour by hour through the inky aisles of fir trees, spiritual understanding came to him. Man is too puny and timid to stand alone in a crisis. Prayer is the agony of his soul in its effort to find contact with the Divine mind and gain strength from an infinite source beyond human intelligence. He understood the cryptic utterance of his mother now. At their parting she had told him he must search until he found God. In the vigor of his young manhood he had never before felt the need of God.

But now he knew. Prayer was man's longing quest for God, who must be found in the solitude of his own heart. When he comes to rely on the source of strength, fear is for the time cast out.

He knew that they might be overtaken by Cockqua's confederates, but he had not a moment's fear for his own safety. He scarcely gave it a thought, his whole consciousness was so filled with the danger that threatened a defenseless girl, practically a captive among filthy Indians.

Multnomah in that night became inexpressibly dear to him. Though he had never seen her in the flesh, yet his heart knew her. Her unseen presence filled her home. He had seen the books she read. All the household spoke of her. Blindly he followed Celiast, praying as he went.

Would the woman never stop? He staggered from weakness. His illness had depleted his strength, and there had been but an hour or two of sleep the night before, and then the long grilling day of the Indian festivities. He felt a sense of hot shame at his fatigue, yet knew that it was gradually overcoming him. Lagging a little behind, he welcomed the brief pauses when Celiast stopped stockstill to listen.

Light was showing faintly in the east when they finally emerged from the timber. Celiast scanned his drawn white face in pity, then lifted the pack from his shoulders as he staggered and sank heavily on the ground, ashamed to let a woman observe his weakness and yet unable to stand.

"We will rest for a little while," she promised, laying a cool firm hand on his aching head. He could only smile his gratitude.

"I must hide you for the day. There may be small bands of my people returning to the lodge. They would kill a white man if they found him in their country. The Nehalems guard the secret of the passes." She took the packs and, leaving Briar on guard, went in search of just the secluded spot she desired for secreting him.

Jim was asleep when she returned. She woke him gently and helped him to his feet, steadying him as they went down into the underbrush where she had spread his buffalo robe on a bed of ferns.

"Rest while you may," she admonished. "You cannot afford to risk a return of the fever." From her opened pack she took a quart flask of blown glass and poured a portion of the thick black liquid it contained into a tin cup.

"Tilki sent the black drink to strengthen you." She held the bitter draught to his lips. "You cannot risk a return of the fever," she said again as he swallowed the nauseous dose. "I must keep on the watch. The river is close. We will cross tonight. My people come and go over the trail."

She covered him tenderly, again laying her hand on his forehead as if to test the degree of fever. How like a gentle mother the Indian woman was, Jim thought, gratefully. She was just like a refined white woman in her speech and manner. Her language was classic in its purity, even though she spoke haltingly, choosing each word with meticulous care. She had been most carefully taught by an educated person. How apt the Indian was at learning. If it were not for her swarthy skin and her buckskin dress she would pass anywhere for an elderly English or American gentlewoman. Multnomah was a young girl. Could she have been her tutor? Hardly. There had been other white people, perhaps a family, in the Nehalem country. The house proved that. In the state between sleeping and waking he reviewed the events leading up to the present moment. Why had neither No-Lie nor Auxica made mention of the others? There was some deep mystery about Multnomah.

Celiast woke Jim late in the afternoon. The change in her appearance and manner distressed him. She was now just an old squaw. Her hair hung in two matted braids over her shoulders. Her face was daubed with damp clay, the sticky gray clay of a stream-bed. Her buckskins were soiled, as if she had lain on the wet earth.

She was going to speak, but paused first to listen, then hastily gathered an armful of the ferns that she had left in making the bed and threw them over Jim and the dog, who lay sleeping beside him. Only a very close inspection would reveal his hiding-place. He laid a hand on Briar's head to keep her quiet, and waited breathlessly.

Celiast had not had a moment to spare. A band of about twenty Indians came swinging down the hill. Jim peeped cautiously through the ferns. What had happened to Celiast? She was running in circles like a crazed thing. She sank face downward on the ground as they approached. She lay inert for a long moment, then uttered a terrible piercing wail, like the cry of a lost soul in darkness. Wail after wail followed. As she fell, Jim had been on the point of going to her assistance, but now he understood.

Celiast was wailing for the dead. The Indians started in alarm at the sound, then stood round her in silence. A young Indian endeavored to lift her from the ground, but she sank back immediately, wailing with renewed vigor. Their manner had changed as they stood about her. They knew there was disaster at the lodge. Again they lifted Celiast, questioning her rapidly. She beat her breast and tore her hair, speaking disconnectedly between her wailing.

Consternation showed in their faces as she sank on her face again. Without giving her so much as a backward glance, they fled down the hill, shouting and gesticulating as they ran.

When he was sure they were well out of sight and hearing, Jim parted the ferns and crept cautiously to Celiast's side. She still lay on her face, uttering her anguished wails. She raised slightly on her elbow, motioning him back to his hiding-place.

"Not yet," she panted in the instant between her shrieks. "There may be stragglers coming."

Jim went back to wait. How helpless he felt. He wished there was something he could do to comfort her. For nearly an hour she lay on her face, uttering her sorrow. Finally she sat up and began unplaiting her hair.

"That was good," she said, grimly, as if congratulating herself on her effort, and yet Jim noted the suffering in her eyes. All the anguish of an old woman's torn and bleeding heart was in those piercing sounds. He was shaken to the depths of his being with impotent pity for her suffering. And yet almost before the echo of the last wail had died on the air she was calmly arranging her hair and smoothing out her dress.

She rose briskly and went to the stream below to wash her face, and on returning opened her pack and took out food.

"What did you tell the Indians?" Jim asked her as he ate the roast venison and camass.

"An Indian woman may wail for her father, may she not?"

"Cassicass was your father?" Jim exclaimed, in astonishment. Tears welled in his eyes as he sensed the emotion under which she had labored before she left the home of Multnomah. Concealing her sorrow, she had traveled all that long night.

"He was my father." She lowered her voice to a whisper. "But I, who am old and sad, having had little else but woe in my long life, wail only with the voice for the dead. After tribulation they go to the Great Spirit. I wail in my heart for the living and there is no comfort."

With a show of unconcern that Jim knew she was far from feeling, she resumed her eating. He noticed that most of her food went to Briar.

"How long will it be before we are out of the Nehalem Country?" Jim asked.

"We cross the river tonight, and tomorrow night we make our way out over the south pass through the mountains. We had hard traveling last night because we had to keep out of sight. We could have come here along the shore in two or three hours."

"Do you think Cockqua will come that way to cut us off before we reach the pass?" Jim asked, anxiously.

"We must be on our guard," she admitted. "We do not know how things have gone in the village. You will be safe once we cross the pass—that is, safe from the Nehalems. They would have no reason for molesting a white man outside their own country, unless Cockqua sends some of his men after us. Anything may happen. We must watch every minute."

"Sleep now," Jim urged. "There will be a couple of hours before it is dark enough to travel. I will stand guard."

"I'll sleep, but with the eye open," she smiled. "White men are no watchers for the Indian country."

CHAPTER FIFTEEN
IN HOC SIGNO VINCES

Jim sat near Celiast, guarding her rest. She slept soundly, like the Indian she was, yet the slightest unusual noise roused her. The falling of a nut from the pouch of an over-greedy pine squirrel or the snap of a twig brought her to instant attention. Now when he slept he died to the things of this world. With all his anxiety, he had not heard a sound during his long refreshing slumber of the morning.

The drowsy peace of the long summer evening was over the quiet land. With his back against a tree Jim looked lovingly over the range of hills. Resolutely he pushed his anxiety to the edge of his mind, the better to dwell on the beauty and contentment of the stillness that carried healing to him. He looked about for unusual specimens. Here was a section of the coast that had never been entered by the naturalist. And yet he must pass through it without so much as pausing to admire the flora.

A flaming torch of scarlet and gold pushed up through a mass of fern-like foliage a few feet below. He resisted the temptation to examine it, deciding that it was a clump of scarlet columbine, *Aquilegia truncata,* a plant common to the Pacific coast. If there were roving Indians about he might be discovered, and then, too, he chided himself severely, he had the bad habit of forgetting everything like a careless child and wandering off when flowers called to him.

This trait he held in common with all naturalists. Present perils were nothing compared with the discovery of a new specimen. With a smile he recalled Thomas Nuttall's irritating way of wandering off alone when they were crossing the country of the Blackfeet, where the white man went at the daily risk of his life. As soon as their boat drew near the shore, Nuttall jumped from it and ran up the bank, oftentimes delaying the party for precious hours while they searched for him. Men who had never known this passion for growing things could not understand. No wonder they had voiced their exasperation.

The stock joke among the mountain men was, "Where is the fool?" Their grinning companions had invariably answered, "Oh, he's off gathering brush."

Every man to his bent. Most of the strife in the world came from a lack of human understanding. To the trader a shrub was just a troublesome thing to trip the foot. How they had laughed and joked at the queerness of a man who knelt in rapture before a tiny plant, even when they were momentarily expecting an Indian attack. But Nuttall had been indifferent to their taunts; and in spite of the danger he had sometimes unwittingly brought them by his delays, they had loved and respected the botanist after their own fashion. And surely, when the final reckoning came, Nuttall had served his generation as fully as they had. He had added nearly a thousand specimens to the known flora of North America. Jim caught his breath at the thought. What more could be asked of a man than that he added to the general knowledge of the world?

He mused there by the side of Celiast and found comfort in his musings. The simple, inoffensive "grass man" might venture safely into a forbidden Indian country, where the trapper with all his bravado and his gun carried conspicuously in the crook of his arm would never dare to enter.

With a body relaxed by rest and soothed by the peace of the evening he went over the whole situation with a clear mind. He lamented the loss of his horses, but their taking had probably come about for his good. Tilki might possibly have had a hand in the matter, knowing that a trader with a pack ready for barter would never be received in friendship by the Nehalems. Only a grass man would stand the least chance of taking Multnomah from them.

After mulling the whole matter over, Jim was not inclined to share Celiast's anxiety over the outcome of an attack by Cockqua and his five or six henchmen. For one thing, there would be a period of nine days' mourning for the dead chief. Even a *skookum* would have difficulty in arousing the Indians to make a decisive move until after the obsequies, and by that time they would be safely out of the country.

If Cockqua should prevail upon a few of his followers to cut them off before they reached the south pass, there was no great occasion to worry. He had noted at the feast the day before that firearms were not apparent in the mountain fastness of the Nehalems. The braves had only bows and arrows and a few small knives that they had secured from the trading-posts. With a gun and the good supply of ammunition that he carried he would have no difficulty in routing five or six Indians. He resolved to kill Cockqua if he ever had the opportunity to draw a bead on him.

That there would be difficulty before the girl, Multnomah, was safe at the fort he could not doubt, still he trusted to the medicine-men to defend her. Her fate was "on the knees of the gods." The way would open somehow. No need to walk down the road to meet trouble. A man who had made two overland trips to the Pacific coast had long since learned not to worry over danger that lay hidden in the week ahead.

His reasoning was sound. He recognized that it was, but over the pellucid surface of his mind shot the lightning arrow of apprehension. Multnomah! The girl was as real to him now as if he had known and loved her always, and supposing he should fail to save her. Cold sweat beaded his forehead. He must! God in Heaven would not allow it to be otherwise.

There was so much of the mysterious in the whole affair and the Indian is so reticent by nature. If he could only prevail upon Celiast to tell him the whole story, instead of leaving him to grope in the darkness. But he despaired of that, though he resolved to keep up a persistent questioning until the whole story would somehow piece together.

Who was Auxica? Tilki would not speak of her, and yet his manner proved that he knew her. Jim started in sudden recollection. Auxica had given him a packet for her mother. How ungrateful he had been never even to inquire about her. He had taken care not to display the bundle when he had made his *potlatch* to the women of the Nehalems; it was still in his pack. He must question Celiast when she woke. He hoped she would not be so reticent, but like as not she would turn the subject just as Tilki had done. Confound Indians, anyway!

He hoped Celiast would talk with him tonight as they traveled. Even an occasional word was cheering, and surely silence and caution would not be so necessary now that they were away from the most imminent danger. Well, he must bide his time if he were to learn the whole story. The Indian woman was bowed down with grief; he must be patient and kind to her.

Celiast rose at dusk, serene and refreshed after a scant two hours of broken rest. She sprang up with the energy of a young woman, smiling radiantly at Jim, as if in her sleep she had dropped off her anxiety, her burden of care, and her deep sorrow. A child-like race, the Indians, Jim thought, living each day to gather its scant joy, forgetting yesterday's grief, with no borrowing of cares from the days yet unborn. The white race had always anticipated the future, and lived today with the next year in view. For a moment he deplored this trait, but after all it had its advantages. The Indian today was just where his ancestors were two thousand years ago. The Anglo-Saxon through his fretting and borrowing trouble had evolved civilization. The arts and sciences sprang from a divine discontent and anxiety.

"Shall I make a cooking-fire?" Jim asked.

Celiast shook a doubtful head, opening her pack to lay out the remnants of food. The haunch of venison and a little of the dried camass would serve nicely if they washed it down with water. Opening his pack for his tin cup, Jim noticed the packet Auxica had sent for her mother.

"Who is Auxica's mother?" he inquired as he picked it up.

Celiast did not answer. He paused a moment, thinking she did not hear his question, but somehow felt restrained from repeating it, as she had turned her back. He put the gift back reluctantly. When she faced him again she held two wax candles in her hand.

"Did you notice our tapers?" she asked.

Indeed Jim had noticed the flood of soft yellow candle-light that illumined Multnomah's home. "Where did you get the candles?" He was all eagerness, hoping to draw her out.

"A long story," Celiast told him as they sat on the ground to eat. "So long ago that we have it only from the old men and women who heard the tale from their grandparents, a ship was wrecked on the beach below the lodge of the Nehalems. You saw the sharp rocks jutting out into the ocean?"

"Yes, there must have been numerous wrecks along the rocky shore." He took one of the tapers and turned it over carefully in his hand.

"See," Celiast pointed.

Near the base of the candle small characters had been stamped in the wax. He turned it about to examine it more carefully in the failing light. IHS, he made out after a little careful study, and the numerals 1679.

"I-H-S," Jim repeated the letters over perplexedly, searching for their meaning. "The numerals must denote the year 1679."

"Multnomah says these tapers were made by the white men to worship their God. We gather these candles still on the beach at low tide. The ship must have carried a full cargo of wax, for there are large blocks of it all along the shore, and the candles are in different sizes. We burn them freely, though my people cannot be induced to come near the lodge if they are lighted. They think evil spirits sent them here to drive the 'great Fire Spirit' from our midst."

Jim took out his flint-and-tinder box to light a taper, studying the other carefully by its light.

"Multnomah loves the tapers," Celiast went on. "She said they were sent here long before she was born to comfort her." She pointed to IHS. "She calls this her sign. She says it is her ray of hope."

Comprehension dawned on Jim at last. IHS, the Christian religion's sign of promise. His rusty Latin, all but forgotten, came back to him. *In Hoc Signo Vinces.* He saw in a vivid flash of lightning the Emperor Constantine's vision, the cross of Christ with the letters of fire, *In Hoc Signo Vinces.* This sign and these burning words had changed the life of the world. Pagan Constantine had embraced Christianity.

"The ship was probably Spanish," Jim said, "blown out of her course. The wax and the finished tapers must have been supplies for the missions in California. She was wrecked over two hundred years ago. Even in the most remote parts of the world the Church sends her light."

Jim looked at the taper again, IHS, faint with washing about on the sands of the beach for nearly two centuries, yet burning as brightly as on the day it was fashioned to serve a Christian altar.

"When Multnomah was sad she burned tapers for cheer. She called them her hope. I think she would have died of grief the last two years if we had not had their light. I could not understand, but then I am just an old Indian woman."

But Jim understood. IHS, the sign of promise to those who held to the faith. And here, in the remote wilderness where no white woman had lived before, a lonely forsaken girl had found comfort and hope in pledge of her religion. His eyes filled with tears that he made no effort to hide.

"I will sing Multnomah's hymn for you," Celiast tried to cover his emotion. In the fluty treble of the Indian she began:

"In the cross of Christ I glory,
Towering o'er the wreck of time,
All the light of sacred story,
Hovers round its head sublime."

Jim could bear no more. He walked slowly down the hill. When he returned he placed the taper tenderly with its fellow in the pack. IHS should be his sign also, coming like a light from heaven in a moment of doubt and discouragement. He would succeed in saving Multnomah; from that moment he would never allow a doubt to enter his mind, come what would.

"So a Spanish ship was wrecked on your coast. Were other ships ever washed ashore, Celiast?" he asked.

"Yes," Celiast answered, "there were other shipwrecks along the coast, but that was long, long ago. So long that only our grandparents told of hearing the stories when they were children. Some time I will tell you of the buried treasure. Multnomah is sure that some day she will find the pirate's chest that my people know lies buried somewhere on Neah-kah-nie Mountain. But she must never make the attempt, lest the pirate's curse fall on her. We have often studied the two rocks with the strange lettering on them, with the arrows pointing up the mountain."

"Then Multnomah came to the Nehalems from a ship wrecked *off* the coast?" Jim was striving to conceal his eagerness.

"No, there has been no shipwreck in our time." Celiast spoke abruptly.

"Tell me, Celiast, who was with Multnomah?" Jim implored.

"There are things of which an Indian may not speak." She was suddenly interested in making up the packs, and the confidences were over.

"I cannot understand," Jim spoke his disappointment.

"Multnomah will tell her story," Celiast assured him. "You will see her soon. You must trust me to take you to her. The twilight is deepening. We will be going now. The night ahead of us is long."

Jim's strength had come back, and with it renewed courage. He felt a leaping eagerness for the journey ahead of him. No matter where Celiast led, he would follow. Only a little while before he had hoped that she would talk with him as they walked through the dark timber. Now he hoped she would not so much as utter a syllable. He would have a long night of silence in which to be the divine thinker of his own thoughts.

The forest was dark and the way rough. Often through the night they were obliged to make tedious detours to skirt precipices. The road leading to the south pass out of the Nehalem country was longer and more difficult than the northern way he had traversed with Tilki as guide, but then they had traveled at their leisure and in broad daylight.

The moon appeared at length, a glorious full moon that made traveling easier, but Celiast with the utmost caution still kept to the shadows. She paused often to listen, and when Jim caught a glimpse of her face, it was drawn and anxious in the cold white light.

"The river is not far now," she assured him as they threaded their precarious way down a steep trail. "There may be bands of my people in camp hereabouts. We must make no sound. There is a boat here for the crossing. I hope it has been left on our side. If it is not, you must swim across and fetch it, while I keep watch on the bank."

The river lay a silver mirror in the moonlight, not a ripple marring its polished surface. They found the small canoe moored in a clump of willows and lost no time in crossing.

"With good fortune attending us we will reach the pass some time tomorrow. Though if there are signs of my people returning we must hide as soon as day comes," Celiast told Jim. "Once we are in the outer country, you will be safe enough. Even Cockqua would scarcely dare attack us openly. We will likely meet bands of Nehalems returning to their village. News travels on the wind in the Indian country, and they have good reason to hurry home just now." She spoke sadly. Jim knew that she referred to the death of her father, the old chief Cassicass.

They clambered up a steep incline from the southern bank of the river, then picked up a trail to the top of a hill so steep that it seemed to Jim to be nearly perpendicular. Looking down, his head swam. They had circled about, but here the bluff overlooked the river, in fact seemed in some places to hang out over it. One misstep and the climber would fall to death on the rocks jutting out of the water below.

Jim, turned suddenly apprehensive, looked to see that his gun was loaded, deciding to hold it ready for instant use. He had been pushed over just such a cliff once because he had foolishly placed his gun out of reach.

"Mind your gun," Celiast warned in a whisper. "A shot will bring Indians on our trail if there are any within hearing. There are no guns in the Nehalem Valley. My people have been afraid, ever since white men came into the country, that some day trappers will find their way to Neah-kah-nie.'

"I know," Jim said, "I'll be careful, but I'll just keep it ready. This path would be a bad place to stand off an attack from above."

They were nearing the top of the hill. The path here converged with another leading up with a more gradual ascent from the west. Many trails that made a network in the Nehalem Valley met in the broad road that led to the pass.

Both were panting with their exertion when they stopped to rest a moment at the top of the hill. Like a flash of lightning an arrow whizzed within an inch of Jim's head. He felt the swift rush of the wind from its flight in his face. Another instant and hair-raising yells burst forth on the still, sweet air.

Celiast, at bay, faced Jim in agony. Below them they caught sight of five swarthy Indians in war paint and clad in their dress of double elkskin with the corset of hardwood sticks interlaced with bear grass. Cockqua and his henchmen had followed them, just as Celiast had feared. From the south came another arrow. They were surrounded. Shooting was not going to be easy. Jim fired below, but the moonlight was uncertain. He could not be sure that his shot had taken effect.

The top of the hill had not even a rock or tree to afford shelter. Celiast ran down the trail leading westward, and Jim followed to a spot where a huge bowlder jutted out near the path. They had scarcely reached this point of safety when they saw Cockqua advancing boldly down the path, his drawn bow in his hand, as if he felt not the least fear of Jim's gun. As he neared their hiding-place he yelled for his companions to follow him, which they did with caution. The *skookum* might think that a gun could not kill him, but, not being *skookums* themselves, they were not so sure. The Indian has no taste for open warfare. He does his fighting always from ambush.

Jim raised his gun and fired at Cockqua just as he was in the act of discharging his arrow. The horrible one fell backward without a sound, his cicatrices showing red in the moonlight. Jim fired again. His aim was better this time. He struck the running Indian full in the back of the head. The others were yelling as they ran. Jim leaped to follow, but Celiast seized his arm to hold him back.

"They are drawing you on to kill you," she whispered. "There are others on the hill. I saw them moving in the shadows. We must run for our lives."

But Jim was stubborn. "They will not attack us now that I have killed Cockqua," Jim declared.

"Cockqua is not dead," Celiast declared. "He has said that nothing can harm him. He has overcome fear."

"He fell," Jim said. "Though I was not certain sure of my aim, I'm sure I killed him." There was a savage exultation in his tone.

"The other one you killed, but not Cockqua. I will know in my heart when Cockqua dies."

With the fleet foot of a deer she flew down the path, motioning to Jim to follow, which he did a little sulkily. A small ravine offered them temporary safety. She turned from the path, drawing Jim after her.

"They will not follow us immediately," she told Jim, her breath coming in great sobs with her exertion. "They are sure we are trapped. They will stop to bury the dead one, and come to take us in an hour or so. We must catch our breath and then haste if we are to live to find Multnomah."

CHAPTER SIXTEEN
CELIAST TAKES A CHANCE

ELIAST had difficulty in restraining Jim Faxon. He sat fingering the trigger of his gun meaningly as she argued gently with him. He felt he had been a puppet in the hands of the Indians long enough. He was a man when it came to fighting, and must make his own decisions. What did an old Indian woman know about warfare? But he listened patiently while they gathered their forces after the strenuous exertion of running.

"We must make a stand," Jim declared, firmly. "We have at least a fighting chance. They have no guns, and if I can pick off one or two of them they will disperse. Now that Cockqua is dead, they will not be so bold. No Indian in his right mind is going to risk his life in an open fight."

"There are more than the five we saw with Cockqua, of that I am sure. The hunting parties are returning, bringing their guns with them. In the valley my people use only the bow and arrow— game is easily taken here—but those who hunt in the mountains use the gun just as the white man does. You must remember that my people mingle freely with the white men and the other tribes in the outer country; it is only at home that they cling to their ancient customs," Celiast told him.

Jim turned the matter over rapidly in his mind before he answered. There might be truth in what Celiast said. Indian eyes are sharper than white eyes. He had seen no evidence of other than the five rogues with Cockqua, but on a main-traveled road it was likely that there would be coming and going. Cockqua could easily invent a tale that would bring them at once to his aid. The very fact that there was a stranger in their carefully guarded country would be enough to enlist them in his cause. Perhaps, after all, the Indian woman knew best, but he admitted this to himself with extreme reluctance.

"If you shoot the gun now you will not come out of the Nehalem country alive," Celiast told him, and her tone carried conviction. "For myself it will not matter. My people will not purposely kill the daughter of a chief, but if I fall by a chance arrow, why grieve? I am old and life has been long and full of bitterness. I would live only to save my little one. If you do as I bid you I see a chance, but a very slight one. Are you willing to heed my counsel?"

"If you see a chance we will take it," Jim promised, shaking his head slowly in agreement.

"Then we will make the effort. If we fail you can still shoot the gun. I may die in the attempt. My people say that death follows the way we are going to take presently, but the white man may not come under the spell. I do not know. Multnomah had no fear of these things, and no harm came to her. If I go to the land of the dead and you escape alone, I must give you instructions for your journey to the sacred medicine mountain where you will find Katoosh and Multnomah. There will not be an instant after we leave this shelter. We still have a few moments here. We must rest, for there will be hard running."

Jim, with his head in his hands, demurred. "White men risk their own lives, but not those of women," he told Celiast. "Show me the way. I will go alone, and you must make your way back to your people."

"I cannot show you, I must lead you," Celiast told him. "The Indian holds life lightly at all times. I have no fear of death. One of my people took this way and he lives. I may be another. Who can tell?"

Jim was busy again with his thoughts. Perhaps Celiast's fear was due to some ancient superstition or meaningless Indian taboo. If Multnomah had no dread, there was no reason for apprehension. If there was a chance, they must take it.

"You have taken the religion of Multnomah, haven't you?" Jim asked.

"Yes, my little one taught me to love the white man's God."

"Then you have nothing to fear. The curses that your people have placed on themselves in their ignorance cannot harm you."

"I have no fear," Celiast assured him. "I must tell you what to do, though, before we go. Life is uncertain always."

"Yes, tell me where to go," Jim assented.

"You are to follow the shore until you come to a grove of smelling trees on a bluff overlooking the ocean. The trail leads east from there. I can only pray that if I am not with you Katoosh will make medicine to guide you. There may be some one waiting there for you. The future I cannot foresee. We go by faith. I myself do not know the way from the grove of smelling trees. The path is forbidden any but medicinemen. Even if I am spared I must wait for a vision to show me what to do. Vision always comes to meet human need if there be faith in God."

Jim made an impatient gesture. "You do not know just where we are going," he said, angrily. "How are you to guide me to Multnomah when you do not know the trail?"

"I am not of the medicine cult," Celiast admitted, weighing every word. "But visions guide all Indians in their need. My people are simple in thought and close to nature. Before now I have been led, and counsel I have received in dreams. Troubles in the days ahead we do not need to fear. The way always opens to those who trust life. All will be well with you even if you must find the trail alone. This I know. If we succeed in reaching the outer country the path is straight, not forked."

Accepting paths on faith was something Jim Faxon had never done before he set out for the Nehalem country. Here he had followed blindly where Indians led him. Again he must go by faith.

They had rested half an hour. Morning was at hand. Not a sound indicated that there was an Indian in the country.

Celiast rose at last and tightened her pack, adjusting it firmly on her shoulders. Jim was rolling his again. She thrust him aside impatiently and attended to it herself, testing the straps to be sure that they would stay firmly in place.

Jim watched her curiously. She had taken the hatchet and the knife that he always carried in his belt and placed them in the roll. "If we are to swim you may lose them," she explained.

She went over them both again, preparatory to starting.

"We will take to the open for a little while. The dead one must be buried before they follow us. They are in no hurry. They know we are trapped."

"Cockqua is dead. They will not be so sure now that they lack a leader." Jim spoke confidently.

"I am not sure Cockqua is dead. I can only hope. The other is dead, we know. My people believe Cockqua when he declares that he cannot be killed by either gun or arrow. He shot himself through the shoulder once with a gun. He pulled the trigger with his toe. He was well in a week."

"He's found out this time whether or not a gun can kill him," Jim said, grimly.

"I do not know," Celiast demurred. "We go."

She moved cautiously out of the ravine to the open trail, scanning the hillside for a moment, then motioned to Jim to follow her.

Up one rise and down another she kept up her flight, with Jim put to it to keep up with her. Briar's pink tongue lolled from her open mouth with the exertion. She slackened her pace a little only when she felt she had put enough distance between them and the Indians to be out of danger from arrows.

The trail led southwest; the last knoll they rounded brought them in sight of a shimmering sheet of water. At the first glance Jim took it to be a lake, but on coming closer found it was a tide-flat. The ebb-tide had left a margin of soft wet sand bestrewn with kelp and slime. The ground was soggy and uncertain underfoot, but Celiast led the way across it without so much as looking back.

Jim paused an instant in hesitation before following her. This was certainly a tide-flat, but cut off from the river. They must be a good mile from the stream they had crossed the night before. Celiast was attempting some foolhardy thing. The ocean must be on the other side of the sheer rock wall that hemmed them in on the west.

Water stood in pools now; farther along, coarse salt grass grew on the hummocks. She was jumping from ridge to ridge until at length she was forced to wade for a stretch, often sinking to her knees in soft sand.

Now there were savage yells behind them. Jim, glancing over his shoulder in his mad flight, saw that their pursuers were running along the edge of the flat, evidently loath to follow them into the water. Arrows whizzed through the air, but fell short of them. He fired a shot at the leader, and was answered by an angry yell as they charged across the tide-flat.

Breathlessly they ran. Celiast kept her feet. Her moccasins gave her a sure footing, but Jim fell and rose, covered with slime, tripped and fell again and again.

His mind functioned with the clarity that often comes with stress. Had the Indian woman gone mad? There was no escape. The water churned madly about the base of the rocky wall. Better, after all, to have followed his plan and made a stand at first. This was what came of trusting such decisions to a woman. There must be a dozen or more Indians crossing the flat. Cockqua's band had met a returning party, then, just as Celiast had predicted.

They could go but little farther. They were fair targets for arrows even now. He paused, intended to reload the gun, but

Celiast called angrily to him. An arrow took his white felt hat off his head, just as a strong undertow swept him from his feet.

Celiast was swimming like an otter, bobbing up and down in the churning waters dashing against the wall of rock. Jim almost lost his gun, but recovered it with an effort, holding it above his head as he swam after his companion. The war party were shouting and gesticulating, waiting with drawn bows for the surge to throw them out where their aim would be sure. Their time had come. The shouting ceased, or had the roar of the water drowned the horrible din?

No, they were standing like horrible open-mouthed stone images, with the rising sun bathing them in its light. Like a man in a dream Jim looked for Celiast. She raised an arm from the water, indicating that he was to follow, and dived out of sight.

Jim waited an instant for her to reappear, then swam closer to catch a glimpse of her. The undertow sucked him downward under the rocky ledge, whirling him round and round. Celiast was only a yard or so ahead of him and Briar just behind.

A terrible force drew him down, down, and then onward. His gun was torn from his uplifted hand. He struggled madly in the seething caldron, feeling himself drawn toward the very center of the earth, but at the same time carried onward.

With aching lungs he rose at last to the surface. A pool of ink was the darkness that he encountered. He fancied once that he heard Celiast scream, but could not be sure; the roar of the water snuffed out all sound. He was alone in a world that contained nothing but darkness, icy chill and noise that ground into aching nerves.

A soft body struck him as he whirled round and round in the maelstrom; Briar had been thrown forcibly against him. There was comfort in the touch of her wet fur. After a terrible interval of being drawn forward at a terrific speed and then thrown back, a hand gripped his hair. Celiast was there, too. He seized her wrist. No matter what happened, he would never loosen his grip.

He was not a man with a physical body; he was just a tremendous will exerting a superhuman strength to keep his hold on an old Indian woman, who clung to him.

For an endless time they were drawn along with a powerful current, then swung about against a rock. The pack on Jim's back broke the force of the impact. He lost Celiast for an instant, then gripped her about the waist.

Something cold and stinging struck him full in the face. Something stuffed but flat and slimy. The sting of the blow infuriated him. Celiast lay strangely inert on his arm. He tried to hold her above water. Horrible slithering bodies swam past him, striking at him viciously. The blows stung like needles, sending curious thrills up and down his spine.

Jim's feet touched bottom. After two or three futile efforts he gained his footing, standing waist deep in water that for a moment was not exerting force to submerge him. The horrid bodies, thousands of them, swam about him in an icy darkness like a Stygian night. A seething hell of roaring sound; this was the place of outer darkness mentioned in the Bible.

The water was shallow now. Jim waded along, holding a limp woman in his weary arms. He broke his way through shoals of the slimy creatures who sought to drag him down, to check his progress with blows that stung and burned.

Celiast made no move. Jim was sure she was dead, but still he carried her. Briar's body brushed his knees. She was dead, too. No, she was swimming. He lost his footing on the varnished rocks. Oh, for a single ray of light! How little he had cherished the warm sun, and he had basked all his life before in its blessed beams.

He was dead now and had gone to the place of eternal punishment, but hell had fires and here was an inferno of cold. The fiends of the pit brushed him. They were sent to torment him. If such a thing were possible, he would think that the roar of the water was increasing. To keep his feet and hold Celiast above the water filled his whole consciousness. The undertow again. He veered sharply to one side with an effort that nearly burst his lungs, and gained a rock, only to be swept off into the churning water.

The limp body of Celiast was snatched from him. One of the fiends had seized her was his last thought before he sank into oblivion.

CHAPTER SEVENTEEN

AUXICA'S MOTHER

BRIAR was licking his face when consciousness returned. She was whining piteously as she pawed at him in her effort to rouse him. Steam was rising from his sodden clothing. He lay on warm sand with the sun beating on his upturned face. He stretched himself and looked about him, then memory returned. He had sunk in dark icy water.

The dog barked joyously as he recognized her, then whined and ran to the edge of the water that seethed over the rocks. She plunged in and looked back, as if expecting him to follow her. Jim sat up dazedly. Briar returned and stood barking. Then he understood. Celiast must be at the base of the rocks or inside that dreadful dark cavern. The whirlpool was the water draining through its subterranean channel at low tide.

There was not a moment to lose. Looking out over the ocean, he saw that the tide would turn soon, and there would be no chance of finding Celiast. With hands that trembled he removed his shoes to insure a better footing on the slimy rocks. Briar frisked about joyfully as she saw that he understood, then plunged into the water. Jim followed her as she headed for the entrance to the cavern.

The ebb tide had drained the water into the ocean and he could now see the opening through which he had emerged. All his force was required to keep from being dashed against the rocks by the eddy, but at last he gained his feet just inside the mouth of the cavern. The light came faintly here. Briar dashed ahead as he worked his way over the slippery rock-strewn floor where water stood in pools. The roar had almost subsided. He heard Briar's sharp bark farther on in the gloom, and made his slow way toward the sound. Horror overcame him as he stumbled over a soft yielding body, cold and smooth to the touch. The same stinging blows that he had experienced before he had to meet again. The denizens of the inferno surrounded him as if to prevent his cheating them of their victim. But Briar was tugging and struggling. He reached down as he came up to her and his hand touched wet human hair. Celiast was lying on the rocks.

With a sudden access of strength Jim lifted her onto his back and made his slow way to the place where light showed at the entrance. Gropingly he toiled over the rocks toward the mouth of the cave. He could see now where to enter the water; its churning had almost ceased—the tide was at its lowest. He maintained a firm grip on Celiast as he plunged into the deep water, and, striking the center of the current, was borne swiftly through the opening into dazzling light. In a moment he had made the sandy shore with his unconscious burden.

Hoping against hope that she was not dead, Jim stooped to examine her. "Celiast is not dead," he told the barking Briar as he rolled her about on the sand to expel the water from her lungs. Thanks to Dr. Townsend, he knew how to go about his work. For half an hour he carried on efforts to bring about respiration before he could detect the least sign of returning life.

He felt in his pocket for his lens, breathing a sigh of relief when he found it. Polishing it carefully on his wet trousers, he held it in the sun to dry. With a wordless prayer he held the glass to her parted lips, uttering a cry of thanksgiving when it came away faintly filmed with moisture. She was alive. He opened the buckskin jacket and felt for her heart, but in his agitation could not detect its beating. Frantically he worked, and was at last rewarded by a slight flicker of the eyelashes as her lax body warmed under his chafing hands.

When Celiast finally opened her eyes, Jim left to build a fire. He had a moment of panic when he missed his knife and hatchet from his belt, but remembered that it had been placed in his pack for safety. He hurried to a sun-bleached piece of driftwood and shaved it into tinder, then held the lens to converge the sun's rays on it. Celiast stirred faintly as the warmth of sun and sand reached her. Reviving her was just a matter of heat to thaw the ice of the subterranean river out of her numb body.

After an interminable interval the wood smoked, charred, and at last he was rewarded with a faint spark which he cheered and husbanded until it became an infinitesimal blaze. In a few breathless moments he had a fire; he piled on dry wood until the blue-tongued flame leaped high, throwing out its intense heat. Blessing on the man who first discovered the burning-glass. The tinder-box was probably water-soaked.

Jim carried Celiast to the cheering warmth, and the flush of life slowly mounted to her face in its ruddy glow. Still he chafed her body, placing her feet to the fire, but she did not speak or appear to notice him, though he called her name tenderly over and over. She just drifted off into peaceful sleep, the sleep of utter physical exhaustion.

Jim left her while he busied himself in gathering fuel and in spreading the contents of the packs to dry. How good life seemed! Warm sun on sand and the breakers far out of reach singing in his ears, with gulls wading out for fish, gave him a sense of security and peace. No Indian alive would dare follow them through that tide-rip. Mile after mile of hard smooth beach stretched away to the south. The way would be easy from here.

In spreading the packs Jim remembered with a pang that he had lost his gun. The seething water at the mouth of the cavern had snatched it from him. He had only his hatchet and clasp-knife and there was very little food left, but they were both alive, and that in itself was sufficient for the present moment. Their worst trials were over. When Celiast was able to travel again they would press on in haste to find Multnomah.

Celiast stirred like a baby rousing from innocent sleep. She was murmuring something in the delicious interval on the borderland of consciousness. Jim ran to her to catch her words. She opened her eyes in bewilderment and smiled at him, then sat up by the fire, running her hands through her steaming hair.

"White man," she said in an awed voice, "how did we make our way through to safety?"

"Briar must have dragged me out of the water," Jim told her.

The dog thumped a joyful tail on the sand at the mention of her name. Celiast laid a caressing hand on her head.

"I have returned from the dead," Celiast told him, her face working weakly.

"I lost you when the suction of the water drew me down," Jim explained. "You were lying on the rocks near the entrance of the cavern when Briar and I went back to find you."

"White man, did you go back to hell to bring an old Indian woman to earth again?" she asked, wonderingly.

Jim grinned sheepishly. "I shouldn't have lost my grip on you in the first place. Briar must have dragged me out onto the sand. She's a dog in a thousand, smart as any man and strong as an ox."

"Smarter than any man," Celiast corrected.

Overcome by the stress of her emotion, she lay down by the fire and drifted off again to sleep.

While Celiast slept Jim busied himself with the preparation of food, filling the cooking-pot with fresh water that dripped from a tiny rill in the rocks and shaving jerked venison into it. They would soon have hot nourishing soup. The sun was directly overhead. He was spent with his exertions, though until now he had not given his giddiness a thought except that the faintness came from the need of food.

Waiting for the kettle to simmer, he wandered down to the point where the water from the tide-rip surged through its course to the ocean. There was a possibility that his gun might have lodged somewhere, and he must search for his hard white hat that the arrow had knocked off his head. This was the second time that that hat had saved his life. It had protected him when Cockqua pushed him over the cliff. There was just a bare chance that the gun and hat could be recovered. Of course the thought of going into the mountains without a gun disturbed him greatly, but the loss of the hat took on the quality of a distinct personal loss, a loss that could not be replaced.

Neither hat nor gun was to be found, but numbers of large crabs were prisoned in the rock-bound pools. Here was delicious food for the taking. With a crotched stick he raked three out onto the sand. They need have no fear of hunger while they traveled near the ocean; mussels, crabs, and clams were abundant and the streams teemed with trout.

Celiast was stirring the broth just as if nothing had happened when Jim returned with the crabs. She nodded gaily and poured the steaming soup into their tin cups, filling the pot with water for cooking his catch before she so much as spoke to him.

"We're safe from Cockqua's band now, aren't we?" Her nonchalance somehow put Jim at a loss. He had expected to nurse her back to health, and here she was going calmly about her affairs, apparently none the worse for her harrowing experience.

"Yes. They'll not follow us through the entrance to the abode of the dead," she smiled, cryptically. "At the next low tide we must dig clams for the journey," she planned. "We must go quickly to the medicine mountain."

They finished their meal in silence. Celiast cleared away the remnants of food and then composed herself by the fire, ready for conversation. Evidently there was much talking to be done, for she did not wait, as was her habit, for Jim's eager questions.

"See." She pointed to the rocks near the mouth of the cavern. Sleek black animals were bobbing about in the water and crawling up to sun themselves on the banks.

"Seals!" Light broke on Jim. "The tide-rip was full of them!" he exclaimed. "And I thought they were some terrible monsters from the infernal regions as they crowded about me and struck me in the face with their flippers. So the cold slimy things were only seals. Superstition doesn't live in daylight, does it, Celiast?" Jim laughed.

But the Indian woman did not laugh. "If you had known what you were daring, Jim Faxon, you would be in the Nehalem country with an arrow through your heart now, and I would be living in my misery and wishing for death."

"That was a trip through hell, sure enough," Jim agreed. "A lake of fire and brimstone could not be worse. I fought like a demon to keep those seals from snatching you away from me. And I suppose a man carrying a torch could go through that tide-rip at low water without wetting his feet."

"I will tell you the story of that passage. No white man has ever heard it before. There are many things that the Indian does not tell to those not of his blood. He has much knowledge and holds in his closed hands many of the dark secrets of nature."

"Yes, I know," Jim assented. "The Indian looks in black rocks to watch the roads, and builds medicine fires to foretell the future in the smoke."

Celiast nodded assent, ignoring the cynical note in Jim's voice. "But one thing the Indian does not do is hold converse with the dead. My people forbid that and punish the practice by death if it can be proven, though in times of great peril the *shamen* sometimes asks advice of their fathers who have gone on. We never speak the name of one who leaves us, neither do we refer in any way to his deeds on earth while those who knew him live."

"But you hold your dead in loving memory?" Jim inquired, thoughtfully.

"Yes, their memory is sacred. We hold it shielded in the heart, counting it sacrilege to speak of it."

"You Indians are a queer, taciturn people," Jim told her. "You are reticent about matters that white folks discuss freely. You have a sixth sense, and see as the animal sees."

"Anyone who differs from the white man is queer." Celiast was a bit scornful. "The Indian lives next to nature's great heart and so is natural. No one has asked the Indian what he thinks of the white man, has he? Your ways seem odd to us.

"But our journey through the passage. I must tell you the story, though what I saw in there I may not reveal to a living soul. When I was a little girl, an old man who had the gift of prophecy and could ward off disease and famine wandered to this tide-flat to pray for the run of salmon. The fish had not come into the river that season and my people were hungry. He saw the water sucking into the hole in the face of the rock and, as he leaned over to look down, lost his balance and was drawn into the cavern. He passed through just as we did. A sea-lion guided him and saved him from the blows of the seals. He told us that he saw and talked with the dead while he was in the darkness."

"If I lived among the Indians I would soon develop superstition," Jim laughed. "I thought I was encountering some terrible demons; their flippers stung when they struck me. I kept fighting them off to save you from them."

This was no laughing matter to Celiast. "Yes," she said, "they were trying to drown me. No Indian can stay up in the water when a seal strikes him. This has always been so. I knew that, like all my people, I would lose consciousness and sink when the first seal touched me in the water. They have always had this awful power over us. We drown if one but brushes us in swimming!"

"And you swam right into that tide-rip!" Jim exclaimed, in amazement at her courage. "You knew that seals lived there."

"There was no other way out," Celiast said, simply. "Multnomah must be saved."

"If I had known your fear I would have fought those Indians," Jim told her.

"Yes, and that would have been the end. But, Jim Faxon, I am not so foolish as you think me. I knew that the seal has no power over white people. No Indian ventures into the ocean, but in spite of warnings Multnomah bathed in the surf. She swam among them without the least fear. She laughed and said our superstitions drowned us, not the touch of any creature on land or sea."

"Yes," Jim agreed. "Your belief caused you to lose consciousness."

"No." Celiast shook her head angrily. "My people are not your people. How can you know the heart of the Indian? The blood is different in color. I can sense the thought of the white man, because my little one loved me and taught me, but at heart I am an Indian and what I know I know."

Celiast sat musing. A blood-red sun was dipping into the ocean. Each alone with thoughts watched it until it sank from view and the golden afterglow threw a subdued light over the quiet land.

At last, as one who hesitates to speak of sacred things, Celiast spoke again: "I have not yet told you of what I saw in the abode of the dead. Of much I may not speak. To do so would bring sorrow to the living. Those I saw and talked with I may not tell you. But I looked longingly for one who is very dear to me. She was not there, neither did I hear her name spoken by the company. You mentioned her name to me and I could not answer. To call a dead child is to thrust a knife in the mother's heart."

"Auxica!" Jim exclaimed. "Now I know why you did not answer me when I asked for Auxica's mother."

"Yes, my daughter Auxica." Celiast's face beamed her happiness. "I know now that she is alive. You have heard of her? I cannot understand."

"Why, of course!" Jim told her. "Auxica is married to a white man and lives near Fort William. She first told me about

Multnomah and led me over the Indian road and told me how
to reach the country of the Nehalems. She sent her mother a gift,
and told me that when the time came I would know her. I asked
Tilki and he would not answer me, and you turned away when
I mentioned her name. So what could I do? You Indians would
save a lot of trouble if you'd just come straight out with answers
when questions are put to you. But wait, I'll fetch the gift."

With a smile Jim handed her Auxica's packet. Celiast rocked
back and forth in her joy as she unfolded the gaudy cloth, smoothing it with a caressing hand, crooning over it and grieving a little
because the water had soaked the pack.

"Now tell me of Auxica," she commanded. "Tell me the
whole story."

Unheeded tears streamed over her cheeks as Jim warmed
to the tale of the snug clean little cabin where Auxica lived so
happily with kind Jed Withers and the little papoose who could
crawl about and was learning to dance when his father held him
up before the fire.

Celiast drank in every word of the story, rocking back and
forth on her heels with the calico hugged to her lean old breast.

"Now tell *me* Auxica's story," Jim begged. "We speculated
about her and wondered who taught her white ways."

"Joy tonight, the sadness tomorrow." Celiast continued her
rocking. "Perhaps when we rest after the day's journey I will tell
you by the light of our fire, but not now. I only rejoice."

But Jim was eager to know more of Celiast's uncanny experi-
ences in the realms of the dead.

"Did you speak with Cockqua when we came through the
tide-rip?" he queried.

Celiast started in dismay, and shook her head. "He was not
among the company I saw, but my mind is somewhat at rest. I
think he will join them soon, but that no one can know."

"You just overlooked Cockqua in your confusion," Jim persisted. "I am sure he is dead."

Celiast shook her head again. "Katoosh beckoned to me from the distance. He, too, can penetrate the wall between the living and the dead. He smiled and I knew that he bade me lead you clear to the medicine mountain. He will point the trail and death will not come to me for my treading forbidden ground. All will be well. I am comforted."

She fondled Auxica's gift, rocking and crooning over it as if it were a beloved child.

Jim sat watching her, but she paid not the slightest attention when he spoke, and at last he moved to the opposite side of the fire and spread his bed, lying for a time watching the stars prick out in the blue dome above. The boom of the waves beating against the rocks soothed him to sleep at last.

Toward morning the screaming of the gulls woke him. Celiast was still rocking and crooning by the fire, crooning to herself alone with her overwhelming joy. Auxica, whom she had mourned as dead, lived in the cabin of the white men and the papoose could dance before the fire.

CHAPTER EIGHTEEN
WITCHCRAFT

I N SPITE of his gnawing anxiety for Multnomah, Jim Faxon found the journey down the seashore a delight. The hard sand made the going easy and rapid, though farther south the stretches of beach grew shorter and less numerous. The stern and broken shore line often forced them to take to the fairly well-marked trails leading along the brow of frowning cliffs that jutted well out into the ocean.

Food was plentiful and easily obtained. They dug the succulent clams which Celiast roasted in the shell. She knew just where to break the shale with the hatchet and bring forth the succulent rock oysters from their hidden cavities. Large trout were plentiful in the streams that tumbled into the ocean and easily taken with her bone hook.

There were rivers to be crossed, but they gave them no concern. The crude raft or light canoe that was the common property of the traveling Indian public was invariably at hand. They were on a thoroughfare that was traversed each season by members of the various tribes on their way to the mountains for roots and berries or to trade their various commodities with the natives living at a distance. The Klamaths, were always glad to barter ponies for the mats, fish nets, and the dried salmon pemmican for which the Indians along the coast were justly famous.

Jim marveled at the swiftness with which they ate up distance. He considered himself a seasoned traveler; thirty miles a day was common enough in crossing the plains. But Celiast led him at least forty miles the days when they could walk on the beach and found the sand smooth and hard. They started with the first light in the east, and halted an hour or so before twilight in order to gather food for the next day's provisioning.

Celiast went boldly, making not the least effort to evade wayfarers. She greeted old friends on the trail with joy, exchanging clams for fresh red huckleberries, or huckleberries or roots for venison or dried camass, according to the supply in hand. If they had nothing to exchange, gifts of food were freely given them. Jim carried a foot of tobacco in his pack and invariably made a *potlatch* of a pipeful to the Indians they encountered.

Jim caught Celiast's mood with an effort. The Anglo-Saxon borrows trouble from the day ahead if he finds none in the sunny hours in which he moves. But the Indian woman was like a light-hearted child enjoying a rare holiday to the fullest.

She gave her whole time and breath to the trotting pace at which she moved along, seldom speaking. But in the evening, as they jerked the venison that they had gained by barter or dug the fleshy roots of sand verbena, the *Abronia latifolia,* to roast in the ashes, she was wont to regale him with quaint stories of the old Indian gods, or explain in minute detail the reason for this or that belief. She had a fund of stories about demons who lived in lakes, and made much of the fate of lovers who dared parental displeasure in fleeing across these enchanted waters to fancied safety.

Jim always listened politely, not much intrigued by the tales of disaster, setting the story down to some tragedy that had occurred in the vicinity. Indian legends always have some slight foundation in fact.

He was always questioning Celiast about Multnomah. What was her real name? Did she know her parents? How old was she when she came? But he never received an answer, only a shake of the head.

"You are too impatient, Jim Faxon," she scolded. "In a few days you will hear the whole story from Multnomah."

"But how old is she and what is she like?" Jim persisted.

"How can I bring up her image before you? You have no visions, but must see everything with the eye before you believe."

"She can read, I know that," Jim said, thankfully. "That her people were gentlefolk I knew the moment I stepped inside the door of her house. She speaks her native tongue faultlessly. How else could you have learned pure, flawless English! I marvel every time you speak."

"I speak as I have been so carefully taught and as I hear Multnomah read from books."

"Multnomah loves books, then?"

"How else could she pass the long winters, if she did not read?"

She was impatient at his stupid questioning, but relented a little at the eagerness in his face, to tell him of Multnomah's childhood, of her play with wooden dolls and her games with the Indian children. To hear Celiast tell it, here was a paragon embodying in her slender form all the virtues. She was fair in her play. She excelled even the squaws in her basket-weaving. She knew the names of the birds and flowers. She could shoot with the bow and arrow.

For days they traveled. Jim lost entire count of the time, but by the drying foliage and the blooming of the summer flowers he judged that August had come. One mid-afternoon they rounded a turn and sighted a copse of olive-green trees upon a promontory overlooking the ocean. Celiast broke into a run, with Jim and Briar close at her heels. She stopped short on entering the grove, and stood for a moment looking up into the interlaced branches, murmuring unintelligible words over and over to herself.

Jim's mind had been so filled with his musing about Multnomah that he had given the flora of the country little more than a passing glance. There had been no time for gathering or classifying specimens and, anyway, his press and papers had been left when Celiast gathered his belongings and brought them to the lodge. But from David Douglas's descriptions he knew that this was the Umpqua country, which up to his time had never been explored by a white man.

The tree must be *Myrtaceæ*. Douglas had spoken of them with rapture, expressing the opinion that this was the identical species of myrtle that grew in just two other localities in the world—the rocky slopes of Palestine and along the shores of the Mediterranean. Jim broke a twig for inspection, distinctly recalling Douglas's description—leaves glossy-green like the bay tree, lanceolate, entire, smooth, studded with numerous receptacles for oil.

He held a leaf up to the light. Yes, the surface appeared to be perforated with pin-holes, due to the translucency of these oil-cysts. The prominent vein running around the leaf just within the margin was a peculiarity of the family, *Myrtus pimenta*. Wood, fruit, bark, and leaves highly aromatic, due to the oil it contains, the tree fitted the English botanist's description exactly. He knew the field book by heart. When rubbed between the hands it produces sneezing like pepper.

Jim began crumpling a leaf in his hand, preparing to inhale the aroma. With a sharp cry Celiast dashed it from him. There was alarm in her face, entirely unwarranted by the simple action, he thought in annoyance.

"Would you call up visions of the dead?" she asked in agitation. "Would you sink to sleep and visit them in their abode?"

"But, Celiast," Jim remonstrated, "David Douglas told me all about this tree. It is one of the rarest things on earth. I never so much as dared hope to examine it. This is *Myrtus pimenta*. No harm came to him when he inhaled the perfume of its leaves. White men take no stock in such things."

"Look into the branches and breathe the sweet air as the wind whispers through them, but do not crush the leaves. None but medicine-men may inhale the fumes. It is forbidden my people."

"No danger in a harmless tree," Jim persisted, impatiently.

"When you are in the Indian country you do as the Indian bids you do." There was a note of command in Celiast's voice that angered Jim. Perhaps underneath the woman was not so gentle, after all.

No harm in humoring her. He turned away, throwing the twig on the ground. But Celiast showed a desire to placate him. She was bending down the branches to gather the tender tips of the twigs.

"We will have tea brewed from the new leaves," she promised. "We believe that if we drink we will gain great wisdom and if we ask the Great Spirit for justice afterward our plea will be granted."

"Then we'll drink and ask that we bring Multnomah safely out of the Indian country. That'll be all the justice we need. Won't it, Celiast?" She laughed and set about preparing the infusion of myrtle leaves.

Without prompting Celiast began the story of Auxica after they finished their meal and drank the aromatic tea which Jim found spicy and good. "Auxica," she said, musingly, "the child I loved best of all. I who have for these last years thought myself childless, rejoice now that she lives and I shall see her again."

Her face took on a look of hate horrible to behold in one so gentle. "Auxica suffered through—Cockqua." She spat the hateful name out of her mouth. "Why didn't you kill him?"

"I think I did," Jim consoled.

"He boasts that guns or arrows cannot touch him, and my people, that is, the younger men—are inclined to believe him. I do not know, but he must die."

"Cockqua is a slave, isn't he?" Jim asked.

"Yes," Celiast said, shortly. "But a slave may be chosen chief if he can but gain the power. Tilki is chief by right. Cockqua will lead my people to destruction. He must die."

"If I encounter Cockqua again I mean to kill him. I hope he comes to his end through some other means, though. I am no killer except when I am fighting mad," Jim said.

"If you had suffered at his hands as I have you would welcome the opportunity to kill him with your bare hands." Celiast spoke in a hoarse whisper. "He wants Multnomah. He will even kill Katoosh and the other medicine-men of our tribe to gain his ends. He is so puffed up with conceit that he does not even fear their medicine. He may defy the Indian gods and go to the sacred mountain. No one, not even a *skookum,* has ever dared such sacrilege."

"Tell me the story," Jim urged.

"Auxica was Cockqua's wife. Day after day he beat her into insensibility. She bore twin sons. My people think that the birth of twins brings a curse on their father. One is always killed at once. Cockqua strangled both, and the birth pangs had scarcely ceased before he beat my daughter nearly to death. Auxica, the granddaughter of a great chief, lay for weeks in Multnomah's lodge. My little one and I nursed her tenderly back to health." Tears streamed down Celiast's face unheeded as she told her story.

"She did not return to him afterwards?" Jim questioned, tensely.

"Fear drove her back, when she could stand. All my people live in terror of that fiend. There was no indignity that a cruel Indian could devise that he did not practice on Auxica. She bears the scars of his torture on her body today. The squaw suffers in silence until she can endure no more."

Jim patted Celiast's shoulder in impotent sympathy.

Celiast's dark face was working with her pent-up emotion. "You have seen the bodies of Indian women hanging to trees? Squaws end their lives when life can no longer be endured. The good Father knows and does not judge harshly."

Jim nodded. Suicide was the only way out for many an Indian woman. Every traveler in the Oregon country had remarked the stark bodies left where death had mercifully overtaken them.

"Your people count such death a sin. Multnomah has declared she will never take her own life. But"—her two fists clenched convulsively—"I will kill my little one before she shall suffer as the Indian women suffer. God will understand. If punishment for my sin is meted, then gladly will I bear it."

"God is just," Jim reminded her, turning aside to conceal his emotion.

"When Auxica went into the mountains with the squaws to gather roots," Celiast resumed, "I knew that she would not return. She meant to hang herself. I grieved but could see no other way. She wandered away, that I know, and kind white men must have found her before she had completed her days of fasting and prayer. No squaw takes her life without praying alone for days and days. The Great Father knows," she finished, brokenly.

"Jed Withers, Auxica's husband, said he found her alone in the mountains in the dead of winter," Jim explained.

Celiast sat crouching by the cooking-fire, with her head buried in her hands for a long time, while Jim awkwardly fingered his lens to cover his helplessness.

She sprang up at last, her face hideous with rage and hate. "I have found a way," she shrieked. "I have learned wisdom from drinking the tea of the smelling leaves. Tomaniwus has at last spoken to me. I have found a way to destroy him. My people will kill me when they know, but what matter? They will be saved from such a chief."

Jim watched her in amazement. No matter how completely the savage came under gentle white influence, she remained Indian in her instincts to the end of her days. In this terrible mood Celiast would burn at the stake and scalp and torture her victim, just as her forefathers had done.

She fairly flew down the tortuous trail to the beach. Jim followed. In this terrible mood she was not to be stayed. He could not understand at first what she was attempting. She selected a spot beyond the reach of the tide and began scooping up the moist sand with her hands. Like a fiend she worked, muttering lurid Indian curses.

When she began molding the sand, he realized. She was shaping a bas-relief figure to represent a man. The form took rapid shape under her deft fingers. She had a peculiar skill in modeling; the result was rather grotesque, but he recognized in it an Indian. She sent Jim to the camp for a knife while she worked on the face, and, when he returned with it, cut off lock after lock of her hair to embellish the wicked thing she had so cunningly created.

Jim watched her intently, thinking perhaps he fancied the resemblance. She had modeled her enemy, Cockqua, prone on the sand. She gave him a terse order to hand her something now and again as she labored in frenzy.

Her task completed, she sent him in haste for the red huckleberries left from their dinner. With these she laid on the red cicatrices covering the chest and abdomen, cursing each as she finished it. For the time being the most diabolical hate had found a home in the heart of the gentle Celiast.

She surveyed her handiwork with a critical eye, and then began a wild dance upon the figure, breaking into a terrible chant that sent the cold chills down Jim's back. He tried to restrain her, to reason with her, but she broke away from under his hand.

Her dance completed, she asked for his lens. She had marveled so often as she watched him draw fire from the sun's rays to start a blaze in the dry wood for their cooking. Helplessly, Jim handed it to her. She gave him the knife and bade him shave dry wood for a fire.

When he brought it she laid a tiny piece of the tinder square on the forehead of the figure and applied the lens. The moisture in the sand prevented the wood's burning. She placed a flat pebble on the spot and tried again, while she shrieked curses never meant for human ears.

Jim watched in dawning horror. Celiast was calling down fire from heaven on her enemy; and while he had the white man's disbelief in witchcraft, it seemed to him that the power with which she uttered her curses must give them potency. At least Celiast believed that she had called the powers of darkness to her aid in bringing about the destruction of Cockqua. While the little flame blazed she began a joyful dance, singing in unholy ecstasy over her triumph.

Jim turned sick with watching her. Her hair looked like the writhing snakes of the Medusa. She had loosened it when hacking off locks to give a life-like semblance to the head of her figure. The face of a gentle old woman distorted with primitive passion was awful to contemplate. He told himself he could kill a fiend just as he could a rattlesnake, but hate like that was beyond any white person.

But who was he to judge Celiast? She came of another race. Her suffering had been long and cruel. He consoled himself with the thought that she had relieved her pent-up emotions and done Cockqua no harm. He would come to his end in good time, if he were not dead. He would kill him if he ever had the opportunity to draw a bead on him. But he started in recollection. He had no gun! He had lost it in going through the tide-rip. Up to now he had not mourned its loss. Well, no use in worrying over what could not be helped, but an unarmed man was certainly at a disadvantage.

Jim confided his forebodings to Celiast as, her diabolical work accomplished, she turned calmly toward the grove of smelling trees. "You'll have no need of your gun," she assured him. "I have killed Cockqua as Tomaniwus pointed the way. He will die soon, never fear."

Jim was loath to believe, but he did not contradict her.

"Witchcraft is forbidden, yet Indian women often practice it secretly. If they are caught, they are killed at once. I know that a squaw made an image of a rival who excelled in weaving mats. She cut off the hand of her figure, and the squaw today has a useless forearm; she weaves no more. But I do not fear. My tribe must be saved from Cockqua, and my thought is for my little one. Never did I think I would stoop to call fire from heaven upon a human being, I who have learned to obey the God of the white man, but I am glad, glad."

CHAPTER NINETEEN
THE MEDICINE TRAIL

CELIAST was strangely reluctant to leave the grove of smelling trees. She made excuse after excuse at Jim's anxious questioning. They must gather and prepare food for the journey into the mountains. They dug clams at low tide and she spent a day washing and drying them, strung on rods suspended over a low fire. She jerked the venison that they had secured the day before. Another day they gathered salal berries. These were dried over gentle heat and pressed into cakes to be easily carried in the pack.

Jim was all impatience to be off into the mountains. Now that they were approaching the mysterious mountain fastness where Multnomah was secreted, he could see no reason for the delay. He felt that Celiast's elaborate preparation of food was just to gain time. She had some real reason for not making a start, and was making weak excuses.

His insistent questioning angered her. She silenced him with a sharp word and an angry glance that conveyed her meaning in an unmistakable manner. He desisted after the first day, understanding that urging only made her the more obstinate. She would not go until she was ready and there was no way of determining when that time would come.

There was nothing for Jim to do but put in the time examining the country, though he had but little taste for plant life; his anxiety over Multnomah filled his consciousness to the exclusion of every other thought. But he was relieved to be away from

Celiast. Usually a bright, cheerful companion, she sulked about her work now with a strange grim expression on her once placid face.

With little thrills of apprehension he noted the signs of the waning summer. It must be late August. The western anemone, *Anemone occidentalis,* that lovely bloom with the covering of silvery wool to keep it warm, so that it often pushed its way through the melting snow and unfurled its creamy flower before the leaves appeared, had thrown up silky akenes. He gathered the waving heads, admiring the delicate whorls of gray-green down. The anemone in seed is even more attractive than the bloom, he thought. But even as he revelled in the new flora, apprehension stalked at his side; the summer was passing on fleet wings and his mission was still a long way from its fulfillment.

He tramped through glades where the virgin's bower, *Clematis lasiantha,* rioted in creamy masses, a fragrant tangle, inviting rest when it made an arbor by swinging from tree to tree. Ordinarily he would have wrung the last drop of unadulterated joy out of days alone in an unexplored country in the summer, but now he had no heart for growing things. Landscape and seascape wearied his vision. The timid "peep-peep" of the sandpiper on the shore angered him. The glint of the sun on the glossy cerulean coat of the mountain bluebird gave him no thrill. The danger to Multnomah grew with the lagging days. If Cockqua lived he may have reached the medicine mountain and overpowered her protectors by this time, and borne her out of his reach forever.

He had trusted Celiast implicitly, but now he was assailed by terrible doubts. All Indians were full of treachery. Since he had witnessed her diabolical actions when she practiced her witchcraft on the beach he had somehow turned from her. She might be gentle and loving to those who did not invoke her anger, but under all the gentleness the cruel savage nature lurked, ready to assert itself on the instant.

But he knew he must await the Indian woman's time. He had not the least idea of the location of the holy mountain where the medicine-man had secreted Multnomah. He was wholly at the mercy of Celiast's whim.

For three endless days she sulked and puttered about the camp in the grove of smelling trees. She kicked Briar out of her way when the hapless dog ventured up for a friendly word or a pat on the head. She refused to utter a syllable, paying not the slightest heed to him, turning an angry back if she so much as caught his eyes upon her.

Jim feared that she had suddenly gone mad. He did not wonder so much at this when he considered the sorrow and the stress of living that had been her portion. He noticed that she was constantly scanning the clouds as if looking for a sign from heaven. He wondered if she slept at all. She wandered off at dusk and did not return until dawn. A flight of birds overhead threw her into a panic. When a band of blackbirds flew through the grove on a harmless errand, she fell on her face, moaning in terror, but when they were followed shortly by a flock of white gulls circling overhead, she took heart of grace and sang and chanted in wild joy.

Her actions drove Jim nearly to distraction. He was in frank despair, and on the point of leaving her and making his way to Fort William. The fear that he would be too late in bringing a party to take Multnomah held him captive.

At dawn the third morning Celiast came into camp with a light glowing on her coppery face. "We go at once," she announced, breathlessly. "I have found the sign. For three days I have searched both in my sleeping visions and in my time of waking, and but now it has been discovered."

"I have searched the country over for Multnomah's sign on the trees, but could not find it," Jim said, in relief.

"The medicine trail cannot be discovered by a white man," Celiast told him.

Jim was all eager impatience. In half an hour they were on their way. Anything in the way of activity, even going in the wrong direction and being obliged to retrace their steps, was better than waiting on a sullen old squaw for he knew not what.

Celiast led the way at the same dog-trot, dipping clear to the bottom of the ravine where only the day before Jim had pierced the tangle of virgin's bower. The trailing vines gave no evidence of having been disturbed by the passage of a party, and Jim had given up the search halfway down. At the bottom they came upon the inevitable brook tumbling over mossy rocks. A little farther up large alder trees interlaced over the water, making a sylvan glade where the sun never penetrated.

Celiast paused before a smooth gray-barked alder tree, and there was the sign exquisitely drawn with some sharp instrument in the soft bark. The outline was brown where the cutting had been done, indicating that it had been made recently. The rose with three wavy lines beneath, they paused to examine it carefully.

"They passed not more than a week or ten days ago, I should say," Jim bent to examine the sign again.

"They followed up the stream. We will find the way marked for us. I fear no more," Celiast said, gratefully.

"We will be on the mountain in a few days now," Jim exulted. "I can only hope that we are in time."

"We'll be in time," Celiast assured him, happily. "I did not know what to do. Tilki told me to go to the smelling trees and wait there until the way opened to me. He could give me no other directions, there was no time, and he only told me because there was danger that I might be obliged to lead you. He goes often to the holy mountain, and the way is plain to him. But no one but members of the medicine cult dare follow the holy trail. I fully expected that Katoosh would send a guide for you and I could return home. When no one came and I could find no trace of the road I was frantic with fear."

"Well, then, why didn't you tell me that you couldn't find the trail, instead of sulking all that time?" Jim asked, in impatience. "I could have put in the time searching."

Celiast ignored his question. "I remember now that Katoosh beckoned and smiled at me in my vision. I should have known that he intended me to come to the medicine mountain, but you shake my faith and confuse me," she said, sadly. "You do not believe in the Indian's vision and in your heart you laugh and sneer, and I, who am simple, cannot dream the dream or see the waking vision that would show me the trail. How can a message come to a woman who is not of the medicine cult and does not know how to induce the vision when her mind is full of fear and clouded with doubt?"

"I am sorry," Jim told her in contrition as he realized that it was his unspoken disbelief that had brought about the sullen resentment in Celiast. Now what was a man to do? He had to think his thoughts and reach his own decisions even if they did interfere with the dreams of an Indian. Rather uncomfortable, this probing of one's secret thoughts. Indians, the country over, are uncanny at divining what passes in the minds of their white companions.

"I'll try not to keep off your visions with my doubts, Celiast," Jim promised, "but if you will only tell me what you are doing we will manage better."

"I can tell you now," Celiast smiled indulgently at him. "We are going to follow this stream up into the mountains. My sense would tell me if this were the wrong direction. We will find Multnomah's sign all along on the alder trees. She is white, but she has lived among my people long enough to have faith in what the Indian tells her. Time and again she has found that we speak the truth and that Tomaniwus does not lie. Katoosh told her that a white man would follow them up the mountain, and you will see by her signs that she believed him."

The traveling was slow, but delightful after the inactivity of those endless hours in the grove of smelling trees. The day turned warm as they drew away from the ocean, but the trees gave shade and the gurgle of the water over its mossy rocks and the ferns and sedges on its borders cooled the still air.

Farther along they struck a well-defined trail, that Celiast declared was the secret way of the medicine cult when they traveled once a year to the holy mountain where their mystic rites were performed. At regular intervals they discovered Multnomah's sign with the arrow underneath pointing to the south and east.

The day waxed to noon, and still they climbed up the watercourse of the stream so graciously hidden by interlacing alders. There is no shade like alder shade. The sun here and there cast great flakes of topaz through the interstices of softly fluttering leaves with their underlining of silver. Cool gray is the smooth bark and the earth beneath soft and dull black. Here and there in the ascent they sighted a miniature waterfall with its delicate fringe of fern and meadow-rue, *Thalictrum fendleri*, whose tassels, hanging in loose clusters, trembled at their passing.

Relieved in his mind, now that they were on the road, Jim always paused to enjoy each rapidly succeeding vista, though he was forced into a run afterward to overtake Celiast, who plunged on without seeing anything but the goal she held in her mind's eye.

When they reached the source of the stream, a large clear spring near the summit of the mountains, they found Multnomah's sign, and below the alder tree a small cairn of rocks. Jim stooped and removed them carefully, one at a time, confident that he would find some message underneath. Sure enough, at last he came on a small buckskin sack, and with fingers, whose trembling he took pains to conceal, drew from it a tightly folded piece of paper.

Celiast watched him as he opened the missive and read:

To the one who is coming for me :
    Katoosh has promised that a white man will come
    to the great convocation of the Medicine-men for the

purpose of taking me to my own people. Make haste when you read this, for I live in mortal terror of an evil Indian who will try to take me by force from Katoosh. The only hope I have in life is that Katoosh is right in promising me that help is coming.

R. B.

Jim stood poring long over the message written in a fine hand with a lead pencil. Celiast asked him at last to read it to her.

"What does the R.B. stand for?" he asked as he finished.

"We never speak the name beginning with R," she told him, angrily. "Multnomah has never used it before. Multnomah is the name my people gave her, and Multnomah she will always be to us, no matter what she wishes the white man to call her."

Celiast's tone angered Jim, but he controlled himself with an effort, having no desire to induce another fit of sullen brooding in his companion. Indians surely lead the world in devising taboos and fool prohibitions, he thought, but he had learned from bitter experience that the effort to draw information from them always ended in his gaining less than if he managed to wait for a communicative mood.

Jim could not wait to solve the mystery of Multnomah. He put the buckskin sack inside the larger one containing the bit of wool delaine and the dainty nightcap, and broke into a run down the incline. Now that he actually had a missive from her, the thought of a white girl living in daily terror of the fiend Cockqua was too much to bear quietly. Celiast and Briar were breathless in trying to follow him.

The character of the Coast Range changes in the Umpqua region, running more to precipitous bluffs and narrow ravines between mountains, though the east side soon merges into gently rolling hills that finally dissolve on the valley floor. In two hours of his merciless travel they cleared the timber, and stood on a hill where the whole magnificent sweep of the country to the south and east stretched before them. Between the two ranges the plane was a gentle undulation. No timber to speak of, just a sea of coppery grass radiating with the heat of the summer afternoon. This was a favorite feeding-ground for bands of deer and elk. They watched them moving like black dots across the sun-warmed prairie.

In his eager haste it seemed to Jim that they could cross the valley and reach the foothills of the next range in a few hours. Celiast had told him that their objective was a peak in this mountain chain. But there were still days of hard travel before they crossed and began their ascent.

While they went on short rations, they did not actually suffer for want of food. Luscious blackberries grew along the creeks in the lowlands, and the foothills yielded red huckleberries lavishly. The streams along their course held salmon trout, and in swales they were able to dig enough camass to provision them until they reached the mountain. They had excellent potherbs in the tender uncurled fronds of the brake and sword-fern and from the tips of the wild black raspberry canes.

Once Jim caught a squirrel in a trap he devised, and another time Briar captured a pheasant that he had wounded with a stone. More and more Jim mourned the loss of his gun. They would have lived on the fat of the land if he but had it. He might have still greater occasion to use it if they encountered Cockqua and his band of rogues.

Each day brought them appreciably nearer the range of mountains, and yet to Jim the days were dragging eternities. "So you think if Cockqua is alive he will follow us?" he asked Celiast, in his anxiety.

"He will not follow us; the way is too long. He will cross the mountains farther north and forestall us. That is my fear. He will try to kill the medicine-men and take Multnomah before we can reach the sacred mountain. After the long period of fasting there will be weakness. How can he become chief of the Nehalems if Katoosh lives to oppose him?" Celiast was thinking out loud.

"I still feel sure that Cockqua is dead or so badly wounded that he had given up following to the mountain," Jim told her, stubbornly.

"If you are sure he is dead, why do you ask if I think he will try to take Multnomah?" Celiast inquired with fine sarcasm. "I do not know. There is so much I may not tell you. Sometimes I doubt if an Indian slave would dare tread the medicine mountain, but Cockqua has conquered fear. They may wait and waylay us as we are returning to the country of the Nehalems, but that is many days in the future. Let us drink in the beauty of the valley as we pass through, for the mountains frown upon us even now."

CHAPTER TWENTY
THE SIGNAI, FIRES

J IM was afraid that Celiast would have further difficulty in finding the medicine trail that led into the mountains, for they had followed no beaten track across the valley floor, always skirting about to avoid swampy ground. He had looked in vain for the familiar sign, but had not been able to find it. He watched her furtively and felt sure that she was at a loss as to the exact direction to take. Their destination as seen from the summit of the Coast Range had been nearly due east, but vistas and a close range view of an area differ very materially.

He hoped against hope that she would not be obliged to undergo another two or three days of sullen delay when time was so precious. Her familiar spirit or whatever it was that guided her surely would not detain them now. But Jim made up his mind to try manfully to keep doubts of her ability in divination from entering even the outer fringe of his consciousness as he turned to sleep the night before they were to start the ascent of the mountains.

But Celiast's morning face glowed with happiness. "I know where to strike the trail leading to the medicine mountain," she told Jim in exultation. "We must skirt those two knolls to the south and then we will find a sharp divide. We'll pick up the path there."

Jim looked his astonishment. "How do you know where the trail is?" he asked. "You slept by the camp fire all night and you admitted that you did not know when we were making camp. I was worried over it."

"My *kawok* [guardian spirit] came to me in my sleep. Three days *kawok* led me up the trail. Katoosh beckoned me. He promised to draw me with his eye, as he has power to do, and to keep us safe. He told me with his eye that I must overcome my fear or I would never reach the great medicine mountain alive. Multnomah smiled and held out her arms to me. She is still safe. This I know. But I fear; I fear. There is terrible peril on the mountain. The chill of it creeps over me even as I speak."

Her face so happy as she began, turned drawn and olive-gray when she finished recounting her vision. Jim, for all he had but little faith in visions, still felt cheered by Celiast's declaration that Multnomah was still safe. They would lose no more time if only the vision proved true.

Full of gay spirits, Celiast led the way around the two knolls, and, sure enough, found the sharp divide with the stream running between it and the next hill. There is a stream of sparkling water in every ravine in the Oregon country.

There was not the least indication of a trail, but with confidence Celiast followed up the right bank of the stream just as she said her *kawok* had led her in the vision. After a mile in which Jim looked anxiously on every alder tree for Multnomah's sign, they came upon the path, and there was the rose with the three wavy lines underneath, showing signs of having been cut recently in the bark.

Jim quickened his pace. Celiast, who had led before, hesitated a little and then fell in behind. She paused occasionally and looked back as if extremely loath to follow the easy trail. She developed an interest in her surroundings that she had not exhibited before when on the march. Jim forged ahead, waiting in annoyance for her to come up with him. The way was barred by a waterfall that dropped in sheer scintillating beauty from an overhanging ledge of solid rock. The path appeared to stop beside

the water. Jim was puzzled at first. He looked about him carefully. There was no way up. The face of the wall was fifty feet high
and perpendicular, but as he ventured closer to the shimmering
spray he noticed the way ran behind the falling water. The overhanging rock roofed a dry chamber.

Celiast stood whimpering like a frightened animal, with her
face turned from the rainbow-colored spray. Jim spoke to her, but
she did not answer, so he passed behind the falling water, coming
out without even being touched by the spray. The path was broad
and well defined on the other side. He moved to a point where he
could beckon to her across the pool below the cataract, but she
was still cowering, and paid no attention to him. There was no
calling to her through the noise. He waved his hand and moved
along the path, expecting her to follow, but was finally forced to
return for her.

"I am just an old Indian woman sunk in fear," she whispered
as he took her hand and urged her forward like a father assuring
a timid child that the darkness held no terrors. "I mean to go,"
she told him, looking piteously in his face. "I try to go, but when I
see the dancing folk in the falling water, I cannot, I cannot." She
covered her face with her trembling hands.

"Nonsense!" Jim expostulated. "There's nothing to harm you
in the water. I went through without even the spray touching
me."

"You cannot see them?" she asked, surprised. "The spirits
who live in the cave behind the curtain of water come out to
dance in the spray when the sun turns it to a rainbow."

"I cannot see the sprites, but if they are there they are friendly
creatures. No evil being could live in pure sparkling water," Jim
reasoned with her.

"You do not see them?" she asked, in bewilderment. She
brightened a little. "Perhaps they are friendly to Indians. I have
never heard. My people love the falling water, but they do not
venture behind it. See," she pointed, "the little creatures are

dressed in blue and yellow and red. How they dance, but they are not noticing us. I will go if you lead me slowly."

"No," Jim soothed, falling in with her mood not to hurry her through the chamber. "If there are sprites and gnomes and undines living in rocks and lakes and waterfalls, I know they are friendly. Men love the beautiful things in nature just as the fairy folk who live there do."

His whimsical explanation seemed to placate Celiast. She straightened her shoulders, seized his hand, and walked through, hugging the wall as far away from the sheet of water as possible. But the effort of will she put forth exhausted her completely. She sank on the rocks with a weak sigh after the ordeal was over.

Jim paused for her to rest.

"There is no way I would not tread if the going would save Multnomah," Celiast said, wearily, as she rose, "but it passes human strength of will for an Indian woman not of the medicine cult to travel to the holy mountain."

Again Jim soothed her as he would an unreasonable frightened child. "A mountain is the most majestic thing in all nature. What can there be to fear on it, besides cold or hunger or wild animals? I am looking forward to reaching an altitude where we can see the whole Oregon country clear to the ocean spread out before us."

"I am not afraid of cold or hunger or wild animals," Celiast declared. "But terrible beings of the unseen world live in mountains. The Indian has always feared the heights. Why should he go there? The medicinemen travel to the abode of dark evil spirits that they may overcome their fears. They have no power over those who face them boldly."

"They have no power over those who do not believe in their existence, either," Jim told her, positively.

"If your eyes were open so that you could see them, would you believe their existence?" Celiast asked, in a tone that demanded an answer.

But Jim parried. "The Indian does not climb mountains because the way is steep. He takes no game there and vegetation is sparse. Because he finds disagreeable conditions he immediately peoples the place with terrible spirits. The white man finds nothing to fear anywhere in nature."

"Yes," Celiast said, sneeringly, "the white man is dumb and blind. He hears only with his ears and sees with his eyes. Can you hear the grass growing if you lie down on a cool sward? Do you know what the birds say as they tend their young in the nest? No," she said as Jim stood silently by. "The soul of the white man is closed to nature. The Indian pities him for being deaf and blind and yet he envies him. There are always terror and suffering as well as joy and peace in the knowledge of the hidden things of life."

Celiast rose and, shaking off her reluctance as she would discard a heavy cloak on a warm day, led Jim up the path. Briar came at her call and kept at her side all the long tiring day, as if each found comfort and strength in the other's understanding. Jim, somehow, felt like a stranger to them, an alien who must not enter the country where they lived.

The faltering and superstitious fear of Celiast troubled him more than he liked to admit. Her seeing things that did not exist was uncanny and disturbing to a man whose nerves were on edge with anxiety, for Multnomah and the strain of the stirring events through which he had passed. He told himself that he would take the perils that were tangible rather than fight with denizens of a world that has no existence in reality.

The trail was well marked and invariably kept to the easiest grade up the mountain. Celiast told him that to make the ascent from the valley floor required three days of easy going, but they had made such good progress the first day, her prediction was that two and a half days would see them at the summit. Jim led the way and quickened his pace accordingly. As the long hours wore away his eagerness to find Multnomah increased.

The rare atmosphere of the mountains takes on a keen chill edge as night falls in midsummer. A roaring fire cheered them. Weary with the day's climbing, Jim rolled himself in his buffalo robe immediately after their scanty meal, but Celiast sat, a huddled figure of despair, moaning and rocking back and forth, through the night. Briar kept the vigil with her and, to Jim's disgust, added her mournful howls to the Indian's woman's occasional muted cries of terror.

They were ready to take the trail before the morning light showed. Celiast seemed to find a relief in motion, though she started in terror at every sound, and passed each tree as if a lurking danger crouched on its shadowy side. A mountain trail as dawn is breaking is an eerie place. Even Jim, stolid as he was where the supernatural was concerned, felt cold thrills down his spine as Celiast alternately screamed and moaned with her hands before her face, then with an effort of will struggled on, as if spirit pushed weary flesh on to its goal.

To divert his attention from her misery he began noticing the formations of the rock about him. The mountain was assuming a different aspect as they ascended. The path, becoming fainter, was often swallowed up in a blur of grayish shale, though search for it was not necessary—their objective, the summit, flattened as if the peak had been cut off evenly, was clearly in view most of the time.

Celiast was plodding on doggedly, panting for breath in the rare atmosphere, working through the mahala mats, or squaw carpet—*Ceanothus prostratus*—that covered the ground with its rich glossy leaves and feathery clusters of blue flowers. She paid not the slightest heed to anything but the way ahead until, overcome again, she shrieked in terror, shrinking behind Jim.

"Do you see it now?" she screamed.

"There is nothing here," Jim assured her in a matter-of-fact tone.

"Yes, yes," she gasped, her breath coming in great sobs. "The spirits of La-o are coming down the mountain. I can go no farther." She froze in terror, pointing a trembling finger. "The giant crawfish."

Jim laughed away her fears and drew her along the trail with jokes and stories. But Celiast's journey up the mountain was a succession of frightful hallucinations.

A second night they camped. Early next morning they would reach the summit. Thinking to ease her mind by coaxing her to talk, Jim questioned her about the objects she had feared through the day, but she spoke only in whispers, telling him that a terrible god called La-o lived on the mountain who had many lesser spirits under his control. These evil entities had the power to change form at any time, becoming dragons or serpents or fierce animals before the horrified eyes of the Indian who dared to attempt to scale the heights.

When Jim inquired whether these monsters had ever harmed an Indian, she admitted that no one knew whether they had or not. No one except the medicinemen had ever dared come near the enchanted mountain, and medicine-men have the power to subdue evil spirits.

"The *shaman* has just learned that these monsters only exist in his own imagination," Jim soothed.

"No, no!" she cried, in indignation. "These horrors are very real to the Indians. We see them. I lived with Multnomah for so long that the sight left me, but the seals in the abode of the dead opened my eyes and now I see clearer than ever before. I shall live in terror again."

"You are tired and anxious now, Celiast. You will not be troubled with visions when you reach home and rest," Jim told her.

"No, the open eye does not close to things in the unseen world about us. I must bear this as I may. Multnomah used to laugh and laugh when my people spent days and days beating on the walls of their lodges with sticks to make a din that drove off the evil spirits. She is white. She cannot see, but every Indian knows that the air is filled with horrible leering creatures who torment him, sleeping and waking."

"But if there are evil spirits, there are also good spirits who love the Indians and protect them," Jim argued.

Celiast pondered this statement deeply before she answered. "That must be truth," she admitted at last, "but no Indian ever thought to look for the good; he can only fear the evil demons that surround him all the time."

"These spirits that the Indians see are not the dead, are they?" Jim wanted to know.

"No. We never mention the dead or any incident connected with them for fear of drawing them to us. No," she continued. "These are spirits that dwell in nature; they were never men as we are."

"Then why are you so afraid of them? No Indian ever tells a story of their doing him any harm but frightening him clear out of his senses," Jim laughed.

But their talk was arrested by a light at the summit of the mountain. The first flare of it lit the whole eastern sky with its rosy glow, then paled and glowed again.

"Katoosh is signaling to us," Celiast told Jim, her voice lowered in awe.

Breathlessly they watched the tongues of flame leap and die, then leap again. Then arrows of fire shot in the air and fell to earth again. Celiast counted these fiery darts as if she read their import. "Three, six, nine," she counted. "The days of the long fast are over. Tomorrow begins the great convocation. To think that I should live to brave the terrors of the sacred mountain and see with my old eyes the signals that begin the ceremony. Tomorrow we shall see Multnomah."

"Tomorrow," Jim said under his breath. "Tomorrow ends the long quest."

"What will the day bring forth?" Celiast questioned, solemnly.

"We can only pray to the God of Multnomah that all will be well."

"Yes," Jim said.

CHAPTER TWENTY-ONE
FIRE FROM HEAVEN

J IM and Celiast hoped to reach the summit of the mountain by midmorning, so they made their usual early start with the first streaks of dawn. Celiast appeared refreshed and fortified for the last lap of her trying journey. She ran on ahead, with Briar leaping joyfully at her side.

To hurry up a mountain is to sink with exhaustion long before the climb is finished. Jim followed a few steps behind her, warning that they must strike a slow, steady pace that could be maintained.

But Celiast turned a glowing face to him. "Katoosh is beckoning to me. With his eye he draws me up the mountain. I feel his strength in my old tired body and will run like a deer to Multnomah. The evil spirits fall away. They fear Katoosh."

Jim laughed, and followed her as rapidly as breathing in the rare atmosphere would permit. He, too, was in high spirits. The dream girl was to be made flesh-and-blood reality today. What if there should be trouble? He felt equal to it in his present mood. Celiast's spirits were high, and this was the mercury that foretold the fair weather or the spiritual stress of the day. Celiast, cheerful, was such a jolly companion. But sullen and full of superstitious fear and foreboding, she took the heart clear out of a man.

The sun came up in flaming angry red and gorgeous but sullen purple. Jim was just a bit uneasy as he watched it. Such a brilliant morning sky might be the forecast of a storm, and a heavy rain at this altitude would be chilling to the most exalted spirit. The morning air was still and intensely cold, but morning and evening always held needles of ice in the rare, thin atmosphere of a mountain-top.

Bounding from rock to rock like a mountain sheep, with Briar close at her heels, Celiast skipped ahead. What a bundle of contradictions the old Indian woman was! At his first meeting he had thought that she might easily pass for a white gentlewoman if it were not for her coppery skin. But the veneer was gone. Under stress she had reverted to type. She had been a true daughter of her race underneath all the time.

Knowing that the climb was an endurance test, he took time every few rods to enjoy the view or to look about him for rare mountain flowers, to exult in the pure stands of black, or mountain hemlock, *Tsuga mortensiana,* with its cones three or four inches long clinging to the upper branches. The way led through forests of noble fir, *Abies nobilis,* the Alpine fir, *Abies lasiocarpa,* and the white fir, *Abies concolor.*

He was struck by the abundance and variety of the bird life. Bluebirds, just waking from sleep, twittered in the trees. Two immense bald eagles winged through the clear air in search of prey for breakfast. And the humming-bird! The Nootka humming-birds frequented Wappatoo Island, but there they appeared in pairs. Here on the mountain they descended in iridescent clouds of ruby red with a metallic sheen, turning from purple to violet and crimson in the light.

The timber grew sparse and low in stature as they progressed, and the whole character of the mountain was changing. The way became barren and sandy. Jim picked up a curious stone and noted its lightness. He gave a loud whistle as the truth came to him. This was pumice. The mountain was an extinct volcano! They would find a crater at the top. Small wonder that the Indians held it in such awe, believing it to be the abode of evil spirits. Their forefathers, like enough, had seen it in action and had handed the tradition down, generation after generation.

Celiast came running down to him in a panic. Her hair flew out wildly as she stumbled and flew like one in danger of her life. She would have passed him but for the narrow path. He stopped her with an outstretched arm.

"Katoosh has ceased to draw me on," she screamed in frenzy. "I must make my way down the mountain. He is struggling with enemies and he can no longer keep the evil ones away from me. They are coming. See! See!" In horror she pointed to something behind a tree.

"Nonsense!" Jim exclaimed. "There's nothing there but a gray rock."

"No," the tormented woman shrieked, "it's a mountain lion, but it has Cockqua's face. Oh no! It's a terrible snake. Beat it off! beat it off!" She cowered at his feet, covering her face to keep out the awful sight.

In pity for her suffering Jim lifted her to her tottering feet and held her firmly when she would have sunk to the ground again. He removed her pack from her back and adjusted it carefully above his own, reasoning that she was exhausted with her mad haste to be off up the mountain. He must help her along and make sure that they kept to a pace she could hold.

Celiast tried heroically to suppress her fear, but after a few steps it triumphed; she made a frantic effort to break away from him. "I will run down the mountain," she declared, her face a ghastly mask of horror. "Even for my little one I cannot go on."

"Come, come," Jim soothed. "There's only a little more climbing. I think I see the summit now. Anyway, there's a broad level space above."

Celiast paused in indecision, listening with strained ears.

"Katoosh is calling again," she told Jim, in relief. "He is drawing me. I go. I go." All signs of her exhaustion vanished as she broke into a run. Jim followed her as fast as he could under the weight of the two heavy packs.

They had climbed the mountain on the northwest side, and, blessed relief, here through a break in the trees was a broad stretch of gray sand sloping but little to the west. Large banks of the last winter's snow stained a dirty gray from the clouds of pumice dust still lay in the hollows. The wind, as they reached the level spot, nearly took them off their feet. The sky between rolling leaden gray clouds was intensely blue. A storm was brewing; it would break in all its fury in an hour or two.

Celiast, her coppery skin a ghastly grayish green, was again showing signs of panic. Jim kept her from breaking away down the trail by placing his arm firmly about her thin, trembling shoulders. With bowed head she dragged along, her lips moving futilely, like one going to the gallows.

But as they cleared the trees an entirely unexpected sight broke upon Jim. They stood upon the rim of the crater of an extinct volcano. And down, down, his fascinated gaze traveled to a sheet of water, a blue lake, so blue that it exceeded blueness and became a thing unreal. The very essence of the blue of the dome of heaven had fallen on earth and was held imprisoned in a lake miles across. He marveled as he gauged the distance with a practiced eye. Five or six miles, perhaps eight or ten across—distance was deceptive in the clear atmosphere—was that lake of blue, held up to the sky in a gigantic chalice of rock rising a thousand feet or more about its placid surface.

Jim led Celiast around the rim of the crater before he noticed that she had never so much as glanced at the water below. He was making for a grove of white-barked pine, where they could rest, sheltered from the piercing wind. She could wait there while he looked for signs of the medicine-men and Multnomah.

Against her will, the water drew her like a magnet. She looked down into the crater, then crumpled up and sank unconscious at Jim's feet. In dismay he looked down at her still form, but in his bewilderment did not try to lift her immediately. His helpless gaze wandered again to the blue of the lake. Could he go down to it for water to revive Celiast? He stooped and began rubbing her hands and speaking to her, thinking dully that she was dead. Drat Briar! She always began that whining and pawing when anything happened, so that he couldn't collect his thoughts.

That blue lake was uncanny enough to strike the life out of anyone who came to its perpendicular edge unexpectedly: a thing some way against nature, but so lovely that it drew the eye and held it. A wooded island rose up out of it, and farther off another that looked for all the world like a phantom ship with sails spread, cruising on a sea of dreams.

The sight of that unearthly sheet of water was enough to kill an exhausted old Indian woman who believed so implicitly in evil spirits that she was sure she saw them. As he bent over her he blamed himself for not having a better human understanding—because he felt no fear of the unseen, he had not even sensed her suffering. He should have sent her home once they struck the trail up the mountain. She would have had no difficulty in making her way alone, and he could have rescued Multnomah.

But he roused from his bewilderment and began working frantically over Celiast. She was not dead, had just fallen into a coma. Tired nature had simply given way under the strain. All efforts to revive her were unavailing. He left her at last and ran to look for water, but could find none. The drop from the rim of the crater to the lake was a sheer thousand feet. There was no way down.

No use. He returned and renewed his efforts to rouse Celiast by chafing her hands. At a low growl from Briar he glanced up. A black head of matted hair and a naked bronze torso showed above the rim of the crater, fifty feet east of where he stood. Then a young Indian clad only in a buckskin loin-cloth emerged into full view. He had in some way climbed up from the lake below.

Jim gazed at him in amazement. The man was in the last stages of emaciation. His skin hung in loose folds over a powerful frame. And yet he seemed to be neither ill nor starving. The eyes in his intent face glowed like two live coals.

Without so much as a glance at Jim, he strode over to Celiast and stood looking down at her. Then before Jim realized what he was about he stooped and raised her limp form deftly to his back and, with a scarcely perceptible motion to follow, led the way over the rim of rocks.

Jim obeyed like a wanderer in the wasteland of a nightmare. For half an hour they worked their way down the sheer wall, following a way that could not be dignified by the name of path. Dropping from rock to rock, the Indian deposited his burden and signaled to Jim to lower her down to him. Never so much as a syllable did he utter, giving his directions entirely by pantomime.

The sky was becoming leaden and the peculiar expectant hush in which all nature waits with bated breath for the breaking of a storm was over all. The morning turned to a dim twilight. Overheated with the rapid climb, Jim shivered in the icy air. His teeth chattered in spite of his efforts at control, and his hands trembled as he lowered Celiast carefully down to the arms of the waiting Indian. Fear all but overcame him when he glanced down the wall. The wind howled and tore at him.

A burst of weird chanting broke through the lull of the storm. He nearly lost his balance, but as he regained his position he realized that he was going where no white man had ever gone before, nor was it likely one would ever go again. He was going into the conclave of the medicine-men of the Pacific coast. This was the spot he had heard of where the *shaman* received his initiation into the great medicine cult. But he had come by invitation and was expected. He felt not the least fear.

At last he made out vague forms in the dim light, and soon his guide led him into their midst on the shore of the lake.

They emerged through a narrow aperture just wide enough to admit the passage of a man's body if he edged his way through carefully.

No setting of nature could be more appropriate for the celebration of the weird savage rites than the one he saw. The blue lake lashed by a furious gale, the sheer wall of stone shutting out the world, gave a sense of unreality to the ceremony that he was to witness. A group of young Indians, naked like his guide but for the loin-cloth, danced and chanted wildly on a stretch of lava-strewn sand near the edge of the water. They circled about a stone platform raised a few feet above them.

The Indian who had borne Celiast down the face of the cliff placed her on the sand to one side and without so much as a backward glance took his place in the circle and resumed his dancing, as if he had only paused for a moment's breathing-spell. The rocky platform was not more than ten feet square and in the center stood a small monolith that served as an altar. There was a smoldering fire upon it, giving off volumes of pungent smoke that veered in a white column with the force of the wind. Jim caught a glimpse of the *shaman* in his ceremonial robes through the wavering smoke.

This personage must be the great Katoosh. His face was covered with a hideous wooden mask, representing some being whose like never was known on land or sea. His robe, reaching to his heels, was made of the skins of the bluebird with the feathers intact, richly ornamented with scintillating bands of the plumage of the humming-bird. A huge top-heavy head-dress of feathers adorned his head, with a circular band of the flight feathers of the bald eagle holding it back from the mask.

The animal and bird life of the mountains hovered about on the sand, drawn, no doubt, by the fire on the altar as they sought refuge from the sudden fury of the storm. A number of deer swam from the island in the lake and paused a few paces up the sandy shore. A smooth-coated black bear kept watch from the rocks above. Weasels, marmots, and minks looked out from the crevices, safe in their coverts. Chipmunks were everywhere.

Golden eagles circled majestically overhead and a flock of great white swans, returning from their migration of the summer, flew back and forth over the churning blue water. Never, Jim thought, had he seen so many varieties of wild life as the storm had congregated in the shelter of the rocks. Clouds of hummingbirds, hawks, jays, blackbirds, both the yellow-headed and the red-winged, water ousels and any number of sparrows, had been lured to the great ceremony. Jim wondered, as he looked about, whether Indian magic had drawn them, or just the fire in the blinding storm. The Indian would say his medicine, but he, being a white man, said natural causes explained the phenomenon.

The chanting and dancing of the acolytes gained in momentum. With both arms stretched above their heads, and faces upward to the sky, the naked Indians turned in rapid circles, uttering their unearthly cries in unison. Jim suddenly felt irresistibly drawn to join them. A gust of smoke blew in his face, and he recognized the spicy tang of the leaves of the smelling tree. Madness lay in inhaling that smoke and yet he felt a power that he could scarcely resist drawing him toward the altar. He longed to throw his arms up over his head and join the emaciated figures with wild ecstasy glowing like fire in their upturned faces.

The thought of Multnomah brought him back to reality. He must keep his senses. He looked about, but could find no sign of her. He felt a vast sense of desolation. She was not there. A gust of icy wind driving needles of sleet into his face nearly took him off his feet. He moved back into the shelter of the cliff a little to one side of the altar, to escape the force of it, noticing as he did so, a recess under an overhanging rock large enough to admit of a man's standing upright. The air had become so thick and dark that objects were blurred and indistinct. He peered into the crevice, and there, safely sheltered from the storm, he thought he noted a huddled form, but could not be sure; perhaps it was just a pile of buckskin garments. His first instinct was for dashing across, but he must pass between the acolytes and the altar, and this was sacrilege. He must wait.

The *shaman* began a chant differing in tone and quality from the rhythmic song of the neophytes, and in breathless expectancy the dancing circle as one man paused to listen. There was an awful dignity about the majestic figure serving the altar.

With his right arm above his head, the high priest paused as if in prayer, then with a swift gesture flung cloak and mask from him, standing revealed in his loin cloth. Jim noticed that his left arm hung shrunken and useless at his side. In a silence broken only by the whistling of the wind, he began a dance around the altar. Twice he circled, then began an unearthly chant that held in its minor cadences all of human longing, all of the soul's prayer to an invisible God.

He paused in silent prayer, then began whirling from east to west, whirling until it seemed to the waiting Jim that there could be no more power of motion in his body. He halted abruptly as if paralyzed. The acolytes paused in their dancing and watched the *shaman* in fascination. Without changing his position, he reached for a large, richly ornamented medicine-bag that lay on the altar, holding it aloft in view of the awe-stricken assembly. They sank to the ground, moaning in an agony of supplication, never daring to raise their faces for so much as a glance at the fetish.

Now the *shaman* was laying out objects on the altar. He took first from the bag twelve polished stones, such as Tilki had used in his divination, placing them in a triangle, with the base to the east and the apex to the west. In the inclosure he put small objects, the nature of which Jim could not determine. Over these he heaped leaves from the smelling tree and kindled them with a live coal from the fire smoldering on the altar.

Thunder reverberated across the leaden sky, followed by a vivid flash of lightning as the flame shot upward. With the flash a woman's shrill scream of horror rang out. Jim turned instantly in the direction of the cry. On the left behind the altar he caught a fleeting glimpse of a face that in that unearthly light he took to be that of an angel, but lost it again as a terrific peal of thunder shook the very sand upon which he stood.

When Jim turned again to the altar the *shaman*, entirely oblivious to the lightning, was proceeding with the ceremony. But as he looked he saw the reason for the woman's terrified shriek. Filing between the cleft in the rock, with their heads just showing above, came Indians. Cockqua was in the lead. Jim cowered, waiting for the next flash to reveal them fully, and saw Cockqua, with a leer of triumph on his malevolent face and his red scars gleaming dully, advance with upraised knife to strike the priest in the back.

In an instant the lightning flash came; the bolt struck the knife and Cockqua fell. Then darkness and another terrific crash of thunder!

The ceremony proceeded. The *shaman* seized a stick and thrust the end into the glowing coals on the altar, calling a name loudly to the prostrate neophytes. One arose and advanced with a firm step. The red coal seared his breast. He wheeled about and plunged into the water. The great swans flew in circles above the assemblage. Dripping, the Indian came and stood on the platform.

Again the *shaman* called a name, and the next neophyte received the baptism of fire and plunged into the lake. With a routine that Jim thought endless the emaciated Indians responded, all except three who lay motionless. He realized that death had overtaken those silent figures.

The rites completed, the great medicine-man calmly put out the fire with his bare heel and turned with a grunt to the prostrate Cockqua, while the initiates gathered about him in an ecstasy of joy, dancing and waving their arms.

Katoosh spoke to them briefly, and with one accord they filed through the opening in the rock and flew up the trail in pursuit of the companions of Cockqua.

Jim turned to search for the white woman whose scream he had heard, and recognized her in the huddle of buckskin in the dry recess under the rock. First he saw two long braids of yellow hair, and then made out a little sobbing figure. With a stride he reached her, and with a hand that trembled lifted a slender young girl to her feet.

Through a mist of tears she looked at him for a long moment, and then, her face on his shoulder, her body was racked with sobs.

"I have come for you, Multnomah," Jim said. "Are you hurt?"

"No," she said, a little doubtfully, "only frightened. I didn't make a sound until I saw Cockqua lift the knife to kill Katoosh, and I couldn't warn him."

She recovered herself a little and drew away, the scarlet flush of embarrassment staining her white face.

"Thank God! thank God!" Jim burst forth in his great relief. Multnomah was safe. Cockqua was dead. A load of anxiety to which he had felt unequal was suddenly lifted from his shoulders.

Multnomah caught sight of the prostrate Celiast where she had lain unnoticed during the medicine rites, and with a cry of mingled joy and pity ran to her and made an effort to lift her. Jim rushed to her side and, gathering the unconscious old woman in his arms, carried her to the shelter of the rock.

During this interval, Katoosh, unperturbed, was collecting the implements of his sacred profession. He finished at his leisure and came slowly into the shelter. The thunder and lightning had passed as the storm broke in fury. The driving sleet had turned to snow.

"Big *shaman,* me," Katoosh said by way of introduction, offering his good right hand to Jim. The left hung limply at his side.

"Celiast is dead," Multnomah sobbed.

"She no dead." Katoosh spoke out of a large unconcern. "Me make sleep. Indian woman die she see Katoosh made big medicine." He pointed to the body of Cockqua lying where it fell. "Me draw Cockqua up mountain for fire from sky make kill. Me show-um trail for come." He grinned in satisfaction as he indicated the forehead. A livid burn showed where the lightning had struck him.

Jim's amazement was mingled with horror as he recalled the bas-relief Celiast had made on the sand near the grove of smelling trees. Here was witchcraft, terrible witchcraft. Celiast had killed Cockqua with his lens when she called down fire from heaven upon him. The spot on his forehead was in just the place she had set the tinder! Then reason stepped to his rescue. The murderous upraised knife had drawn the lightning. Coincidence, simple coincidence. Had he been so long among superstitious Indians that he was coming to believe in their voodooism? His mind was a chaos of seething unrelated thoughts. He did not know.

But through the seethe in his brain there shot like a beautiful ray of light the knowledge that Multnomah was safe. A holy joy filled his soul. She was, in that unearthly flash when he had his first glimpse of her, a celestial being, white and holy like the angels singing around the throne of God. Now he saw her in reality. She was just a simple, straightforward young girl about eighteen years old, rather embarrassed, yet happy beyond measure that he had come for her. The reality transcended the vision. He preferred every-day girlhood to white angels any time.

Katoosh brushed Multnomah aside and shouldered Celiast as if she had been a baby. He was a powerful man in spite of his infirmity.

"We go," he announced and led the way out into the raging storm without so much as a backward glance at the body of Cockqua or the three neophytes who had failed in the medicine test.

Jim dreaded the ascent for a tender white girl. He helped her up the rocks when he was not handing Celiast up to Katoosh. But Multnomah did not need assistance. She climbed easily from rock to rock up the steep incline.

When they reached the level, they made swiftly for a huge fire that burned brightly in a grove of trees in a hollow shut off from the wind. A number of tepees were set up, and sixteen proud young medicine-men clad warmly in buckskins lounged in the warmth.

Multnomah shuddered as she pointed to the bodies of Cockqua's companions a little distance away. "They have killed them all." Her tone carried mingled relief and regret. "Cockqua is beyond troubling. We have nothing more to fear. My days of terror are over. The white man I saw in my dreams has come to take me to my people."

"Yes," Jim answered her.

Katoosh had placed Celiast by the fire and was making mysterious passes and pressing his hands hard against her chest, while he blew his breath in her face. Multnomah and Jim watched him anxiously and were rewarded shortly by signs of life. The *shaman* then wrapped her warmly in fur robes and left her to sleep by the fire.

Food was passed around—huge chunks of jerked elk meat and cakes of camass. The nine days' fast of the young medicine-men was broken. They ate in silence.

Katoosh, no longer a high priest, but a man eminently pleased with himself and the day's ceremony, ate his food and laughed and jested.

"What you t'ink, you see me draw fire from sky for kill Cockqua? What you t'ink you see me call birds and deer and bear for watch medicine fire?" he asked Jim.

"Big medicine," Jim approved, heartily.

"Me draw you up mountain for find Multnomah. Me make-um sleep," he pointed to Celiast.

Jim, watching Multnomah narrowly, saw a faint smile of good-natured tolerance curl her lips. "I was afraid your medicine would fail. I have been horribly afraid for a long time," the girl told Katoosh.

He laughed in fine scorn. "Medicine no fail. Nehalems happy people now. Cockqua gone. Him ver' bad Indian. All time make-um trouble. Multnomah happy, too," he said, with a significant glance at Jim, who colored to the roots of his hair.

"Now we sleep-um," Katoosh ordered. "Tomorrow down medicine mountain. Multnomah tell story tomorrow."

Jim was greatly disappointed. He had hoped to have the opportunity to talk with Multnomah. Tomorrow was a long time off. He wanted the story of Multnomah's life that night.

CHAPTER TWENTY-TWO

THE SUN RISES ON CRATER LAKE

THE Indians paid not the least attention to the howling of the storm, sleeping peacefully through the night with their feet to the fire. Jim found his tepee warm and comfortable. Toward morning the wind dropped and cold stillness descended on the mountain-top. The summer blizzard of the higher altitudes departs as suddenly as it appears.

Jim Faxon was too happy to sleep despite his weariness. He spent the early hours of the night in living over the events of his stirring day, placing Multnomah in the vivid setting in which he had first glimpsed her. In the days when he had first heard the story of the white girl, half believing in her existence, he had built up her image in his heart and loved her as every man loves his highest ideal of womankind. Then when he was certain that she lived, he experienced a dread of meeting her, at the same time being hardly able to restrain his eagerness.

Now he had seen her, had held her hand and spoken with her, and the stuff of dreams had resolved itself into reality. He acknowledged to himself that for the first time in his life, he was in love. Multnomah was simple and unaffected and sweet. He marvelled at her beauty. No wonder the Indians had named her Rose-on-the-Water, but now she was a pallid rose from her days of terror and misery. He pictured her with pink in her cheeks, and the dancing spirit of mischief in her blue eyes, and bubbling laughter on her lips, and then cursed himself for a fool. Who was he that he dared hope to marry such a radiant creature? His case was hopeless. His unworthiness overwhelmed him. In the next instant he determined to move heaven and earth to win her love. Such is the way of the young man hard hit with his first great passion.

He made all sorts of high resolves. He would be just and fair. After he had heard Multnomah's story he would see that she reached her people. She must have a chance to judge men by comparison. He was, in all probability, the first young white man she had ever seen. The least hint of love would not be honorable until she had had the opportunity to adjust herself to her changed condition.

Then high resolves were thrown to the wind. He determined to win her love before she met other men; that was his only chance. Wavering from the noble to the base viewpoint and back again, the night passed. He slept in the early morning hours, waking to find his problem just where he had left it.

Faint light shone through the opening at the top of the teepee. Jim raised the flap and looked out. The mountain wore a snowy mantle, serene in the peace that it imparted. Indians, one or two of them, were stirring about the fire, replenishing it and making preparations for breakfast. Jim rose and stole out, without their even turning to notice his departure. Dawn and the white mountain and a glimpse of the enchanted blue lake would cool his fevered brain, weary with making high resolves and breaking them. He told himself he was happier than he had ever been in his life before, and then in the same breath acknowledged that he was sad and torn with fears, fears worse than any he had ever known.

He listened for a stir in the small teepee a little aside where Multnomah and Celiast had passed the night, but there was no sound. So he hurried from the camp, knowing that the company would start down the mountain very soon after sunrise. He told himself that he wanted to be alone in the cold, still morning to collect his scattered thoughts, then wished with all his soul that Multnomah were with him.

Turning up the incline to the edge of the crater, he started with joy. Small moccasin tracks led upward. They were Multnomah's, he knew at once. The Indian toes-in when he walks. He broke into a run in his eagerness, then slowed down to a decorous gait as he realized how ridiculous he would look to the girl. But his step quickened in spite of himself; he hoped that she would think he was moving briskly on account of the intense cold.

He found Multnomah standing on the rim of the crater. She turned and ran toward him with a joyous welcome, holding out both hands to him just as a child would have done. There were a complete absence of self-consciousness and a directness and simplicity about her that put him at his ease. At home he had never been without an uncomfortable shyness in the presence of young ladies, but he had not seen a white woman for two years, so perhaps this accounted for his lack of embarrassment in Multnomah's presence.

The exercise in the cold morning air had whipped roses into Multnomah's cheeks. Her dress was the simple Indian jacket and skirt of buckskin, fringed at the seams and nicely beaded. She wore leggings and moccasins. Her hair was like new buckskin, just as Auxica had told him. Her eyes drew him. They were clear and blue, like the blue of the lake below them, and yet in their depths there lay signs of recent suffering, that hurt him, tightened his throat, as he realized the terror and loneliness through which the girl had passed. In the moment that her hands lay in his, he told himself that no woman should be allowed to undergo such suffering. He wondered if ever in his long life he could do enough to recompense her for the years of agony.

But Multnomah's clear laugh rang out, and a set of even white teeth flashed. "I do not know your name yet, white man," she said.

"I'm Jim Faxon from Fort William. I'm an American. I came to the Pacific coast with Nat Wyeth."

Multnomah shook a doubtful head. "I have not heard of Fort William," she told him. "Father always thought that there were English or American traders somewhere to the north, but we had no means of finding them."

"Then your father was with you?" Jim asked, relieved that she had not been alone among the Nehalems.

"Father died about three years ago," she told him, with tears near her eyes. "I have been alone with the Indians since that time. Katoosh promised father, just before he died, that he would find a good white man to take me to my people. You cannot know what it means to me to see you. I believed in your coming, and yet there were times when I couldn't believe. I am hardly sure now. I might wake and find you just a pleasant dream."

"Be sure now," Jim told her, joyfully. "No-Lie—er—Yallup, told me that there was a white girl among his people. I only half believed him, but came on the chance that he spoke the truth. Curious, reticent people, the Indians, aren't they, never telling a story completely, just hinting and evading? Even Celiast turned the subject or refused to answer when I asked about your parents."

"Celiast is an Indian and queer, but she's been my mother ever since we came here. I can just remember my own mother, but father talked constantly of her, to keep her memory green, he said. The Indians never speak of the dead or refer to them in any way after they are buried; that is the reason you could not learn our story from them."

Her eyes suddenly swam with tears that she made a heroic effort to keep back. "My greatest grief after father died was that I could never mention his name," she said, and her pathetic effort to smile clutched Jim's heart.

Jim sought to divert her by changing the subject. "But tell me how long have you been on the mountain?" he asked.

"I have been here ten days. This is the tenth sunrise I have seen and they were all different. What makes the lake so blue?"

They had walked rapidly to keep warm, and the sun was just rising over the eastern rim of the crater, tinting a cloudless sky with its glowing colors and casting its rosy reflection on the snow.

"I think heaven must be blue and crimson and gold like this. I mean to remember these hues so I can put them on canvas some day when I go to my people and really learn to paint. I can only draw now, and that not very well; there has been no one to teach me."

"Of course you will learn to paint," Jim assured her.

"No wonder the *shaman* keeps this lake a secret," Jim mused. "But tell me, Multnomah, do you see spirits everywhere as the Indians do? Do you think they really see things that are hidden to white people, or is it just their imagination?"

"I do not know," Multnomah answered, thoughtfully. "Father told me not to think too much about it. I have never seen a spirit, other than the spirit of beauty that lives in nature. It may be that the Indian's power of sensing the unseen is greater than ours. They live in deadly fear of evil spirits all the time. The medicine-men are the only ones who ever really overcome their dread of the supernatural."

"Do you think that Katoosh caused the lightning, as he declared he did, and drew the birds and animals to the altar?" Jim asked.

"No," Multnomah smiled, "but we must not show that we doubt his power. Father studied Indian magic very carefully, and he found much that completely baffled him; but he said that no human agency influences the wind. Of course the birds and animals were frightened by the storm and the fire drew them. They are not afraid up here. A bow has never been shot on the medicine mountain."

"Do you think that Katoosh really drew me out of the company of white men at Fort William by his magic and brought me here to take you away?" Jim persisted, as they walked around the rim of the crater.

Multnomah shook her head doubtfully. "Katoosh has power," she admitted. "He has always kept his promises to us. I love and trust him implicitly. He told father that he would bring a good white man to care for me, and that he would come without the knowledge of other white men. He sent Yallup away the next year on his mission, and I have had faith that you would come, though the waiting has been long. About the magic I do not know."

"I never would have believed No-Lie's story but for the cloth with the pink rosebuds on it and the nightcap that some woman had sewed so daintily. Even then I had grave doubts," Jim told her.

"The cloth was cut from a dress of my mother's," Multnomah explained. "I gave the little bag to Yallup so that the man he chose would know that he was not lying to him."

"We must go back to the camp," Jim urged, noticing that Multnomah's teeth were beginning to chatter with the cold. "Breakfast will soon be ready and the Indians will be on the march."

"Yes," Multnomah agreed, a bit reluctantly. "There is so much I must tell you. It was hard just now to speak of father. He left a letter for you. I brought it with me for fear something would happen to his papers while I was away."

She took a carefully wrapped packet from the pocket of her skirt and handed it to Jim.

"You are the man father intended this for," she said with a little smile. "There are other letters and documents at home that will prove the story."

One of the young Indians came in search of them, grinning and motioning toward the camp, then ran back. They both smiled as they noticed that he kept his eyes carefully turned from the lake.

"You'll have to read as we march, and I'll tell you everything. There is so much for you to know." The girl sped over the snow to the camp, Jim close behind.

There was hot soup and an abundance of camass awaiting them. The packing had been completed. The medicine party would be on the march in a few minutes. They were feverishly impatient to be off. The Indian abhors the cold, though he bears it stolidly; and then, too, once his mission at the haunted lake is fulfilled, he does not tarry an instant longer than necessary in a spot so terrible to him, even though he has overcome his fears.

Celiast sat huddled by the fire, and Multnomah ran and put her soft young arms about her neck. Tears coursed down the tired old woman's face as she gathered her in her arms and smoothed back the soft hair from her face with an adoring gesture.

"My little one is safe now," she said, brokenly, to Jim. "Cockqua is dead. Jim Faxon, didn't I tell you fire from heaven would strike Cockqua?"

Katoosh came up to the group, waving his good right arm in his triumph. His eyes glittered like the eagle's and there was a power about him that commanded attention, and yet he was childishly boastful of his magic, taking great credit to himself for everything that had happened.

"Katoosh say you no worry." He turned to Multnomah. "Katoosh promise white husband."

Multnomah blushed painfully, and Jim turned aside to attend to his pack and to give her time to recover from her confusion. He was furiously angry with Katoosh for his sally. The Indians met it with gales of wild laughter.

CHAPTER TWENTY-THREE
MARTIN BRAINTREE'S LETTER

THE trail the homeward-bound medicine-men took led down the south slope of the mountain. Multnomah told Jim that Katoosh was the head *shaman,* the high priest who ruled the medicine cult, whose members were drawn from the various tribes on the Pacific coast. These young men who had endured the test would now return to their own country, where they would serve their people.

Katoosh was a power in the Indian country. Multnomah called Jim's attention to his withered arm, telling him that he had at some time in his early youth been struck by lightning. The Indians believe that if the victim of fire from heaven lives he can ever after command the lightning and rule over the forces of nature. He is revered as little less than a god.

The descent was much easier than the steep path leading up from the west, and now there was no need for haste. The sixteen new-fledged doctors of Indian medicine formed a V-shaped vanguard to ward off the evil spirits and keep the way clear for the white people and Celiast, Katoosh told Jim. According to his account, the spirits were fleeing in terror before them, while as Celiast and Jim ascended the mountain they had rushed at them and expended their mysterious dark forces to keep them from reaching the lake in the crater where they had their abode.

Celiast showed not the least fear, trudging along cheerfully under the protection of the mighty Katoosh. The air, stinging cold and clear as crystal at the summit, gradually grew warm and balmy. In two hours they had left all traces of snow behind.

The way led along the edge of a gorge, where a torrent, probably fed from underground by the waters of the lake, tore at its rocky banks in the headlong journey to the valley below. This cut in the earth was fearful of aspect. The water had worn its way through rocks and sand. Pinnacles of rock stood out on the sharply sloping sides, looking in the distance for all the world like men turned to stone with the everlasting winds blowing over their defenseless heads.

Katoosh pointed them out and told the initiates that these were the bodies of neophytes who in former times had failed in the medicine test. Soon three more columns would appear. The three aspirants who now lay dead by the lake would take their places among the company.

The young Indians, on hearing this, set up a mournful dirge for their lost comrades, in which there was a note of triumph at their own success in enduring the nine days of fasting alone on the haunted mountain and the ordeal of initiation. The ceremony at this awesome spot occupied the better part of an hour.

Jim was eager to read the letter Multnomah had given him. He drew her a little apart, and together they broke the seal on the missive.

"Father died the day after he completed this letter," Multnomah told Jim. "Writing was an effort for him at the last, but he could not rest until he concluded his message. He used the last of his ebbing strength in finishing it."

Jim opened the packet and, with Multnomah watching his face and commenting from time to time, he read the letter to her:

THE PACIFIC COAST, *November 7, 1833.*

To the White Man into Whose Hands This Message
Shall Fall:

This is the last writing I may hope to do. I can only
pray God that the man who reads this is a gentleman
and willing to discharge the sacred trust I have imposed
upon him with honor.

I am Martin Braintree and this letter concerns itself
with the future welfare of my beloved daughter, Rosaltha
Braintree, known to the Indians as Multnomah. In my
blind foolishness I have put off making an attempt to
take my daughter out of the country of the Nehalems,
until now, I realize that it is too late. I know that I am
on my deathbed and at best have but a short time to live.

Now that I am slowly dying with consumption, I am
full of fears and terrible forebodings for my daughter's
future. Her fate rests in the hands of Katoosh, my faithful friend. He has promised that he will do his utmost
to find a responsible man of my own race willing to
assume the guardianship of Rosaltha until she reaches
my people in England. I realize that this may take two or
three years. Should she reach the age of eighteen before
a guardian can be found, she will then be able to make
her own decision in the matter of marrying or returning
home to my people.

That she will be largely guided in her decision by
Katoosh is my great consolation. The *shaman* will keep
his word, and I know of few Englishmen in whom I
repose a greater faith. While he judges by Indian standards, his estimate of a man is sure and accurate. The
man whom he chooses will merit his opinion of his
honor and integrity.

My story is a long one and sad. As I look back over
the years since I made the rash decision to explore the
Indian Country to study the native races, I see that I was

blinded by my own folly in attempting to take a delicate woman and a defenseless child into a region where no white man had gone before. What is done is done. I can only regret my shortsightedness. I blame myself, as only the dying can blame, for my neglect to make an effort to find my way to the settlement in the north. There are white men somewhere in this country, of that I am sure; a year or two ago we might have reached them in safety, and I would now be in good health and able to protect my daughter and conduct her safely to civilization.

I believe that there is a trading-post not many hundred miles from here. The Nehalems have been making yearly trips to the north with their peltries, returning with guns and such objects of trade as are supplied by the Hudson's Bay Company or the American companies.

The Indians refuse to enlighten me in regard to white men's activities, fearing that our escaping to them would bring in trappers and traders who would speedily destroy their elk and beaver and drive them from their homes. So while we are treated with the utmost consideration we are virtually the prisoners of the Nehalems. They are a tribe apart, never having allowed other Indians to cross the two secret mountain passes that secure their country from invaders. I realize the justice of this prohibition of theirs, and wish to protect them in their rights to this rich valley. The Indian has no reason to trust the white trader and trapper.

Katoosh promises to send Yallup, a trusted member of the medicine cult, who will search for a white man whom he deems worthy of the trust to be imposed upon him. This is to be done on condition that the secret of a white man and his daughter in the Nehalem country shall be kept inviolate.

Rosaltha is to leave the Pacific coast without the knowledge reaching the trading-posts, and this is to be accomplished as soon as possible. In my weakened condition I can only pray that she will be placed on ship and reach friends in safety. I have the word of Katoosh upon which to rely. I can but trust his judgment. We have had nothing but the utmost kindness and consideration from the Indians since we landed among them eleven years ago this fall. In spite of the seeming dangers, I rest secure in their wisdom and kindness.

The story of the Braintree family is a singular one and filled with sadness. I realize now more than ever that it was my own folly that brought death and sorrow upon those I love. But that this was due to the hand of fate, and not to be avoided after the first step was made, is my only consolation in my last days.

The seat of the Braintree family is near Liverpool. Upon my father's death the entailed estate went by right to my eldest brother, John. My patrimony was small but adequate to our simple needs. I was always of a studious turn; in my days at Oxford, ethnology had been my delight. My young wife shared my joy in the study of primitive races. Now that we had funds sufficient for our study, we decided at once to make a year's sojourn among the Indians of the Pacific coast, with the view of writing upon their manners and customs. My wife was an artist of no mean ability. She hoped to depict Indian life by means of the brush and crayon. Our little girl, Rosaltha, we were loath to leave in England, so after much deliberation and not without some misgivings as to the wisdom of exposing a tender child to the dangers of a remote uncivilized country, we at length decided that she should accompany us.

We foolishly kept our plans a secret from our families, who were wont to consider us impractical and dreamy on account of our devotion to our studies. We could see no particular danger in our journey of exploration. True, men did not take their women on such expeditions, but my wife was strong and well and felt herself capable of enduring hardships if she could but keep me company. Too late, I realized how criminally foolhardy I had been.

Desiring to find a spot on the Pacific coast where we might encounter the Indian unspoiled by contact with the white race, we determined to sail with my life-long friend, Captain Robert Maddock, master of the Bark *Linnet*, engaged in the fur trade on Nootka Sound, far to the north. Captain Maddock was not without misgiving at first, but, seeing that we were determined to pursue our course, he at length assured us that he knew of a small cove on the Oregon coast where a bark could land at high tide. So far as he knew, no white man had ever visited this part of the country, as the nearest post was Fort George at the mouth of the Columbia River, a distance that he estimated as between one hundred and fifty and two hundred miles to the north.

Accordingly, I made arrangements to sojourn among the natives for the period between his trading voyages, or longer if we saw fit. I left England with my beloved wife and little daughter, April 2, 1821 with an ample supply of building material such as glass, nails, and tools for the erection of some sort of habitation, as well as books and provisions to make our stay comfortable.

The *Linnet* was delayed by storms after rounding Cape Horn and we were not able to make the tiny harbor called "Smuggler's Cove" until late in October. A great sorrow came upon me two weeks before we landed. My beloved wife died of a heart ailment, brought on, I feel sure, by the rigors of the long, tedious voyage. We buried her at sea.

Captain Maddock implored me to continue the voyage to Nootka with him, or at least allow him to put in at Fort George, where passage could be taken in a ship bound for the Sandwich Islands; from there we could sail for England in a few months' time. I was broken-hearted and desolate over the death of my wife and longed for strangeness and solitude in which to overcome my first great sorrow. I feared for the life of my little daughter if she were forced to undertake six months or more of difficult ocean travel. So against his better judgment, I determined to be put ashore to await his return from his voyage to Nootka Sound.

With many misgivings Captain Maddock set us ashore. He promised to touch at Smuggler's Cove in a year at the outside. The Indians, he assured us, were friendly and kind, having had no dealing with white men to make them bitter against the Englishman. I had no apprehensions in going ashore with my little girl.

The tribe welcomed us joyfully and did everything in their power to make our stay with them a pleasant one. Celiast, a slave woman, belonging to the household of their chief, Cassicass, I bought, according to their custom, and installed her as Rosaltha's nurse.

She deemed this a post of great honor and was faithful and eager to learn our ways. I set about at once to teach her English methods of housekeeping. I gave much of my time that first year to teaching her to speak the language well, in order that Rosaltha might not fall into slovenly habits of speech and deportment. I did my best to instruct the Indians, at the same time learning their manners and customs. They readily learned enough English to make living among them easy.

In return they taught us their dialect as it is spoken in its purity, a feat, perhaps, never before accomplished by the white man. The Indians guard their language as sacred. At the end of the year we began looking for the sail of the bark *Linnet*. But no ship has put in at Smuggler's Cove in all these long years. No word of Captain Maddock has ever reached us. Too late I came to realize that some disaster had befallen him. I am rather inclined to the belief that the *Linnet* was wrecked in a terrible gale that lashed the coast in late November of that year, though there is a possibility that she may have fallen into the hands of the Spanish pirates who infest the waters of the Pacific. That he was lost at sea I am satisfied, for otherwise he would have delivered instructions for our rescue to those in responsibility.

Papers and documents which Rosaltha has been instructed to give you will verify my statements and instruct you in the method of procedure in communicating with my family. My manuscripts, two complete treatises on the manners and customs of the North American Indian, are to be delivered into your hands. They contain directions for their disposal. It is my belief that these will prove of great value to ethnologists, as they have been written after a close study of the subject.

My daughter, Rosaltha, has inherited her mother's talent for sketching; and, while entirely self-taught, her drawings, which are to accompany the manuscripts, are admirably adapted for illustrations. I wish to caution in regard to these; the Indians believe that a likeness of them gives their spirit into the keeping of the person who made the picture. They consider any delineation of their features to be witchcraft, and deal sternly with its practice. No one but Celiast knows of these sketches and she can be relied upon to keep the secret, though she had many misgivings while they were in process of execution, and lives in constant fear that they will be discovered.

My strength fails rapidly. I have been a long time in writing this letter. I feel it to be entirely inadequate; there are so many instructions I would give and so much that I would relate. My dear daughter must supply the details that have escaped my trembling pen.

I have made constant endeavor to educate Rosaltha according to English standards, and to instruct her thoroughly in the traditions of her people, so that she may take her place among my family without embarrassment. Our books, while necessarily few, have been most carefully chosen, and I venture to assert that she has done more solid reading than most girls of her age. In addition to this she has gained a certain health and grace from the free outdoor life she has led.

Contrary to general opinion, the Indians have many traits which their white brethren would do well to copy, and in strict justice I must admit that Rosaltha has learned from them as much as they have from her. She has developed the honest, straightforward nature of the Indian woman, entirely devoid of sham or affectation. In many ways I rejoice that she sees life through Indian eyes as well as through English eyes.

Though I speak with a father's doting fondness, I believe my daughter promises to develop into a woman of beautiful character as well as one with grace of manner. She has been well grounded in religion and is entirely free from the taint of Indian superstition.

My days, perhaps my hours, are numbered. I turn faint with fear when I think of her fate if she be not rescued by an honorable white man. Her fate, if married to an Indian, is too terrible to contemplate. She will soon reach the age when her only safety will be in marriage with a white man or a return to my home in England. I would not stretch out a hand from the grave to bind my daughter; her judgment is sound. If she is of age before help reaches her, she will make her own decisions with the advice of my trusted friend Katoosh.

With my last breath I pray for her safety and happiness. As death nears, my sorrows are more than I can bear, though I comfort myself with the knowledge of God's infinite goodness and the belief that there are many upright, honorable men in the world.

Yours in deepest trust,

MARTIN BRAINTREE.

The last pages of the letter required their combined efforts in the deciphering. Martin Braintree had exerted his dying strength to finish his message to the unknown protector of his daughter.

Multnomah's tears flowed freely as they finished reading. "I have been sorely tempted to break the seal on father's letter," she confessed. "He told me if no white man came for me, to read it, but I resolved to wait to see if Katoosh was right in promising that you would come to the medicine mountain for me."

Her tears broke out afresh. Briar thrust her black-and-tan muzzle between the interlaced fingers covering her face to offer doggish sympathy. Jim longed to comfort, but could say nothing, just waited with tears in his own eyes until her grief had spent itself.

"Poor dear father," she said at last. "He was so gay and cheerful at the last, trying in every way to comfort me. I am sure that he instructed Celiast to kill me if she saw that I must fall into the hands of Cockqua, or any of the other young Indians who wanted to take me for a wife."

"That would never have happened," Jim told her, decisively.

"No," she said, "not while Katoosh lives and maintains his power over the Nehalems, but that power has been waning lately. Cockqua was gaining the ascendency."

They went to join the Indians, who had finished their ceremony. Jim was thoughtful as they moved along down the mountain. Katoosh had risen to a place of respect in his estimation. He had risked the wrath of his Indian gods in taking a defenseless white girl to the sacred mountain, where no woman had ever gone before. His plans for bringing a white man into the country without the knowledge of the *attachés* of the forts and the execution of the plot would have done justice to an English or American diplomat.

Now he understood No-Lie. He had been willing to bear the ridicule of the white men to inquire into their private affairs. His nosing was not prompted by idle curiosity; he had a very definite purpose. He was weighing each man in the balance, and he, Jim Faxon, the joke of Fort William, had been found worthy of the sacred trust imposed upon the Indians by a dying man.

Jim felt a sudden warm glow of pride, as if somehow knighthood had been conferred upon him, then he swore in his secret soul to be worthy of the honor that was his. He would keep faith with the Indians. No white man should know of the country of the Nehalems. He would spirit Multnomah, or Rosaltha—he dwelt lovingly on the name—out of the Oregon country on the *May Dacre* when she sailed for Boston on her final voyage in October.

He strode along beside Multnomah with a mind full of bright plans for the future, wondering if he could ever be kind enough to her to make up for the suffering and loneliness she had known in the last three years.

CHAPTER TWENTY-FOUR

BANG-UP AND
EARLY PIETY

THE return trail proved a delightful one. The slope here was gradual, and after the lava-flow near the summit had been passed the way led for miles through a magnificent stand of *Pinus ponderosa,* or Western yellow pine, whose straight poles towered heavenward without a branch for three-fourths of their majestic height. To Jim Faxon the path led through an enchanted forest with a golden-haired fairy princess by his side. With Multnomah he was always straggling a bit behind the company, who were in haste to complete the tale of miles.

"There Klamath country," Katoosh told them, pointing to the great grassy plain that waved and billowed in the summer heat far below them. "Much deer. Much elk. Big medicine feast, then go to own country."

With shouts of joy the medicine-men broke into a run, Katoosh following with leisurely dignity, until they reached a level space that bore evidence of many such medicine feasts. Bones of deer and elk lay bleaching in the sun and a sunken spot bore ashes from last season's cooking-fires. The young men were fitting arrows to their bows almost before camp was made. They must go on the hunt before the feast could be spread.

"They are fairly famished," Multnomah told Jim. "Katoosh brought plenty of food for me, but the young men came into the camp on the mountain only the night before the ceremony. For nine days before the great medicine at the lake they had been fasting alone in the mountains to the north, fighting the demons. Fasting and running in circles until they are exhausted is part of the test of the neophyte. Their endurance is marvelous. You remember how we suffered from the cold during that terrible storm? Think of braving it without clothing, after going without food for nine terrible days."

"I can hardly believe it," Jim answered, "and they are all but three of them alive and apparently well and happy."

"Now they will feast and dance, and then," Multnomah said, rather wistfully, "we will hurry home. I am all impatience to reach my home. There is packing to do if I am to go with you." Jim thought she was just a bit confused when she spoke of accompanying him.

Inside of an hour two fat elk and three black-tailed deer were borne into the camp on the shoulders of the hunters, and in the dusk the great feast began. Jim remarked that the medicine-men were not the gross feeders that the ordinary every-day Indian is. They were breaking a long fast, taking food sparingly and afterward dancing in joyous abandon to celebrate their entrance into the great medicine cult.

Jim and Multnomah were impatient to leave at once in the morning, but the hunters went out again as soon as daylight came. Meat must be secured and jerked for the long journey to their various homes. When the party reached the great Klamath plain below, they would disperse and go their separate ways. Representatives from most of the large tribes of the Oregon country had come to receive the great medicine test. One young man from the Nehalems, Wyack, had accompanied Katoosh and Multnomah.

For three days they worked at hunting and curing the meat, gathering quantities of roots and berries. There would be no time to stop to secure food on the trail, for summer was fast giving way to fall. Jim was anxious to be on the way, but he made the most of the time to rest. He told himself he had never, not even in crossing the Great American Desert, lived through such days of strenuous travel, and yet he felt no ill effects from it.

He was full of apprehension for Multnomah. Two weeks of keeping up the steady Indian pace was an endurance test of a strong man inured to the life, but she showed not the least sign of undue fatigue, adapting her gait to the ambling trot of Celiast and Katoosh with the ease of the Indian woman. Cheerful and happy always, she pointed out the beauties along the trail, reveling in the wayside flowers, telling Jim their Indian names and learning botanical terms in turn from him. She never tired of examining stamens, pistils, and pollen under the lens. Jim had long since lost his shyness in her presence; she was simple and natural, displaying none of the feminine arts and wiles intended to bring a man to her feet.

On the fourth day they came to the parting of the ways, and with a great deal of handshaking and many protestations of friendship and good will the young men strode off toward their homes. The Nehalems veered about sharply to the northwest, where their country lay.

Celiast had been silent since her experience at the blue lake, but she was cheerful and answered them readily if they addressed her. She had formed the habit of keeping Briar at her side and talking to her in low tones as they walked. Jim and Multnomah exchanged anxious glances as they noticed her lagging steps toward nightfall. They realized that she was put to it to keep up with the party, though she made a heroic effort to conceal her fatigue.

Two days more and Jim and Multnomah walked one each side of her, giving her help over the rough places. She shook them off angrily as long as she could manage unassisted. Never a word of complaint did she utter, though her suffering etched deep lines in her tired old face.

Katoosh appeared not to notice, but each night he brewed strong evil-smelling potions that he pressed to her lips, making passes over her body and uttering weird cries as she drank. Jim found his fear reflected in Multnomah's eyes as she spent her evening soothing her old nurse, crooning lovingly to her as she smoothed the head pillowed on her knees.

"Help come," Katoosh declared one hot bright noon when they had paused a couple of hours for Celiast to rest. "Come heap soon. Me hear-um." But for once it seemed that the *shaman* had erred in his predictions; there was no one in sight and the plain stretched for miles.

"We must camp a few days," Jim told Multnomah, and she nodded in assent. Katoosh caught his whispered words and pointed an angry finger westward.

"You t'ink me lie," he declared in righteous indignation. "You t'ink Katoosh no can make medicine. Look-um."

Appearing like ants on the western rim of the horizon they distinguished a band of horses traveling northward. They counted twelve, two of them bearing riders. Katoosh lifted his right hand to the heavens and began uttering seducive calls that reverberated on the still, hot air, but the riders were too far away to hear. Again and again he called, then began whirling rapidly in circles, ran toward them, whirled again, waited, and called louder than ever.

The riders paused at last, as his cry reached them faintly, or they caught sight of the whirling figure. They wheeled at once and came toward the medicine party at a strong gallop.

"Me draw-um," Katoosh declared in triumph as he waited for them to approach. "Tomaniwus no strong like on medicine mountain."

Jim could hardly believe the evidence of his eyes as they neared. A comely young Indian girl and an awkward Indian youth were driving the horses. "Wopcelia!" he exclaimed. Wopcelia threw back her head and laughed in her joy at seeing him again. She was mounted on Pite, his cayuse renegade, and her companion rode in state on Bang-up, Nat Wyeth's beloved saddle horse. Jim ran to look Bang-up over, and Pite by way of welcome rolled his eyes until only the whites were visible and nipped him on the arm with his ugly yellow teeth.

Jim's joy turned swiftly to resentment. "So *you* stole my horses, Wopcelia," he charged.

Wopcelia turned somber black eyes on him in reproach. "Me no steal-um horses," she protested. "Me pay beaver skins. You no need-um horses. You no take-um pack into Nehalem country for trade-um. Nehalems keel, you come for trade-um. Wopcelia friend. Wopcelia know."

Briar, tired and worn as she was, was bounding with joy at meeting Wopcelia. "Briar her know," the girl explained. "Heap smart dog. She give-um horses. She no bark. Know more as mans." She threw a buckskin leg over the side of the restless Pite and slid to the ground to caress the dog.

Her young companion had almost dismounted and was shaking hands and laughing loudly to cover the embarrassment of the moment.

Recalling the amenities of the occasion, Wopcelia introduced the young Indian to Jim with a backward jerk of her thumb in his direction. "Kamoox, him my mans," she announced, with wifely pride in her voice.

"But, Wopcelia," Jim ejaculated, "your father married you to Cultee. I attended the wedding, you remember."

Wopcelia and her bridegroom laughed and laughed. The girl assumed the attitude of a bent old man, imitating to the life the walk and manner of the aged Cultee.

"Cultee give-um papa six herses for marry with me. Me no like-um Cultee; him old mans. Him mean, him ver' bad mans. Me like-um young mans. Give-um papa much cayuses." She indicated the band of horses grazing under the watchful eye of Kamoox.

Jim laughed as he saw the situation, then frowned. "So you got away from Cultee, and you've spent the summer stealing horses in the Klamath country, and now you're on your way to give them to your father so you can have your new husband, are you?" he asked. "I left No-Lie swearing vengeance on Cultee for stealing back the horses he had given him for you."

Wopcelia was indignant at Cultee's perfidy. "Cultee steal-um papa's horses! Him *cultus* [bad] Indian." She stamped an indignant foot. "Kamoox heap good Indian. Papa like-um Kamoox. Papa him heap glad me get away. Papa laugh beeg when see much fine cayuses."

"But you stole those cayuses from the Klamaths," Jim reproved.

A roguish twinkle in the black eye of Wopcelia and loud laughter from Katoosh and Wyack were his answer. Even Celiast revived enough to smile. Multnomah made an effort to frown severely on the offenders, but did not succeed very well.

The bridegroom, feeling that Wopcelia was receiving rather too much attention, jerked roughly at her sleeve and bade her look to the cayuses, who were threatening to stray. Here was a husband to Wopcelia's liking. She meekly obeyed her lord's command.

"Bang-up and Pite have arrived just in time, anyway, no matter what we think of horse-stealing," Jim told Multnomah. "I began to fear that Celiast would not live to reach home."

Wopcelia, counting horses, cut three strong cayuses from the band and proffered them to Katoosh. She handed Jim the tethers of Bang-up and Pite. They were to ride into the country of the Nehalems.

"You give-um cayuses papa when see," she admonished Jim. She had no time for bandying words, but must be on her way to give her marriage offering to No-Lie and show off her new husband.

Jim had difficulty in persuading her to wait until he had written a note to the commander of Fort William telling him that he would return there shortly and asking him to delay the sailing of the *May Dacre* if he should be a few days late in making his appearance.

CHAPTER TWENTY-FIVE
THE "GRASS MAN" RETURNS

C ELIAST recovered rapidly when the strain of traveling on foot was removed. She rode the easy-gaited Bang-up with a great show of pride. Katoosh urged them forward at the top of their horses' speed. "Tilki need-um help," he said with a noncommittal shake of his wise old head.

Multnomah handled one of the half-broken cayuses with the ease of the Indian horsewoman, and Wyack took a delight in subduing Early Piety. The days passed swiftly and pleasantly.

Jim and Multnomah showed a tendency to lag a little behind the others. There was so much to tell. The girl relieved her pent-up emotions in relating all she could remember of her life in England and of her childhood among the Nehalems. She gained comfort from speaking of her father to a sympathetic listener. Through loneliness she had been given to introspection. Jim marveled at her broad outlook on life.

As he grew to know her he was torn with conflicting emotions. Just what was an honorable man to do under the circumstances ? Her father had given directions for her return to England, but since then she had come of age. She was free to choose her husband, but in asking her to be his wife, wasn't he rather taking advantage of her? She had known no white man except her father. How could a girl under such conditions know whether she wished to marry him or not. If he spoke, gratitude might be her only motive in accepting his love. He paled as he thought of this, and resolved that, no matter what the cost to him, even if he risked losing her to some other man, he could only maintain his silence and comply with her father's wishes. After she was safely at home with her own people, then he would tell her of his love for her.

But Katoosh and Celiast showed a great lack of delicacy. In their blunt directness they were a constant source of annoyance to both of them. Troubled by no fine points of honor, the pair made it perfectly clear that Jim was to marry Multnomah.

The salmon run had begun in late August in the Nehalem Valley. The camp was in gala dress, with the split salmon looking like vivid red flannel underwear as it hung on the racks to dry in the hazy Indian-summer air. The whole tribe had returned from their various expeditions and were all busily engaged in fishing and curing the catch when the medicine party returned.

The stench of the offal from the fish offended the nostrils. Jim and Multnomah hurried Celiast directly to their lodge, where the wind would not waft the odor to them. Celiast bustled about like a New England housewife, preparing food and setting the place to rights after their long absence.

She fairly radiated joy. She was going soon with Jim and Multnomah to pay a visit to her daughter, Auxica, but it was not Auxica of whom she spoke. She could hardly wait to see the papoose, speculating daily as to whether he could walk and how soon he would learn to talk.

Multnomah was eager to learn the news of the camp. There were two new papooses to be admired. She sighed when Katoosh, coming in, told of Tilki's plight. Fearing he was dead, she had not dared to ask, knowing that if he were her question would not be answered.

"Tilki much hurt. No die. Soon well," Katoosh told her.

"Cockqua did try to kill him, then," Multnomah whispered to Jim. "I knew he was terribly injured, else he would have guided you to the medicine mountain."

Katoosh would say no more. Speech might involve a mention of the dead. Just what had happened after Jim ran from the village on the night of the great feast could never be learned. But he led them to the tepee where Tilki lay on a pile of new mats. He greeted them joyfully. He could not rise, but assured them that he was well on the road to recovery, though one eye was blinded and his face was a mass of half-healed bruises.

"Tilki heap big chief now," Katoosh grunted, in satisfaction. "Me save-um life."

"How I wish we could learn just what happened," Multnomah mourned to Jim with unsatisfied feminine curiosity.

"Do you really think Katoosh lured Cockqua and his followers to the mountain with his magic?" Jim asked Multnomah as they walked up the hill toward her lodge.

"No," she doubted. "Father always said we must look deeply into causes when judging Indian necromancy. One event does not necessarily spring out of the event preceding it, as the primitive savage believes. Cockqua's own conceit led him to his destruction. He had no trouble in finding his way across the mountains. His ability to bear pain without flinching made him bold to defy his gods. Coincidence explains a great deal, father declared."

"But the witchcraft Celiast practiced on the beach," Jim demurred. "Cockqua bore the mark of the lightning on his forehead just where the lens burned in the image."

"Coincidence, again," Multnomah insisted. "When the white man cannot explain he says 'coincidence,' and there the matter rests. I do not know. Often father was puzzled, for the Indians' powers are not the powers of the white race." She dismissed the subject with a shrug.

"Cockqua was shrewd," Jim admitted. "He could easily have killed the medicine-men while they were spent with fasting. Only a kind fate intervened in our behalf. We will let it go at that."

"The Nehalems have learned a lesson, at any rate," Multnomah said. "Never again will they resist their medicine-men. Rest assured, taboo or no taboo, Katoosh will somehow find means to spread the story of the fire from the sky that he drew down upon his arch enemy. The Indian fears nothing more than he does the lightning."

They had reached the lodge in the mellow fall afternoon. Multnomah led Jim up the hill to show him her garden where the late blooms of the broad-leaved arnica—*Arnica latifolia*—bloomed in golden profusion. She had skillfully naturalized the wild flowers and by cultivation had brought out the best in each. There were quantities of fall asters and a goodly colony of ferns in the deep shade. A sunny bank that earlier in the season must have been ablaze where the fireweed, or great willow herb, *Chamœnerion angustifolium,* was now opening its cylindric capsules to scatter silvery floss through the quiet woods.

The earlier things, many of them, were bearing ripened seed. Jim was delighted. "You will give me seeds to round out my collection?" he asked. "We will take them with us and the plants will remind you of your home."

"Yes," Multnomah agreed. Then turned away sadly. "I am finding it hard to leave my home. Couldn't you stay here with me?" she asked, timidly.

Jim faltered and colored to the roots of his auburn hair, then looked directly into her eyes. "We would be obliged to marry if I remain," he said, slowly, "and I cannot bring myself to ask that of you until you have known other men and had a chance to judge them."

Never having known the wiles of the white woman, Multnomah neither blushed nor faltered. "I am willing to marry you, of course." She was searching his face with clear blue eyes devoid of guile or simulation.

"But," Jim faltered—the words were very hard to utter—"women of our race choose the men they marry because they love them and not for the sake of expediency. I have hoped hard that you will learn in time to love me. I know just where I stand. I loved you before I saw you—that is, I loved the image I had made in my heart—but I only knew what the love of a man for a woman meant when the lightning flash revealed your face to me there behind the altar near the blue lake."

"I knew, too," Multnomah faltered, trembling a little.

But Jim was not to be swerved. "I have seen the women of our world, and so I know, but you must take time to make your decision. Your whole future happiness depends upon your decision. I will guard that even if it means my great loss." With a groan Jim Faxon buried his face in his hands.

Multnomah drew his hands away and forced him to face her. "Of course I love you, Jim Faxon, in spite of your stupidity. How could I help loving you when you were willing to risk your life because two Indians hinted that there was a white girl living among them? I, too, made an image, and it was more accurate than yours, for Katoosh told me what sort of man he was bringing for me."

Jim, fighting manfully as he listened, was suddenly overcome. He took the girl in yellow buckskins in his eager arms and kissed her upturned face again and again, a face that Auxica had told him was like a wild rose on the water.

"How stupid you have been, Jim!" Multnomah chided him, laughingly. "You know nothing of women, even if you have spent your life among them."

"No," Jim faltered, kissing her again, his face lit with his great joy. "No man knows women. Here I've worried over this situation and intended above all things to act honorably, and you had it settled in your mind all the time."

"Yes, I had it settled if you loved me, and I have been sure that you did, since that first day," Multnomah admitted, candidly. "From books I know that women wait to be chosen, or rather pretend to wait, but I am like the Indian woman. She chooses her mate, most generally, though it may appear that she is sold like merchandise—that is, she does if she is clever."

"And she is generally clever," Jim admitted.

Multnomah laughed. "Wopcelia did the choosing, in spite of Yallup. No man, not even an Indian, is likely to win a wife against her wish. He'll rue it to his dying day if he does."

"But I still maintain that you do not know me well enough to make a wise decision." Jim was stubborn.

"I make my decisions just as the Indian does," Multnomah told him, firmly. "I know that you are kind and gentle. Celiast has told me of your consideration for her. You are not a coward; you went back into that terrible tide-rip to save her life. You set an Indian child's leg when you were on the road to the Nehalem country."

"How did you know that?" Jim was wondering if Katoosh or Tilki had been making medicine again.

"The family have returned, and the boy walks with scarcely a limp," Multnomah told him. "Your goodness has gone before you. The Nehalems are going to adopt you as a member of the tribe. We will go with their blessing, and will be welcomed home gladly if we ever return, and I hope we will some day." She looked about her wistfully. Leaving the only home she had ever known and going to a strange new country brought its sadness.

"But you will go gladly with me now?" Jim persisted, seizing her hands and looking into her eyes.

"Yes, 'tis best. Father would have had it so. I feel as if his hand is stretched out from the other side of life to guide me, now that I can speak of him to some one who loves me and understands," Multnomah told him.

"We will go first to my mother, and then settle up your father's affairs as he directed, and after that we will return to live in the Oregon country. I was leaving because I wanted a wife to share its loveliness with me," Jim confided. "Missionaries came across the plains with us. Settlers will follow the missionaries. In ten or twenty years at the outside there will be women and children living on farms in the rich valley of the Willamette."

All things settled so happily between them, they set about making preparations for the journey to Fort William. Multnomah gave a *potlach* that was remembered for years by the tribes. Every man, woman, and child received some little gift for remembrance.

Katoosh consented to the taking of Martin Braintree's manuscripts, saying that he wished the white men to know what a great *shaman* he was by the "talk on paper." His medicine failed him completely for once. He gained no inkling of the sketches that Multnomah had made. Celiast with secret misgiving hid them among things she was packing to take away.

The *shaman* was overjoyed when Multnomah gave him her lodge for his home. He planned to use it for the medicine lodge of the tribe, declaring that he would perform most wonderful magic within its walls.

The Nehalems provided a great feast and a harvest dance, after which Jim was formally adopted by the tribe with appropriate ceremony and given the impressive name of "Kloske Tipso Skookum," the highest title they could confer. In their dialect it means "Brave Grass Man."

"I must be called Rosaltha when we reach the country where white people live," Multnomah told Jim. "The Nehalems were angry if they heard father call my name. To please them he called me by the name they gave me when they were about."

Jim shook his head doubtfully, "I'll try," he promised, "but I'm afraid you will always be Multnomah to me."

"I will not be obliged to wear buckskins when we come to your mother's house," Multnomah confided happily to Jim. "You will not be embarrassed by bringing home a wife who looks like a young squaw. Father insisted on keeping mother's things until I was old enough to wear them. I'm a bit smaller than my mother was, but they fit me well enough. I have her shoes and hat and black silk shawl."

The Nehalems wished to celebrate the marriage according to their tribal custom, but Jim and Multnomah were adamant on that point. They would be married with the Christian ceremony. Katoosh agreed reluctantly when Jim told him that the white priest, Jason Lee, who had come to the Oregon country to teach the Indians, would marry them as soon as they reached Auxica's cabin. He promised to swear him to secrecy and to take Multnomah to the ship that would bear her away without the knowledge of other white men. No one would notice a girl in buckskins if she remained in Auxica's cabin.

They left one crisp fall morning with a company of very proud Indians who were going to help Jim raise his *cache* and to return with the goods which were to be the bridegroom's special *potlach* to the Nehalems. Celiast, all impatience to see the papoose and Auxica, rode with them, and Jim led the other horses loaded with the bales of prime beaver skins that were Multnomah's marriage portion. In their pride they never would send the daughter of their white friend away without some remembrance.

They found Auxica anxiously awaiting their arrival. Wopcelia had hurried to her with the good news. The cabin was freshly scoured and young Jed Withers attired in new beaded buckskins in their honor. No-Lie was on hand, proud of Wopcelia and his new son-in-law and ostentatiously displaying the horses she had brought him.

Multnomah was much concerned about her wedding dress. Nothing but the wool delaine with the pink rosebuds would answer. Celiast very carefully set the piece back in the flounce so that the darning, done with ravelings, was hardly noticeable.

"I snum!" Jed Withers ejaculated as he saw the bride in the flowered dress and the white silk stockings, a little yellow with age, and the dainty black slippers with the silver buckles on them. "I snum! Ef I'd jist 'a' knowed thet thar secret o' the Nehalems' in time, I shore 'ud 'a' found the pass inter thet thar kentry."

There was just one more detail to be attended to before the *May Dacre* sailed. No one had given Briar a thought. She had just trudged faithfully along beside Jim all the way home. He laid a caressing hand on her black head in parting. "Briar is Wopcelia's *potlach*," he said. "She has always loved my dog. She tried time and again to trade baskets for her."

Wopcelia screamed in her delight. Her cup of joy was fairly overflowing. She had secured the bridegroom of her choice and would soon return to the Nehalem country to live out her happy days. No-Lie's mission among the whites was fulfilled, now that he had found Multnomah a suitable husband. All of the Nehalems were quietly returning to their lovely valley with no one the wiser. The goings and comings of Indians are not noted by the lordly white man.

"Now me not called No-Lie never no more. Me named Yallup," No-Lie told Jim. "Me no lie. Me tell-um trut'. White man not know ever't'ing. Jim Faxon, him know me no lie, me no steal."

And so it came about that to this day the secret of Rosaltha Braintree is not known in the Oregon country. Jason Lee kept faith and the *attachés* at Fort William were not returning to Oregon. They swore to a man never to mention the matter, though where Jim Faxon found the white girl was a mystery far past their solving.

Just before the *May Dacre* cast her anchor, news was received at Fort Vancouver of the safe arrival of Marcus Whitman and his bride, Narcissa, and the Reverend Mr. Spaulding and his wife at Fort Walla Walla early in September. They would reach Dr. McLoughlin's home late that fall.

"What did I tell you, Rosaltha?" Jim said to his bride when they heard this delightful bit of news. "The missionaries have brought their wives across the Great American Desert. Other families will follow in a few years. We will return. The great

Oregon country will draw us back. Once live in the green land and there is no home anywhere else on the earth."

"Yes," the bride answered, "I shall find myself counting the years until we return home."

THE END

www.ingramcontent.com/pod-product-compliance
Lightning Source LLC
Chambersburg PA
CBHW021219260626
47172CB00002B/508